SHW

Love,
Louisa

Also by Barbara Metzger
in Large Print:

Wedded Bliss
A Worthy Wife
The Primrose Path
Saved by Scandal

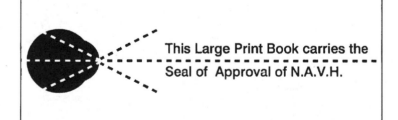

Love,
Louisa

❧

Barbara Metzger

WHEELER
PUBLISHING

Published in 2005 by arrangement with Harvey Klinger, Inc.

Wheeler Large Print Hardcover.

The text of this Large Print edition is unabridged.
Other aspects of the book may vary from the original edition.

Set in 16 pt. Plantin.

Printed in the United States on permanent paper.

Library of Congress Cataloging-in-Publication Data

Metzger, Barbara.
    Love, Louisa / by Barbara Metzger.
      p. cm.
    ISBN 1-58724-992-8 (lg. print : hc : alk. paper)
    1. Triangles (Interpersonal relations) — Fiction.
    2. Seaside resorts — Fiction. 3. Hurricanes — Fiction.
    4. Landowners — Fiction. 5. Large type books. I. Title.
    PS3563.E86L67 2005
      813′.54—dc22   2005005045

To Louisa, I miss you still.

As the Founder/CEO of NAVH, the only national health agency solely devoted to those who, although not totally blind, have an eye disease which could lead to serious visual impairment, I am pleased to recognize Thorndike Press* as one of the leading publishers in the large print field.

Founded in 1954 in San Francisco to prepare large print textbooks for partially seeing children, NAVH became the pioneer and standard setting agency in the preparation of large type.

Today, those publishers who meet our standards carry the prestigious "Seal of Approval" indicating high quality large print. We are delighted that Thorndike Press is one of the publishers whose titles meet these standards. We are also pleased to recognize the significant contribution Thorndike Press is making in this important and growing field.

Lorraine H. Marchi, L.H.D.
Founder/CEO
NAVH

* Thorndike Press encompasses the following imprints: Thorndike, Wheeler, Walker and Large Print Press.

Chapter One

On the night of their engagement party Louisa cracked up her fiancé's car. The relationship went downhill after that, but not as fast as Howard's beloved Porsche went down that steep, icy slope. The Porsche might have fared better if not for the garbage truck at the bottom of the hill, and the engagement might still have flourished, if not for the money, the wedding, and Howard's mother.

"My mother? How the hell did my mother get into the discussion about paying for the car?" Howard was pacing the Manhattan apartment they shared on East Fortieth. Out one tenth-floor window you could almost see the FDR Drive and the East River; from the other, the new condo being built across the street. Howard jerked the verticals shut on the construction, offended by the disorderly scene. He was not much better pleased with the sight of Louisa in her sweatpants and faded T-shirt, with her yellow-pad lists of wedding guests spread all over the table. "She wasn't the one who backed her piece of Japanese junk into my Porsche."

Of course not. If Irene, as Mrs. Silver insisted her future daughter-in-law call her, had tried to back her huge Cadillac down that ridiculously long, icy Great Neck driveway, she would have flattened the Porsche. Louisa refrained, quite nobly she thought, from mentioning again that if Howard had had the hand brake on his car fixed, the damn thing would not have budged at a mere tap from a Toyota, which piece of junk, incidentally, hadn't sustained so much as a scratch. Louisa also stopped herself from pointing out that if Irene had not spent the engagement party finding fault with Louisa's dress, hair, and friends, Louisa just might not have been in such a hurry to leave. What she did do was point at the four yellow pads with her pen. "It's the wedding, Howard. If your mother didn't insist we have such a big affair, I could afford to help pay what the insurance won't."

The insurance company, it seemed, did not have as great an appreciation for Howard's classic sports car as Howard had. What they were offering was book value on a totaled wreck, not payment for painstaking rebuilding. The decision rankled Howard, but not as much as his asking for her money rankled Louisa. He earned a lot more, had more money in the bank and the mutual funds, and wasn't paying nearly enough toward the wedding his mother wanted for her only son. His mother had offered plenty of advice, but she hadn't offered to pay for anything except the flowers — if she got to pick them out. Louisa's widowed mother was buying the extravagant wedding gown — that Irene insisted on helping select, since Louisa's own mother was living in Florida. On a fixed income.

"You know I can barely pay for that orchestra your mother wants. If she adds one more name to her list, we'll have to cut back on the sushi bar."

"Mother only has our best interests in mind. Those people can be a great help to my career."

Howard was already a successful tax attorney, working long days, nights and weekends. If he were any more successful, Louisa would never get to see him at all, except at the law firm, the same one where she was personnel director. They'd had that argument before, too, so she did not bring it up again. "I don't see what the issue is here, anyway. In two months what I have is yours, and vice versa. So all this talk of who pays for what, the wedding or the car, the rent and the honeymoon, is silly. Isn't it?"

Howard fiddled with her notepads, making neat stacks out of her scraps of paper. "I've been meaning to talk to you about that pre-nup thing again."

Louisa barely glanced at the table, knowing she'd have to start all over again, now that he'd put her lists out of order. "I thought we decided we didn't need one?"

"Yes, but I've been thinking. It might be best, you know, to protect you."

"Me? You're the one with investments, profit sharing and pensions. I'll be out of a job when we marry."

The company's policy did not let married couples work together, so Louisa was already training her replacement.

"You'll have no trouble getting another job," he answered, which was no answer at all, of course. He moved to stare out the window, the one that showed a corner of the East River, if you craned your neck around the dark Con Edison plant.

"I'll never make half your income."

"Exactly. If we have a contract, you won't have to worry about getting your fair share of my earnings, in case we get a divorce."

"Howard, we're not even married yet and you're thinking about a divorce?" Louisa put her pen down and went to

10

join him at the window.

"Don't be ridiculous. I just want things to be aboveboard, with no confusion." He did not turn to meet her eyes, though.

Louisa put her arms around him from behind and rested her head against his back. "You do love me, don't you, Howard?"

"Of course I do, sweetheart."

Howard loved Louisa so much, he saved her from a bad marriage. He didn't show up for the wedding.

Louisa knew there was a problem when Irene's flowers did not arrive at the North Shore Inn that afternoon. Neither did Irene, the groomsmen, or the ring bearer, Howard's cousin's son. The photographer kept glancing at his watch. How many pictures of the bride checking her frilly garter could he take? Louisa took the silly, scratchy, useless thing off so she could pace better, almost mowing down her mother and Bernie, her mother's Florida boyfriend. Louisa would not think about where those two had spent the last night. Bernie in a tuxedo instead of his Bermuda shorts was enough of a revelation.

Louisa's brother-in-law Jeff was drinking, her sister Annie was nagging at her kids to stay clean, the kids were picking on each other and whining . . . and Louisa was pacing. "Stop that," her mother ordered. "You're making me dizzy. Besides, you'll get sweat rings under your arms. How will that look?"

Louisa listened to her mother as well as her niece and nephew did to theirs. She kicked her gown's trailing satin train out of her way as she turned and headed back across the room adjoining the reception hall.

"How did Howard seem yesterday?" Annie wanted to know, or else she just wanted to distract Louisa. "Maybe he got sick and he's in a hospital somewhere. Should we call his mother's house?"

The implication that Howard would have called his mother from the emergency room instead of Louisa was not lost on anyone. Louisa scowled at her sister and snatched a glass away from her nephew before he could drink his father's cocktail. "He was fine in the afternoon, getting ready for the bachelor party. I am sure someone would have notified me if he'd had a heart attack or something."

"So he could have had too much to drink and overslept?"

"Mama, it's four o'clock in the afternoon. No one oversleeps that long, not on their wedding day."

12

No, Howard hadn't had an accident on the Long Island Expressway, hadn't fallen down in a drunken stupor and broken his head, and hadn't run off with some hired stripper. He must have spent the whole day calling his friends and business associates, for none of them showed up at the catering hall. Only Louisa's friends and family arrived, huddled together on one side of the big wedding parlor while, behind a screen, the Itzhak Perlman–priced violinist played over and over the same pieces Louisa had selected four months ago. For what she was paying him, Louisa thought the maestro ought to know more than three songs. She sent her niece and nephew behind the screen to tell him to play something else.

The baby's breath in Louisa's upswept blond hair was gasping its last when the inn's manager finally brought Howard's message. The poor man was pale and shaking, wringing his hands — and that was before Louisa threw up on his feet.

Howard thought she deserved better. He thought she'd be happier without him. He thought Louisa would come to agree with him.

Louisa thought she was going to die. Right there, in front of her nearest and dearest and a dozen waiters who couldn't hide their smirks. Her mother was weeping in Bernie's arms — at least one of them had someone to comfort her — and Annie was apologizing to the violinist for the spilled ginger ale. She was sure his violin could be wiped clean. Annie's husband Jeff pressed a glass into Louisa's hands. "If you love me, this is hemlock," she told him.

It wasn't. It was the pricey champagne that was supposed to be the wedding toast, the one thing that could have been returned if it was unopened. Louisa drank it down without admiring its bouquet or bubbles. Then she pulled the veil off her head, jerked the buttoned train off her gown, and marched into the big room and down the white-runnered aisle, by herself, to *The Flight of the Bumblebee*. It seemed appropriate.

Despite the lump in her throat and the tears flowing down her cheeks destroying what the professional makeup artist had applied hours ago, Louisa ordered the rest of the champagne bottles opened and served. "As a . . . as a t-toast to my l-lucky escape," she managed to get out before collapsing into the arms of the judge who was to have performed the wedding ceremony. His black robe was now smeared with the remnants of her makeup, but at least she hadn't thrown up on him too, she thought proudly, accepting another glass of champagne after he helped her to a seat.

Everyone was watching her, but she couldn't look back, not to see the pity there. They were all expecting her to crawl away, she knew, to weep and moan and have hysterics. She would not give him — the absent, abysmal ass Howard — the satisfaction. Louisa wiped her eyes and raised her chin. She'd paid for the damn wedding, and, by god, she was going to hold the damn wedding, even if it killed her. She could have a nervous breakdown tomorrow.

She turned around and held up her glass while the waiters scurried about with trays of stemmed glasses. Jeff, thankfully, shouted, "To Louisa, who was too good for that mama's boy anyway."

Everyone cheered, and again, when she had the head waiter announce that the reception was going on, with hors d'oeuvres being served on the terrace.

The food was superb, as artfully balanced on the plates as a Calder mobile. Louisa did not eat.

The music was lively, with no YMCA's, horas, or macarenas. Louisa did not dance.

The champagne kept coming, replaced by two kinds of wine and then cordials. Louisa did not let a pourer pass by.

The company was friendly. After all, they were mostly related, or had known each other forever. The few strangers, escorts and such, were soon made welcome by the small group. Louisa did not mingle. Buffered by her mother and sister, insulated by her brother-in-law and Bernie, she sat with a smile frozen on her face, her heart frozen in her chest. Her mother frowned at the glass clenched in Louisa's hand and told the waiter to bring hot tea. With lemon.

"Hot tea isn't going to fix this, Mama."

"Neither is falling down drunk in front of your friends. Think what everyone will say: that Howard was right to call the wedding off, rather than marry an alcoholic."

"Mama, you know I barely touch the stuff. In case you haven't noticed, this is not a usual event."

"And you haven't eaten anything all day, either. You'll get liver failure or something, like those college boys."

Before her mother could expound on binge drinking, or extend her lecture to Annie's husband, Jeff interrupted and said, "I know a guy who knows a guy who can take care of the bastard for you."

Louisa did not have to ask which bastard her brother-in-law meant. "Take care of Howard?"

"Yeah, you know, old-fashioned revenge. Teach the jerk he can't treat you like this. He breaks your heart, we break his head. I'll help pay."

Louisa was tempted, but she was sober enough to know not to trust her own judgment.

Besides, this could not be happening to her. She'd wake up tomorrow in Barbados happily married. But not to Howard. He was not in sight, so not in her befogged imagination.

What had she done to deserve this? Louisa had done everything he and his mother wanted for the wedding, and it had not been enough. It was never going to be enough. She had to face the facts. No, she did not have to. Not today. She pushed aside the tea and picked up her wineglass again.

Annie wiped chocolate off her daughter's face and hands. "I think you ought to write the creep a letter, telling him you're pregnant with his child. That ought to shake him up enough."

Louisa looked over to where her ten-year-old nephew was licking sugar roses off the wedding cake. She shuddered. "I'll consider it."

"No, you ought to sue the bum." Bernie

seldom spoke, in recognition that he was not really family, but he did now, patting Louisa's mother's hand. "Money. That's the best way to get back at someone like Howard, hit him in the pocketbook. Go for big bucks, for breach of promise."

"Do people still do that, Bernie?"

He shrugged his thin shoulders. "I don't know. Ask a lawyer."

There was silence at the table. Everyone knew Howard was a lawyer.

"What I think," Mama said, "is that living well is the best revenge. Our Louisa can get on with her life, and be happier without Howard than she would have been with such a two-faced, lying cad." (Mama read a lot of paperback romances.)

Jeff raised his glass. "To getting even."

Bernie raised his cup of coffee. "To Louisa and a better life tomorrow."

Annie raised the question: "But how?" Louisa had no job, no home, not much money, no husband, no lover — and that bright tomorrow was sure to bring a hangover.

"I don't know," Louisa replied in as firm a voice as she could find, "but that's what I'll do. I'll make a better life for myself. As soon as I come back from my honeymoon."

Chapter Two

She'd held the reception herself. She could damn well go on the honeymoon by herself. What else could Louisa do, anyway, go back to Howard's apartment?

First she hid in the bride's anteroom while her mother and sister stood at the inn's door, hugging and kissing all the head-shaking, tongue-clucking guests good-bye. Then, still in her wedding gown, Louisa made her brother-in-law drive her and the leftover food into the city, to every soup kitchen and food pantry they could find. At least someone would get to enjoy what was supposed to have been the happiest day of her life.

Happy? In all her twenty-seven years, Louisa could not remember being so miserable, so angry and hurt and numb all at the same time. Her father's death when she was nineteen had left a sad gap in her life, almost as sad as when he'd moved out and away to Oregon when she was twelve, but not quite. That was like living with one damaged kidney. You survived. This, though, was like having your heart squeezed out of your chest by your own pet boa constrictor, then eaten by rabid baboons with purple behinds. No one could live through it. No one should have to. She curled up on her bed when they got back to the inn, in the room where she was to have spent her wedding night. Room, tomb, what was the difference? Womb, with Mama and Bernie across the hall. No groom. Lost her bloom. Doom.

The phone rang. The baboons were playing bongos inside her brain. "Mpf?"

"Good morning, Miss Waldon. You asked for a wake-up call."

How could she wake up when she'd never gone to sleep? "Hnuh?"

"Have a lovely day."

Good thing Louisa's mouth was filled with sawdust or she'd have told that chirpy voice where to go with her lovely day. She did drag herself off the bed, though, and stood under the shower for ten minutes. Then she took off her wedding dress and took a bath.

"I am never going to have another drink. Never going to have another wedding. Never going to trust another man. Never —"

"Don't be ridiculous," Annie said. "Jeff

20

knows some very nice men at his office. As soon as you're back from your honey—vacation, we'll have a barbeque at our place."

Hot dogs, hamburgers, baked beans, insurance salesmen. Louisa's stomach churned. Annie'd insisted on driving Louisa to the airport, rather than have her spend the money on a limousine. The children were, thankfully, home with Jeff. Louisa kept her eyes closed as Annie navigated the LIE and the Belt Parkway, over potholes and construction plates.

"You'll be fine," her sister was saying, reaching over to pat her shoulder, crossing into the lane of an oncoming Army transport Jeep.

"— Never going to drive with you again."

"And we'll all stand by you."

Except that Mama and Bernie were leaving tomorrow to visit his married son in Arizona, and Annie hadn't suggested Louisa come stay at her place 'til she found a new apartment.

"I'm sure you can get your old job back."

"Annie, they threw me a shower. My replacement gave me a picture frame, the partners gave me a huge bonus. And

21

Howard works there. I could never go back to that office."

"Well, you'll find something better, then. You always had all the brains and looks and the luck in the family."

That's what Louisa needed right then, her sister's resentment. Annie was older, heavier, and cut her own hair. With a manicure scissors, it seemed. She wore too-tight old blue jeans and Jeff's too-big old shirts. Her children were spoiled and her husband was . . . a decent man who would never walk out on her.

"No, it's you who has everything," Louisa said as she got out of the car at the airport terminal. "Make sure you appreciate it."

Annie leaned over, while taxicabs beeped at her. "Are you sure I shouldn't come in and wait with you?"

"Yes. You know you want to get to your exercise class, and I have one of Mama's books to read if the flight is delayed. What's the worst that can happen?"

"Howard could decide to go to Barbados, too."

Louisa ripped up his ticket. The worst thing, though, was that they wouldn't let her on the plane. The ticket said Mrs. Howard Silver and her driver's license read

Louisa Waldon. The tickets had been paid for with Howard's credit card, besides. The line of would-be passengers behind her grew, dragging suitcases and golf clubs and oversized pocketbooks and attaché cases that would take hours to get through security. Louisa tried to explain about the canceled wedding to the ticket clerk, and got a "Gee, that's too bad," instead of a boarding pass.

The head ticket agent was more sympathetic, wanting to tell Louisa about the rat she herself was married to, but rules were rules. For all the FAA knew, Louisa could be a terrorist who'd done away with Mrs. Silver, and she'd blow up their precious airplane next. With her perfume atomizer? Louisa demanded to see the manager or supervisor or the pilot, for God's sake. Someone who could understand that rules were to protect the people on board — not keep innocent travelers from getting on the darn planes.

A thick-waisted, gray-haired black man in uniform eventually appeared through a door at the rear of the counter. He explained the safety policy again, in short words, simple sentences, and soft tones. Louisa felt as if she were back in elementary school, in the principal's office. She stumbled and stuttered through her explanation one more time, but Captain Roundtree ("Security, not flight crew") just shook his head. The lines of passengers were thinning, everyone heading for the gate and the plane. Everyone but Louisa. In desperation, Louisa dumped the contents of her purse on the counter; Captain Roundtree stepped back and reached under his jacket for a cell phone — or a gun. She fumbled through her wallet to find a picture of her and Howard, a letter with his name on it, a receipt, anything. She came up with gold: a wedding invitation, the one she'd carried around for luck.

"You see?" Her lip trembled. "My name, Howard's name." Her throat closed up again until she could barely stammer: "The N-North Shore Inn, yesterday's d-date." Tears splashed on the heavy card stock. "The p-pleasure of your company," she finished with a sob and a wail, against Captain Roundtree's broad chest.

They held the plane for her.

Not only did she have her boarding pass and clearance for the connecting flight to St. Jerome's, but she got swept through security, got a ride in the ground transport cart straight to the plane, and got an upgrade to first-class.

The man she was now supposed to sit next to did not get up from his aisle seat. He pointedly looked at his watch before collecting his belongings, newspaper, laptop and trail-biking magazines from her seat, and managed to move his legs a half-inch so she could clamber past. He looked at her swollen eyes, reddened nose, blotchy complexion, and sneered. "What's the matter, honey, your fingernail break?"

Enough was enough. No, it was more than enough. Louisa was not going to apologize, and she was not going to tell her humiliating story one more time. She dabbed at her eyes with Captain Roundtree's now sodden handkerchief, and sniffled a couple of times before telling Mr. Frequent Flyer that no, her fiancé had had a heart attack while biking in a charity triathlon. He wasn't expected to last through the night, and she only prayed she'd be in time for a last farewell.

The stewardess had tears in her eyes. The First-Class ass muttered an apology. Louisa made sure he was sincerely sorry by shaking her head and adding, "Yes, and he's just about your age too."

The Seafarer Resort at St. Jerome's turned out to be a couples-only place.

Louisa fit in about as well as a collie at a cat show. The first night she stayed in her room anyway, sobbing and sleeping, sleeping and sobbing. By the next morning, she was bored, hungry, well-rested, and almost as angry with herself as she was with Howard. She went down to breakfast on the hotel's patio, overlooking the pink beach and the turquoise water. The only person to speak to her other than the waiter was a blond Adonis who looked like a surfboard advertisement. He turned out to be the resident tennis pro and gigolo. If ever there was a woman who could use a little gigging, Louisa decided, she was it. She just might take him up on his dinner offer, and dessert, too. First, though, she was going for a walk to clear her head, to come to terms with her anger and grief.

On reflection, with the glare reflected off her sunglasses, she decided she was more angry than grief-stricken, more humiliated than heartbroken, more shocked than saddened. How could she have been so wrong about Howard's character? How could she have trusted a man who could do such a thing to a woman he swore to love? How could she get even with him by sleeping with a tanned boy toy?

No more tears, Louisa told herself as she kept walking along the shore. No more self-pity. Now she had to think about what she was going to do with the rest of her Howard-less life. She had to think of the future, not the past. Instead she thought of every tired cliché about when life gives you lemons, and lessons learned, and opportunity knocking. When the going gets rough . . . she kicked a rock out of her path and kept walking down the beach.

Louisa covered almost half the coastline on her hike, never noticing the seashells, the sailboats, the other tourists or the fishermen. She walked for five hours.

Her sunscreen lasted for two.

The man sitting next to her at the emergency clinic was a local woodcarver. At least he had been before the accident. He showed her a bowl carved out of the native cwehee trees — that's what it sounded like to Louisa, anyway. Even with her eyes swollen shut, Louisa could see that the wood was exquisite, the workmanship superb. Now here was something she could do with her life! Not sit on an island carving objets d'art, but selling them for the native people. She could set up a Web site, put them on the Internet, spread beauty and prosperity through cyberspace.

Become an entrepreneur. Yes!

To get started, she bought outright, for cash, two crates of bowls, plates, and goblets, all of which were instantly confiscated at the airport when she left, after five days of ice packs and misery. The baggage inspector sternly informed her, before he returned the bowls to his brother-in-law to dupe another gullible gringo, that the cwehee tree was an endangered species.

So were honest men.

Louisa could not get into her apartment — Howard's apartment — in Manhattan. The locks had been changed. All of her belongings, though, were carefully boxed and labeled at the concierge desk, along with a note from Howard. Louisa didn't know who was more mortified, the deskman or her. She crossed to the other side of the lobby to read what sorry excuse Howard had come up with to explain his desertion. *Louisa,* he'd written, no dear. *I understand you might be angry* — hah! — *and might even think you have just cause for a lawsuit.* So Bernie was right after all. *I have enclosed a check which should show my remorse* — more like his fear of losing his shirt, his job, and his reputation. No apology, no excuses. He thought money could repay her?

A check could clear his conscience? *You can keep the engagement ring, too.*

Louisa hadn't even thought about the engagement ring until now. She'd worn it for over a year, after all, so it was almost part of her. She took it off, having to lick her finger first, and stared at the large stone, the garishly large stone, in its tacky, flashy, raised setting that caught on everything. She didn't even like the ugly thing anymore. Most likely his mother had picked it out.

After a few lines about returning the wedding presents and gift certificates, he concluded: *you'll consider us even. H.*

H? Hero? Hamlet? What did he think she was, his secretary?

Louisa wished she was upstairs in his fancy apartment with its white leather sofa — and her red lipstick. Instead she replied on the back of the check, before she wrapped it around his ring. She wrote: *We'll never be even, Howard, because I am a better person than you will ever be. Love, Louisa.*

Chapter Three

Homeless.

How in the world had it come to pass that Louisa Waldon, age twenty-seven, was homeless? She'd studied hard, worked hard, lived a decent life — and now all her belongings were wedged in an old gray Toyota. She could not even put the front seat back to sleep, if she could find a place in the middle of Manhattan to take a nap. The only consolation she could give herself, meager though it was, was that not a quarter of the stuff would have fit in Howard's Porsche. And she wasn't a bag lady.

No one would rent her an apartment, not without a job. A decent hotel would have gobbled what remained of her savings — and the thousand-dollar wedding gift Bernie told her to keep, because she'd need it now more than she ever would have with the bastard supporting her. A not-so-decent hotel would have been slightly less voracious, but less safe. She could find a motel out of the City, but she'd still be going through her bank account at a prodigious rate — and be far away from job interviews and employment agencies. She knew better than most, having handled the personnel department at her company, how long it took to find a decent position and how many other applicants there were. Résumés had to be checked, senior department heads had to be consulted — and what could she answer when they asked why she'd left her last position? Because she was a fool? That was sure to win high points at the interview.

She didn't want another job like hers anyway. Or a stale-smelling, insect-harboring walk-up like her apartment before Howard. Or battening herself on her friends.

She could have crashed on someone's couch for a few days, Louisa knew, but she was too humiliated to ask. Why should her friends suffer for her own lack of judgment, or Howard's lack of scruples?

Louisa didn't know what she wanted. What she did not want was the noise and confusion that surrounded her, the dirty air, the dirty looks from the cab drivers. She didn't want a high-pressure job, even if it came with a high salary. She didn't want singles bars, blind dates, personal

31

ads, or waiting to see if Howard ever called her so she could not answer.

She mightn't be able to go home again — not to Howard's apartment and not to the old house in Queens her mother'd sold years ago when she moved to West Palm — but she could go to the summer house. It was almost May, anyway, so it didn't matter that the old beach cottage had no heat. There was a fireplace, and she could burn the furniture when she ran out of money, like an old-time heroine.

Yeah, Louisa decided, she'd get on the Long Island Expressway and drive almost until she ran out of road. Paumonok Harbor was a little village on the edge of the toney Hamptons. Not yet discovered by the mansion-builders, it still had potato fields and fishermen. Her family had owned the cottage since her grandparents' time, and she'd visited every summer when she was a kid. Her mother used to spend time there, but now she preferred her friends and card games in Florida. Annie sent her kids to camp — for self-preservation, most likely — so they'd been renting the cottage out. This year they hadn't. The real estate agent had said she couldn't rent it, not in such dilapidated condition, except to college kids working out east for the summer. What the kids would pay in rent couldn't pay for the repairs.

Well, those same repairs would be a lot less costly if Louisa did them herself. She could paint and hammer and re-grout the bathroom. Grout was the stuff that went between the tiles, wasn't it? What she didn't know she could learn, Louisa told herself, thinking of old man Redstone, who used to look after the cottage. He wasn't the brightest bulb in the pack, and he'd managed, before he retired. She refused to consider that if the old handyman had been a bit handier, the house wouldn't look like an abandoned fishing shack. Her mother was going to have to pay someone anyway if she wanted to keep getting the rental income. She was willing to buy materials and stuff for Louisa to do it.

"Are you sure you want to go so far away, Louisa?" Her mother's voice was full of doubt when Louisa called her from the McDonald's on the Manorville Road. "It's so . . . so empty out there."

Empty sounded good to Louisa right now. Empty, quiet, peaceful. "I'm sure. Just 'til I can decide what I want to do with my life."

"But there are no men out there for you."

"If there's an electrician and a plumber to do the technical stuff, I'll be happy."

"That's not what I meant, Louisa. You shouldn't be alone. Go to your sister's."

Annie's? Alone would be heaven by comparison. "I'll be fine, Ma, I just need to be by myself for awhile, a little solitude."

Well, there was plenty of that at the old house. Not much pressure in the shower, after she begged old man Redstone to come turn the water on for her, and not much light through the creeper-covered windows, or heat, with a squirrel nest falling down the chimney when Louisa opened the damper. But there was a lot of solitude. According to the guy at the post office, when she went to change her mailing address, she was the only current resident of Whaler's Drive. There were only three other houses along the unpaved street anyway, one for sale, one waiting for summer renters, and the Mahoney place that was boarded up. The old couple were still getting their mail forwarded to Florida, but word was Mrs. Mahoney'd had a heart attack, so no one knew if they'd be back for the season at all. The rural carrier, whom Louisa interpreted as the mailman, wasn't going to be happy to add another one-stop road to his route, and an unpaved one at that.

She hadn't been here two days and someone was mad at her already? Louisa almost volunteered to rent a post office box and pick up the mail herself every day, until she remembered all the times she'd volunteered to pick up Howard's dry cleaning, Howard's resoled shoes, and Howard's mother's repaired jewelry and watches. Her postage stamps were paying for free delivery, damn it, and Louisa was going to get free delivery, even if she did have to install a mailbox a truck-convenient distance from the curb, exactly forty-eight inches high, on a sturdy post, and set in concrete.

"Else the kids'll knock it down every Saturday night."

The hardware store had everything, plus a few snickers when she came back for a bucket to mix the concrete in. And a shovel to dig the hole. And screws to attach the effing black box to the effing crooked post, after she got the concrete off her hands so she could dig the wood splinters from the post out of the blisters from the digging. At least she had a screwdriver. And she hadn't had to ask anyone for help.

As soon as her hands healed a little and her back stopped aching, she'd start in on the overgrown vines and shrubs, then scrub the windows so she could look out at the view. The bay was two blocks away, but all the houses on Whaler's Drive faced an undeveloped wetland parcel. When they were children, Louisa and Annie'd called it the woods, where they'd go berry-picking, tadpole-catching and turtle-watching along the deer paths. Through adult eyes, Louisa could see that the woods were not that extensive, with low scrub trees and wild grasses and prickly briars, not some enchanted forest. Still, she'd be hearing birdsong instead of traffic, and smelling growing things and water instead of bus exhaust. She wouldn't be looking at steel and glass and brick, thank goodness.

At night, she'd be looking at . . . nothing. There was not a single light through any of the front windows, even the ones with no blocking foliage. Nothing. Lions and tigers and — no, she would not let her imagination run amok. This was the country. But what if something happened to her, if an axe murderer, say, should creep out of the woods? No one would hear her screams. No one would even know if she lay dead on her dusty rug, not 'til the catalogs started to pile up in her shiny new black mailbox. How long before the mail got forwarded? Who was going to write to her anyway?

Axe murderers, she reassured herself even as she lit every lamp in the house, were, thankfully, few and far between. Knocking over mailboxes was about the extent of the crime rate, according to the local weekly newspaper. That and a couple of drunken drivers. This was not a high-crime area, even in this day and age. Why, Louisa'd bet half the Harborites still left their doors unlocked. Hers, of course, were locked and bolted.

No matter how confident she tried to be, Louisa couldn't sleep. Now the lights were in her eyes, the house was too quiet, her bed was too empty. No, she wouldn't think about Howard or any other mean, ugly marauder. Instead, she'd keep her mind busy with all the things she had to do to-morrow, after the man came to clean the chimney and put a screen guard across the top. She'd find out how to sign up for cable so she could watch old movies all night, get a library card and take out an armload of books the way she did when she was eleven. She'd buy new garden shears, and gloves this time, and she'd get chains for the doors. No, she'd get a dog.

Howard hated dogs. Too much responsibility, he'd said, too much dirt and drool. He didn't want dog hairs on his upholstery and he wouldn't let one in his car, if it could have fit in that four inches behind the front seat. Cats got on the counters and birds made too much noise. All Louisa had was a pair of goldfish, still with her sister, if Annie'd remembered to feed them, and her kids hadn't eaten them.

But a dog, all her own. Louisa smiled at the thought, and thought she hadn't smiled since before the would-be wedding. Yes, a dog was just what she needed. In the face of such trauma, such personal upheaval as the loss of one's sense of self, sense of direction, sense that she ever had any sense whatsoever, some women went shopping. Others went to the medicine cabinet or the local bar. Or on food binges. Louisa went to the pound, eating a chocolate bar along the way. The chimney guy'd been so late, she barely had time for her other errands.

There was an arrow across the street from the hardware store that pointed toward the animal shelter, room in her front seat, and no Howard telling her no. Definitely a sign from God.

"You're not wanting a pet for the summer, are you?" the stocky, raspy-voiced woman in a tan uniform at the shelter asked after introducing herself as Jeanette, the adoptions counselor. Also the animal control officer, kennel manager and cage cleaner. "We get crowds in here every spring," she went on as she led Louisa through the empty building to the outdoor pens, "wanting a dog or a cat to keep the kiddies company at the beach house. Then they dump them on our doorstep when the kids go back to school. Or they just leave 'em on the streets. That's why we make you sign a contract, pay for the license, and swear to get the animal spayed or neutered. Some other places, they make you have a fenced-in yard, and they go inspect your house to make sure you don't live on a bad corner, or run a dog-fight ring in your cellar or something." She shrugged. "You look decent, and I figure our dogs need homes too bad to be too fussy. 'Sides, I know where you live."

Louisa felt as if she were making the wedding vows she hadn't had the chance to speak. Do you, Louisa, take this abandoned mutt, 'til death do you part, in sickness and in health, to have and to hold on a leash . . . ?

She did. She would. She'd think later about finding a Manhattan apartment that permitted dogs.

Well, if Louisa'd been looking for love to replace the louse, she'd come to the right spot. The dogs were throwing themselves against the bars of their cages, yipping their eagerness to go home to her run-down cottage, to stick their heads out the window of her old Toyota, to eat whatever kibble she could provide, even if it wasn't a premium brand. Louisa was an angel to them, a goddess, a best friend.

Now all she had to do was pick one. She walked up and down outside the cages, reading the tags. Not a puppy; she didn't know how to train one. Not an old dog; she couldn't bear the thought of someone else leaving her. Not too big to fit in the car, not too small in case Annie's kids came to visit, nothing that looked like it would get into fights, chase cars, or need a lot of grooming. Not the one who cowered in the back of its cage, or the one who almost climbed the chain links of the outdoor run. She would not ask what would happen to the dogs she did not choose.

Jeanette was looking at the clock in the kennel. "We close soon, you know."

Louisa bet the woman took longer to choose from a dinner menu than she was giving her to select a lifetime companion. "I'm just not sure," she said, over the din.

"Then come back tomorrow when you can take them out for a walk, see how they handle."

Go back to that dark, empty house alone? Louisa walked toward the cage that held a big reddish hound with soulful eyes.

"Howls, that one does. Wants to be on the scent, too. Take your eyes off him a minute and he'll follow his nose to the next county."

Louisa didn't want a dog that wasn't going to be loyal. God knew she'd had enough of that. "What about this one?"

"The golden? She's a handful." Jeanette looked at Louisa in her size-five jeans. "You're not up to her weight, unless you want to pay for a trainer."

Louisa kept walking.

"Goldens shed bad, anyway."

Louisa stopped in front of the pen of a slightly smaller, dark grayish dog with matted curly hair, and a short tail that was barely wagging, as if the dog were not willing to expend a lot of energy on yet another fruitless effort.

"He barks a lot, according to the woman who brought him in. That's why she couldn't keep him. Her apartment neighbors complained."

"That's what I want, a watchdog."

41

Jeanette shrugged and started to unlatch the cage. "Sad story, this one. Lived with an old lady, he did. They say a nephew bought him for her, to ease his conscience, I guess, for leaving the woman alone. But she tripped over him, broke her hip, and landed in a convalescent home. The neighbor found the dog wandering in the street — that's why he looks so ratty — but the old woman said she didn't want him back, just to trip her up again. Then she died at the home, with no relatives coming at all. Sad way to go."

Jeanette reached for a leash hanging next to the cage door. "The neighbor left messages with the nephew, the bastard. He never called back." She shook her head while opening the cage door and hooking a leash to the dog's collar. "Here. Take him around back. You'll see he's been trained. A real gentleman. Some kind of terrier, we think, Kerry blue or maybe giant schnauzer. Something like that. Never got his name, either."

The dog put his bearded muzzle in Louisa's hand, then took his place on her left side, looking up with big brown eyes, waiting for a command, waiting for a decision, waiting for yet another person to walk out on him.

"I know what it's like to lose someone, too," Louisa whispered, her choice already made. The dog was tall, dark, and handsome, so she called him Galahad. Every maiden in distress ought to have a knight in shining armor. Or matted fur.

Louisa didn't sleep well that night either, despite the dog on an old blanket at the side of her bed. Galahad barked at every branch that scraped against the side of the house in that evening's wind and rain storm, and every time the hot water heater kicked on. And he had fleas. Which meant that Louisa had fleas, because the dog didn't stay on the floor for long.

Worst of all, for Louisa's peace of mind, was that the dog, her guardian protector against things that went bump in the night, had to go o-u-t. On a leash. In the wind and the rain and the spooky, scary, pitch-black dark where things hid in the woods.

Lions and tigers and bears, oh, my.

Chapter Four

Fences were good.

Robert Frost liked them, the dog pound lady liked them, and Galahad would just have to get used to them in the backyard, when he got back from the vet where he was being bathed and neutered on the same day. Louisa felt bad for putting the sweetheart through another ordeal when he was hardly over the last, but the bugs and the balls had to go. Maybe he'd blame the adoption people instead of Louisa.

A fence was a good idea in other ways, besides eliminating midnight dog walks and keeping rabbits out of the garden she was planning. The barrier was symbolic, Louisa convinced herself as she struggled to get the rolls of chicken wire out of the car without shredding her shirt and her skin on the edges. She'd be marking her territory, like Galahad. This was her place, the mesh was going to tell the world, with her dog to defend it. She'd be safe inside, where no one could come along and steal her peace of mind again. Just a girl and her four-legged friend, against the world. No trespassing, not on her seedlings or her sore heart.

Granted, Louisa knew she was asking a lot of four-foot-tall chicken wire, but that was all she could afford. Besides, she could put it up herself, nailing it to the old split rail fence along the property line. A thief could cut it, a deer could jump it, rabbits could burrow under it, especially where Louisa hadn't pulled the roll of wire tight enough, but she had her enclosure. She didn't think Galahad would try to get out, for the dog had seemed content enough to stay by her side, not letting her out of his sight in the house. He suffered from insecurity, she supposed, and understood it well.

Louisa even figured out how to make a gate of sorts, with hook and eye latches from the hardware store. Hell, she was getting so good at hardware, maybe she'd get a job at Home Depot when her money ran out.

Which might be sooner than she supposed, after the vet bill. No one ever told her how expensive keeping a pet could be. Her goldfish cost what? Five dollars a year? Galahad's bill was two pages long: surgery, anesthesia, bath, brush out, inoculations, blood tests, pills to prevent heartworm, and some stuff to put behind his neck to keep fleas and ticks away.

"Is this stuff safe?" she asked the white-smocked girl at the desk who was processing Louisa's credit card into catatonia.

"Safer than Lyme disease and the allergies dogs get to flea saliva. Oh, and you better take some of this flea spray for the dog's bedding, before they start breeding in your rugs."

Louisa tried not to scratch at the bites on her legs and paid cash for the can of insecticide. "But you're worth every penny of the cost," she told the still-groggy dog on the ride home, patting his head that rested on her thigh. "And you're even more handsome than I thought." He smelled a lot better too, but she didn't want to hurt his feelings, not after what he'd been through.

Did dogs know? she wondered. "Jeanette at the dog pound made me do it," she told him, in case. It would be a hell of a note if her own dog, her own suddenly expensive-investment dog, didn't like Louisa any better than her expensive ex-fiancé did.

Galahad licked her hand.

"Good doggy," Louisa said, and sniffed back a tear. Someone loved her.

Louisa woke up the next morning feeling better rested than she had in weeks, both she and the dog having had a good night's sleep. The dog had been drugged, and Louisa'd been exhausted from the unaccustomed physical labor. Besides, she had her fence, and the satisfaction of a job well-done. As soon as she had her shower, her breakfast and walked the dog, she'd start on the yard work.

Right after she renailed the section of fence that had come down.

With pad and pencil in hand, Louisa did a survey of her new kingdom. The outside of the house looked worse than it was, Louisa told herself. Once she cleared the vines and brambles off the windows and the weeds off the front walk, trimmed the bushes and gave the wood trim a scrape and a coat of paint, it wouldn't look so much like a handyman's special. Some flowers along the split rail fence, fresh curtains in the windows, a new coat of tar in the grass-cracked driveway, and the old place wouldn't look like she felt, old and uncared-for. Those things she could do herself, and a bunch of the inside jobs. She had one of those how-to-fix everything books, didn't she?

Louisa threw herself into the job, making lists, buying supplies and more home-repair books in equal numbers. She woke up early, worked 'til late, read 'til she fell asleep — and went whole hours without thinking of Horrid Howard.

When she took breaks, Louisa took Galahad on long walks, mostly on the beach. The bay was two blocks away, but the ocean was less than a ten-minute drive. She'd forgotten how exciting the ocean could be, how changeable the scenery near the shore. Every day, by different light, the water took on another color, a different texture. The horizon was so far, the waves so endless, Louisa couldn't help being reminded of her own insignificance in the grand scheme of things. And if she was small in the universe, her misfortunes were positively petty. Besides, the dog was thrilled with the beach. How could anyone be miserable watching a silly mutt play tag with the waves or chase a seagull or roll on a dead fish? Louisa kept looking over her shoulder in case Jeanette from the animal shelter caught her letting the dog off the leash to run loose.

Despite "Born Free" echoing off the dunes, Louisa was careful to clean up after the dog, remembering Manhattan rules and Manhattan mess when dog owners didn't. Here, little by little, she learned to listen for the surf instead of sirens, and wake up to birdsong instead of the screech of tires. When she went back to the city, back to the real world, Louisa decided, she'd have to come out to the Harbor on weekends more, just to refresh herself in this slower pace, this newfound quiet. No makeup, no panty hose, no dry-clean-only suits — and no men.

The males she did get to know were the bald old guy at the hardware store who had been there before sponge brushes were invented, the cigar-chewer at the lumber yard, and the belly-over-the-belt plumber who came to fix the leaking pipes. They were enough. This was Louisa's make-believe escapist fantasy. Who wanted trolls in Never-Never Land?

Louisa kept to herself in the little village, not ready yet to confront old friends or make new ones. Just a girl and her dog, sufficient unto themselves. She didn't need anyone — except the stooped pharmacist at the one drugstore who showed her what poison ivy looked like, too late.

She did discover the joy of yard sales, though. She bought new pillows for the living room sofa, and a new lamp for her bedroom — for pocket change, it seemed. All the stuff in the world was out there, and she could afford it! She replaced the chipped juice glasses and the rickety stool and the ripped patio umbrella. She even bought a weed whacker that only needed a new cord, the people assured her, for two dollars. Heck, she could fix that easily. Bill at the hardware store had taught her how, after she ran over the electric lawn mower's power line the third time. She could find almost anything she wanted at garage sales, stuff she desperately needed, and stuff she never knew she wanted 'til she saw it. Howard hated stuff. Clutter, thingies, knickknacks, junk, tchotchkes, he belittled anything he didn't like or couldn't see a use for. Louisa'd thrown out boxes of belongings when she'd moved into his apartment, never considering that she was tossing away bits and pieces of herself. Well, she was starting over with a blue pottery vase to put flowers in, a ficus tree taller than she was, and salt and pepper shakers in the shape of penguins, just because they made her smile. She doubted there was anything whatsoever in Howard's entire apartment that cost under a dollar, and nothing that gave him as much pleasure.

Louisa also found new satisfaction in

growing things. Pansies, geraniums, impatiens, all found spots around the house, along the fence, on the porch, climbing the mailbox post. The books she took out of the library said marigolds were easy to grow from seeds, and by god, they were. So were peas, sprouting an inch a day, it seemed. Louisa and Galahad made notes on their walks, studying other people's yards and window boxes, then buying more seeds, more plants, another package of Miracle-Gro.

Slowly but . . . slowly, the house was getting ready to face the world, and so was Louisa. Well, at least she could now face the pudgy teenager at the gas station without worrying that no man was ever going to find her attractive again.

Louisa had her work — and her sore muscles to prove it — her dog, and her library books. (The chocolate was a given.) While she wouldn't go quite so far as to say she was happy, she hardly shed a tear anymore, and was getting more satisfaction out of her roses and her re-bricked front path than she ever got out of conducting interviews and reading résumés. The only flies in her ointment — once the exterminator said the bugs in the kitchen were ants, not termites — were the neighbors.

The Mahoney house on Louisa's left was still vacant, as was the one for sale, but the house on her right was rented. Louisa had no idea who held the lease, but she was pretty sure there were laws forbidding so many people congregating in one place every weekend. If there weren't, there ought to be. Somewhat younger than Louisa, at least five couples appeared every Friday and partied with at least fifty others, it seemed, until Sunday. They played their music too loudly, parked their cars all over the street, and yelled at Galahad when he barked at the slamming doors and outdoor conversations. Worse, they sat on the fence that separated the two properties, breaking the top split rails and knocking down her chicken wire. They ran over her geraniums trying to fit so many vehicles in the driveway, and took a chunk out of the old oak tree at the sidewalk.

The village clerk told her to talk to the police, the police told her to talk to the code enforcer, the code enforcer was in court being sued for the selective issuance of warrants. Louisa couldn't figure out if the guy was a Republican ticketing Democrats, or a Democrat going after contributors to the Republican mayor's friends. She didn't give a rap, either. Those raucous, disrespectful renters next door had to go.

A caretaker came by the place twice a week, picking up the stray beer bottles from the lawn on Mondays, and bringing the empty trash cans back from the curb on Thursdays. Louisa made a point of waiting for the fellow after the last weekend, and her last geranium-based fence post became so many toothpicks. He was a dark-haired, tallish guy, without the paunch so prevalent in the handymen she'd been calling for estimates on the roof. In fact, she supposed some women might call him handsome, in a coarse, T-shirt and blue jeans kind of way. Then again, some woman thought the rat-faced roofer she hadn't hired was handsome, for the jerk boasted of his six kids.

This house-watcher needed a haircut, a shave, and a lesson in manners. He didn't bother turning around when Louisa walked over and said, "Excuse me." Maybe he didn't understand English, for many of the workers in town seemed to be Spanish-speaking, so Louisa tried *"Buenos dias?"*

Nothing. Granted the jerk was fixing the screen on the front door of the rental house, where one of the partyers had likely put his fist through it, but he could have nodded or something.

53

"Excuse me," she said a bit louder. "I need to get a message to the owner of this house. Could you give me his phone number?"

The man put down a razor-cutter knife and another tool with a rolling wheel in it. Louisa would have liked to ask that one's purpose, but the man's scowl, when he turned, did not encourage polite conversation. He straightened up, proving even taller than Louisa had estimated, tanned, kind of weathered-looking. He also looked somewhat familiar to Louisa, but that could have been because she'd been seeing so many of these rough-and-ready sorts of workers. He didn't take off his sunglasses, and didn't smile a welcome. In fact, he just stared at her rudely. Or she thought he did, through the dark shades.

"The owner?" she repeated, almost shouting by now. "I'd like to inform him about the conduct of his tenants. Unless you already have, of course." She indicated the torn screen. "Precluding the necessity."

The man still didn't speak. Lord, had she used words of too many syllables for the uncouth cretin? She pointed to her broken fence. "His renters are ruining my property. Do you understand?"

At least the workman looked toward the

fallen rails, which were, admittedly, old and rickety. He just tilted his head to the side.

Louisa took a deep breath and tried again. "Please tell the owner that I would like to speak to him. My name is —"

"Louisa Waldon."

"You, ah, know me?" Perhaps she'd met him all those years ago when she summered here with her grandparents. Or maybe he was one of the garbage men, moonlighting.

"Vivian Rivera," was all he said, naming one of her mother's old friends from summers at Paumonok Harbor. Aunt Vinnie had even been invited to — Oh, God. He knew. Louisa damned herself a million times for the blush she could feel spreading across her cheeks. "Then if you know who I am, I suppose you know about the . . . the wedding."

He nodded slightly. "Damned shame."

She tried for a smile and a shrug. "Life goes on."

"I meant the Porsche."

Chapter Five

Louisa had to look away. At her flowers, her dog, the weeded drive. Here she was making a new life for herself, finding simple pleasures she never knew existed — and her old life was taking out the trash next door. For a minute she wanted to cry, experiencing the pain and humiliation all over again. Then she wanted to strangle Aunt Vinnie's scrawny neck. How could her mother's old friend gossip about Louisa's utter mortification — and with a handyman, no less! Granted she should have gone to visit Aunt Vinnie when she got here, or when she got a little more settled, but Louisa hadn't been ready to face anyone who knew her before, to hear their commiseration and see pity in their eyes. But a handyman? If this . . . this person knew about the wedding, chances were everyone in the town knew. He looked just the type to sit around bars on weekends, laughing about the summer people and the rich renters, while he didn't return their phone calls, showed up late for appointments, and charged exorbitant fees. Well, this ignorant, arrogant bastard wouldn't laugh at her.

Louisa raised her chin. "I prefer not to speak of that matter. In fact, I'd prefer to speak to your employer about the renters and the noise and damage they create."

In answer, the redneck removed his sunglasses, finally. She recognized the expression he wore, for she'd seen it at the hardware store and the lumberyard, when the carpenters and plumbers and masons looked at her as if she were too dumb to know which end of the hammer to use. This guy's eyes were a remarkable shade of blue, though, somewhere between sapphire and summer sky. With his dark hair and the black stubble on his tanned, chiseled cheeks, the man looked like he'd stepped off the cover of one of her mother's romance novels. Maybe that's why he still looked familiar, though she was positive she'd remember meeting such a deliciously handsome man. And didn't the devil just know it, Louisa'd bet. Well, she wasn't hungry.

She raised her chin another notch, trying to appear taller. "What do you intend to do about my fence? My sister and her family are coming for Memorial Day weekend and I want the place to look nice.

Besides, I need the fence for my dog."

The man looked at the fallen fence, the fou-fou dog, and the self-righteous female. He sneered.

Dante didn't like fences. All the rich new homeowners were installing gates and high hedges around their properties, as if they were too good to be seen by the common folk. They didn't care about community or friendliness, only protecting their privacy — as if anyone was going to peep in their windows. Who cared what a bunch of Wall Street Waldos did on weekends? Even low fences ruined the natural look of the neighborhood, besides chopping up the landscape into little boxes.

He didn't like trophy dogs, those purebreds with pedigrees longer than their tails that the tourists were all dragging around at the end of their monogrammed leashes. One summer the renters all showed up in Mercedes convertibles; the next they all had SUVs to carry the babies and the dark-skinned nannies. This year they all had Hummers and high-bred dogs. Maybe the dogs ate the babies. Hell, if they lavished as much attention on the kids as they did on the dogs, they wouldn't need the baby-sitters. This particular animal was groomed to an inch of its curly coat, with a ridiculous mustache. That's why the poor mutt barked all the time, Dante supposed, because it was too embarrassed to stand and be stared at.

Most of all, what Dante Rivera liked least was women like Louisa Waldon. Oh, he knew all about Paumonok Harbor's newest and most notorious resident. He knew all about the sports car and the aborted wedding, when the bride was too drunk to recognize her own guests. He knew that her wedding dress cost more than his sister spent on three years' worth of clothes, and he knew that she'd been here nearly a month without calling on Aunt Vinnie. She was a beauty, he'd give her that, if a man liked that brittle, sharp-boned, blond look. In his opinion, the lady looked a lot better now, with some natural color to her cheeks, and her hair gathered back with one of those elastic things, instead of piled on her head in stiff, sprayed sausage curls. And her legs, well, a man could dream at night about those long, smooth tanned legs, rubbing against his, wrapping around him.

Dream was all a guy could do, Dante knew, taking his eyes off her denim cutoffs and what they cut off. The woman was a man-hater. He'd heard it from Bill at the hardware store, how she wouldn't give any of the guys the time of day. Okay, maybe she'd been burned, but she wouldn't go to the PTA Game Night or the fire department's pancake breakfast, either. They weren't good enough for her around here. He put his sunglasses back on so he wouldn't have to notice the heightened color from his rude staring. Well, no Big City spoiled beauty was good enough for him to waste his time on, either. Even if she did have pretty green eyes and a cute little nose. Why, if the haughty bitch raised that nose in the air any higher, she'd fall over on her cute little ass. He went back to fixing the broken screen.

Of all the arrogant jackasses, Louisa thought, this one took the prize. For sure he'd never get a job where she was personnel director, no, not even as under-janitor on the night shift. She tapped her foot and cleared her throat. "About the renters."

Dante didn't like the renters any more than he liked fences and fancy dogs. A friend had called in a favor though, and he was stuck with them. "I'll talk to them," was all he said, his back to the impatient, demanding female.

"And what about my fence?"

Damn, she was a persistent broad, kind of like one of those kamikaze mosquitoes. Dante put down his tools, cursing her for the time he was wasting, and looked at the tangle of wire mesh and wood between them. He walked over and picked up a fallen rail, pulled the bent chicken wire off it with the merest tug, and snapped the post in half. "Rotten."

Louisa gasped. "But that's my fence."

"Then fix it. The weight of your chicken wire pulled it down, that and all the vines you've got growing up it."

The runner beans were getting a bit thick, Louisa supposed, but if the visitors next door hadn't sat on the rail, she was sure it wouldn't have broken, and she told the top-lofty laborer so. He just shrugged and kicked at one of the uprights, which promptly uprooted itself and keeled over. "Rotten," he repeated.

Louisa bit her lip. There was no way on earth she was going to be able to dig more fence posts. At least twenty, she thought, looking around. The mailbox construction had almost killed her. Besides, she couldn't afford all new posts and rails. But she needed that fence. Maybe she could just string the wire up with tomato stakes? She furrowed her brow in concentration.

Cripes, the woman wasn't going to cry, was she? Over a lousy fence? Dante hated weepy females more than anything. "I'll, uh, see what I have lying around."

She brightened immediately. "Would you? And I'll pay you to make the repairs."

Louisa knew she'd just told herself the lout was unemployable, but at least he seemed responsible. He showed up on time to gather the empty trash cans back from the curb before they rolled in the street, like hers did the rainy morning she'd put Galahad out in the backyard and gone back to sleep. Gally's barking at the noise would have woken the neighbors for three blocks away.

"No, you couldn't pay me enough."

The going rate for carpenters and such was steep, but Louisa guessed she could match Aunt Vinnie's price. "I'm sure I can pay whatever you get from Mrs. Rivera."

"I'm sure you can't." The last thing Dante Rivera needed in his life right now was another difficult, demanding woman. He already had his aunt Vinnie, who was forgetting things, and his cousin Francine, whose husband kept forgetting he had an ex-wife and kid waiting for the support checks. He also had an ex-wife of his own who was making outrageous requests for his time and money and — No, he wouldn't even consider what else Susan wanted from him. He did not need yet another needy woman.

He'd seen this one struggling with an old wooden ladder. It was a miracle the antique hadn't collapsed with her on it. And he'd seen her trying to mow the grass with that relic of a mower, when anyone could have told her it needed the blade sharpened. He was not getting involved. He didn't know what the blonde was trying to prove, but he wasn't going to encourage her by helping, the way some turkey'd encouraged Susan and her new lover by telling them what good parents they'd be. No, the sooner Ms. Louisa Waldon had her fill of playing house and moved back to the city, back to *Bride's Magazine* and the rest of that crap, the better all around. Otherwise, before he knew it, Dante'd be mowing her damn grass and reshingling the roof for her! No, he was not getting involved, not with this ruinous female who had no business being here in the first place. No way. Never.

"I'll think about it."

"Were we that bad?" Louisa asked her sister.

Annie poured another glass of iced tea and looked over the rear porch to where her darlings were fighting over who got to throw the ball for Galahad. "Worse. We always wanted to play with the same dolls, at the same time. My two usually have different interests."

Yeah, Louisa thought, Alex was into shoving and Lisa was into screeching. Neither of the kids wanted to be here, away from their friends, the malls, their own TV, telephone and computer-equipped bedrooms. Louisa's gardens were suffering the consequences, and poor Galahad was faring little better. He'd been waiting ten minutes, his tongue hanging out, for one of the brats to throw the tennis ball already. The kids hadn't looked twice at all the games and jigsaw puzzles Louisa'd bought for them at yard sales, the games she and Annie had played for hours. Alex only wanted to play games on the computer, and Lisa pleaded to try on makeup. Louisa locked her bedroom door. She only wished she were on the other side of it.

"Why don't you tell them to go play in the woods? We spent hours in there, hunting for salamanders."

Annie looked at her as if she'd grown another head. "You really don't like my children, do you? I told Mama you didn't."

"How can you say that? I love your children. They're my only niece and nephew, aren't they?"

"Well, you might as well tell them to go play in traffic, though God knows they'd be safe on this block. But those empty lots are full of ticks carrying a hundred different incurable diseases half the doctors in the world can't recognize. Besides, who knows what kind of perverts hang out in there?"

Louisa did not want to hear about lurkers in the woods across the street from her house. "Oh, come on, Annie. The worst that ever happened there was when you pushed the Mahoneys' grandson in the swamp for trying to steal a kiss."

Annie rattled the ice cubes in her glass and smiled. "I wonder what became of old Jimmie."

Most likely he was bald and soft-bellied, Louisa speculated, just like Annie's husband Jeff the insurance salesman, who was watching a car race on TV. A car race, for heaven's sake, when the beach was two blocks away.

"Speaking of Jimmie," Annie said, "what do you hear from Howard? No, don't get mad. Mama told me to ask."

"Why? She asks herself every time she calls. Howard and I are not in communication, if it is any of your business."

"Don't go getting all huffy, Lou, we just worry about you."

"You can all stop worrying. I am doing fine."

"Yes, but what is it that you are doing out here? I mean, you're not working, not even sending out résumés, Mama says."

"You can't tell what I've been doing? All the flowers and the fixing? I've been making the house more presentable for next year's renters, that's what I've been doing." She tossed one of the new chair cushions at Annie.

"You think the place looks better with pigeons on the pillows?"

"Those are doves, and yes, I do."

Annie threw the pillow back. "Well, maybe you could take over for Martha Stewart. But, Lou, you're out here in the back of beyond. How are you going to meet any men?"

"I meet lots of men. There's Bill at the hardware store, and Ralph the mailman. I'm not sure about the bank manager's name, but he was very nice about transferring my account. The garbage man is my favorite, though. He whistles."

Annie made the snorting noise that had always annoyed Louisa. "That is not the kind of man I meant, and you know it. I meant the marriageable kind, educated, refined, successful, not some backwater, blue-collar bozo."

Reminded of blue collars — and blue eyes — Louisa asked, "Do you remember how we all laughed when Aunt Vinnie asked if she could bring an escort to the, ah, to the wedding?"

"We were all guessing how old her companion would be. Aunt Vinnie must be pushing seventy-five."

"So who did she bring? I can't quite recall."

"I'm not surprised you can't remember. I was only surprised you could still stand, after what you drank that night. We all thought Jeff would be driving you to the hospital to have your stomach pumped."

"Aunt Vinnie?" Louisa prompted, to get the conversation away from that night.

"Oh, she had her nephew drive her in so she wouldn't have to take the train and taxis from the — You slyboots, you. You've been seeing Dante Rivera, haven't you?"

So he wasn't just a common laborer, Louisa acknowledged; he was Aunt Vinnie's nephew, likely one of those locals who never managed to extend their horizons past the county line. "Tall, blue eyes, kind of nice-looking?"

"Kind of? Are you still in an alcohol fog? It's no wonder you didn't see him at the catering hall, 'cause your bridesmaids were stuck to him like mailing labels." Annie pounded the pillow. "This is perfect! Mama will be thrilled."

Oh, lord. "For heaven's sake, I just met the man, Annie. He's working at the house next door, and he's rude and condescending."

Annie was grinning. "And divorced, I hear."

"Most likely some divorce attorney took him to the cleaners — or the laundromat, in his case — and that's why the man hates women."

"Seemed to me as if he liked them just fine. Jeff and I were making bets as to which of your friends he would have gone home with, if he didn't have to drive Aunt Vinnie. I picked Sarabelle Delehanty."

"Sarabelle is overweight and — and I am not interested. I am not in the market for a man, and if I were, a conceited clod like your Dante Rivera is the last one I'd choose."

"Now I am really worried, Lou. If you

can look at a hunk like Dante and not go all shivery, then you really have retreated from the real world."

"Why, because I want to make a place for myself, by myself? What's wrong with that?"

"What's wrong is you'll never find a husband that way, never have a real home of your own, or children. You do want kids, don't you?"

Louisa didn't answer. She was too busy watching the two brats in her backyard toss clods of dirt and marigold seedlings at each other while the dog barked in an agitated frenzy. "You do hate my children!" Annie wailed. "I told Mama you did!"

Chapter Six

By the end of the long weekend, Louisa felt the way her fence looked: miserable, mangled, and dragging on the ground. They'd both been trampled on, and she couldn't blame it all on the obnoxious renters next door. She waved good-bye to her sister and her family with tears in her eyes.

"Don't cry, Lou. Mama will call every night. And we'll come back real soon."

That's why she was crying.

Now she had to see about fixing the fence for Galahad, who was on a tie-out rope, wrapping himself around the bushes, the porch furniture, and Louisa's legs. Either that or she'd have to go walk him at eleven o'clock at night, with a flashlight. No flashlight was bright enough for that.

She thought of putting the dog out in back without a rope, because he always came when she called him, but what if Galahad chased a rabbit or a cat? Worse, what if he went after a raccoon that could tear him to pieces? The idea of losing her dog, of seeing him injured, was wrenching.

In such a short time, the mutt had become an indispensable part of her life, so much so that she wondered how she'd managed without him. And he returned her affection tenfold. He'd romped with the children, but never close enough to be stepped on. He'd taken food from Jeff, but never wagged his tail after Jeff yelled at him for barking during the sports scores. He'd let Annie scratch his ears, but never rolled over for belly rubs the way he did for Louisa. He liked her best. For sure Howard had never given her half the love, the constant devotion she got from Galahad. The dog listened better, too.

So she'd get his fence fixed, if she had to give up chocolate and yard sales, both.

The renters next door — she never found out their names, or which couple actually held the lease, or if they were even a couple — might not be entirely to blame for the wrecked fence, but one of the jerks in a mile-high Suburban had definitely snapped off another huge branch from the old oak tree at the corner of the two properties. At least the branch had fallen on their side of the yard, but not, to her regret, on the effing car.

They'd destroyed her sleep again with their all-night parties, too. So Aunt

Vinnie's nephew was going to talk to them? Hah. She had a thing or two to say to the man herself when she saw him. Then she remembered he might agree to work for her and tried to get a rein on her aggravation. The man was a boor — a beautiful boor, granted — but he said he might have some old lumber around. You had to cut some slack to a guy with tools, if he ever showed up.

He didn't. Another man, shorter, older, dark-skinned, came to drag back the garbage cans. Then he returned a half-hour later with a chain saw and started to hack up the thick oak branch, tossing the pieces to the back of an old pickup.

Louisa didn't see how she could get the logs to hold up the split rails, but oak burned in a fireplace, didn't it? Louisa waited 'til the worker stopped to put more gas in the chain saw, then went over.

"Excuse me, I was wondering if you are just going to throw out that wood."

The man grinned at her. "Mr. Dante, he says to take it away before the lady next door beeches."

Bitches? So he thought her a complainer, did he? Louisa pasted on a smile. "I am not complaining. In fact I am pleased you are taking care of the mess so quickly. I would like some of the wood, though, if no one else wants it. I guess I'm half-owner of the tree." Not the half that had to dispose of the heavy branches, thank goodness.

"Mrs. Louisa, yes. Mr. Dante, he says so."

"That's Miss Waldon, or just Louisa. I'm not married."

The man grinned wider. "Mr. Dante says that, too. Me, I'm Rico."

If blabbermouthed Dante Rivera worked for free, it was too much. Louisa turned her back on Rico and the free firewood. "Just tell Mr. Da— Mr. Rivera, that I would like to speak with him, when he gets a moment of time."

The sarcasm was wasted on Rico, who just kept smiling. "I'll tell the boss, Mrs. Louisa. He'll find time."

Dante was not thinking of Louisa at all. Not of her fence, at any rate. He figured that if he put off fixing the cursed thing long enough, the annoying female would be back in the city with her tight-ass lawyer. So what if she and her sister had stopped by Aunt Vinnie's at last, with a pot of geraniums — a pot that he'd have to plant? One visit didn't mean the Waldon woman could walk on water, the way Aunt

Vinnie was singing her praises. Of course, with those incredible long legs . . . No, he didn't have time to waste thinking about any transplanted hothouse bloom — and he didn't mean the geranium.

What he had to think about today, between getting three other houses ready for tenants, his nephew to Little League practice on time, and getting his boat in the water, was his ex-wife and her expletive-deleted baby.

"What do you mean, you won't sign the release and waiver of paternal rights?" Richie Newhouse, Dante's lawyer and driving range partner, yelled across the tees. "Susan and this C. A. Chalmers are promising you freedom from child support."

"I read the damn contract. An abrogation of all rights and responsibilities in perpetuity."

"Well, hell, Dante, isn't that what you want?" Richie hit another ball and cursed when it hooked left. "I mean, you don't want any six-year-old dumped on your doorstep calling you Daddy when Susan's latest relationship sours, do you? Worse, she could sue you for college tuition in eighteen years, for a kid you've never seen. Or the kid could claim part of your estate when you're dead. Sign the damned papers already."

Dante set down his golf club and watched his friend hit another hook. "But it's my kid."

"Christ, it's your sperm, nothing more."

"What if those two aren't any good as parents? What if they screw the kid up?"

"Then they'll have to pay the shrink bills, not you." He teed up another ball. "What do you want, visitation rights and the rest of that crap? Susan won't go for it."

"But I might never have another kid. What if it's a son?"

"Sons aren't all they're cracked up to be. You think Junior's going to be your fishing buddy? Think again. He'll be out drinking, driving too fast, giving you gray hairs as soon as he's out of diapers. You want a son? Take one of mine."

"A daughter, then. A pretty little girl."

"With braces and ballet lessons and you'll never see your bathroom again. Trust me, you're better off out of it. Besides, who says this is your last chance at paternity? You're what, thirty-five? Damn, you've got a half-century of potency ahead of you, maybe more with the new drugs. You'll find some sweet young thing sooner or later who'll put a ring through your nose. Pardon, she'll put your ring on her finger, and then she'll turn into a goddamn maternity ward, just like my second wife."

"I'm not interested in any twenty-two-year-olds now. I can't imagine having anything to say to one when I'm forty-five."

Richie waggled his eyebrows. "That's the secret, my friend. You don't talk to them. But, hey, didn't I hear you have a knockout new neighbor over at Whaler's Drive? One of the Waldon girls?"

"Yeah, Louisa. She's trying to fix up the old place."

"Isn't she the one with the vanishing groom? How old is she, anyway?"

"Don't even think about it, bub."

Dante wouldn't think about it either, as he drove to his next appointment. He wouldn't imagine any golden-haired little cherubs with Louisa Waldon's green eyes, no way. Hell, that woman gave off such a chill she made Susan look warm and cuddly, and the last time he'd snuggled with his ex-wife was a heck of a long time before the divorce. He'd bet the belligerent blonde was as cold as a winter flounder, and that was why Louisa's tax attorney had taken a walk. Either that or she had a drinking problem. He pulled into a parking space thinking, Thank god

Louisa Waldon wasn't his problem.

Susan was.

He was here, he was going to do it, give Susan what she wanted, the same as always. She'd wanted to get married, even though he knew they were way too young, so he'd given her a ring. She wanted to be an artist, so he'd built her a studio. A potter. He'd built a kiln. A sculptor, or was it a puppeteer next? Then she'd wanted a divorce, so he'd given her that too, along with the real estate office he'd started. Now she wanted a baby, and he was going to give her that, damn it. How could he refuse when she looked up at him with those pansy-brown eyes? He hadn't been able to say no to her when he was twenty, why should he start now?

The Waldon woman's eyes had fire in them, he'd give her that. Not an ounce of whiny wheedling in them. Damn, why couldn't he get that fence-crazed female out of his mind? Susan was the one begging him to say yes to her latest hobbyhorse. The only difference was this whim couldn't be stuck on a shelf with the art supplies, gathering dust. Unfortunately, Susan was thirty-five too, the same age as Dante, and she was running out of time for motherhood, no matter what miracles modern medicine promised. Besides, she swore she was going to do it, with or without his help.

"Oh, say yes already, Dante," she'd said. "You wouldn't want me to have some pimply college kid's sperm father my baby, would you? He might lie about his intelligence or his health or his psycho uncle."

Of course Susan had managed to say no to him at least a thousand times during their marriage. She was still saying no.

"Why don't we make your baby the old-fashioned way, for old times' sake?" he'd asked.

"Over my dead body," was her answer.

Yeah, that would be just like old times.

At least there was a male attendant at the sperm bank, a skinny black guy in a white lab coat, very efficient, no smirks.

"Magazines and videos are in the room," he told Dante as he walked him down the hall and handed him the labeled vial.

"What, no topless dancers?" Dante joked, trying to appear nonchalant, as if he did this every day. No, he didn't want the attendant to think he did this every day.

"That'd be extra."

"Extra?"

"You'd be surprised what some of our clients request."

"No, I mean extra, as you're charging me for this?" He walked back to the front desk. "You can just keep your damn jar."

The attendant was confused. "Well, someone's got to pay for the lab work, and storage. I mean, we can't run this place for free, you know." He looked as if he was ready to push a button calling for security or something.

"I didn't mean you should. I'm not paying, is all. I'm willing to give my wife — my ex-wife — my all, but I sure as Hades am not going to pay for it. She wants this baby, she can cover your expenses. The woman got half my bank account, she can afford it."

The man clucked his tongue in sympathy and took out another form to write in the new billing address. "Susan Johnson Rivera. Your ex-wife, huh?"

"And her new lover, if you can believe that. C. A. Chalmers. Get that on there too."

"So why doesn't this Chalmers dude, uh, you know?"

"Why isn't he here, being mortified to death?" Dante took back the vial with its new label. "Because the frigging C.A. stands for Cora Alice."

The African-American attendant whistled.

Then he winked at Dante. "Want I should fill your bottle? Now that'd be justice."

Dante was still chuckling when he went into the little room. He flipped on the VCR, paged through the top magazine, and then he did what he'd been trying so hard all day not to do: he thought about Louisa Waldon.

That worked.

Chapter Seven

When Louisa got back from walking the dog, the oak branches were neatly stacked along the side of her house. They were on the cosmos seedlings, but she wouldn't quibble. Somewhere in one of her books, she was sure, was how long she had to wait before burning green wood. Proud that she knew what green wood was, and that you shouldn't put it in the fireplace, she didn't want to sound dumb — again or still — by asking at the hardware store. Aunt Vinnie's nephew would know, naturally, but it would be a cold night indeed before Louisa asked that condescending creep for advice. She supposed he was still "thinking" about working for her.

Rico seemed nice enough, so she could ask him, if she ever saw him again, and if his English was good enough to understand the question. For that matter, she might even ask him if he'd do some of the heavy work for her. Then she could tell Mr. Dante his services weren't required and he could stop thinking. She'd never

been above hiring another firm's employees, so she shouldn't have scruples
now about hiring away the handyman's
helper. Meantime, she ought to tip Rico
for stacking the wood for her. He could
have just left it dumped out by the sidewalk. Ten dollars? Twenty? But if she gave
him that much now, he was liable to think
she could afford higher prices later, which
heaven knew she could not. Besides,
Louisa could never figure how much to
give the doorman at Christmas; that was
Howard's job.

"What do you think, Galahad?"

The dog looked up, hope in his eyes.

"Good idea. We'll bake him some cookies."

Regrettably, Louisa had no idea how to
bake cookies. Aunt Vinnie would, though.
Delighted to have company, Aunt Vinnie
dragged out a dozen cookbooks and a shoe
box filled with index cards and magazine
clippings.

"I keep telling myself I have to organize
all of these someday," the older woman
said, over the noise of the morning talk
shows on TV. "But I never get around to it.
I don't know where the time goes, I swear
it. Hours just seem to fly on by."

Louisa would be happy to give some of
her own excess hours, especially after

dinner and before bed. She could keep Galahad out walking only so long before she had to face that empty house. The shows on summer television stank, even with the cable hookup, and renting tapes every day was too expensive. She had signed up for free Internet service through the library, but her access code was still being processed. If she read one more book her eyes would cross, and none of them, mysteries, biographies, best-sellers, held her interest anyway. Last night she'd started one of the jigsaw puzzles she'd bought for the kids at yard sales. Tonight she might have to try playing computer solitaire. Unless she learned how to make cookies.

"Now these are Dante's favorites," Aunt Vinnie was saying, after she reshuffled a stack of newspaper cuttings.

"Yes, but I want to make cookies for Rico, his helper."

Aunt Vinnie shook her head, sending hair clips flying. "Oh, do I still have these silly things in? I'm sorry, Annie."

"It's Louisa, Aunt Vinnie, the younger sister."

"Of course you are. Couldn't get to be the older one at this stage, could you? Now where was I?"

"Rico."

"Oh, yes. You don't need to be making goodies for Rico, dear. He has a girlfriend, Marta, who works at Osprey Hill." Aunt Vinnie leaned a little closer and whispered, so Rosie or Oprah or whoever was telling women how to lead their lives today wouldn't hear: "And a wife in Colombia."

"Yeck."

"Oh, yes. He's shown me pictures of his children. At least he sends money home all the time."

Then Louisa had to listen to the woes of Aunt Vinnie's daughter Francine, who'd married a no-good bum who was always late with his child-support payments. That led to the local doctor who ran away with his nurse, one of the schoolteachers having an affair with the principal, and that last minister whose daughter got pregnant at Bible camp. Aunt Vinnie might not remember the name of her visitor, but she knew the personal lives of four generations of Paumonok Harborites. And their favorite cookies.

Louisa didn't mind that every recipe seemed to call up a new memory, because she was enjoying the comfort of the old woman's company as much as Aunt Vinnie was happy to have a new listener. They had tea and that morning's freshly baked blueberry muffins. Louisa got the recipe for them, too.

Then it was time for her to leave, before she ran out of excuses why she couldn't stay to supper. Dante would be bringing his nephew Teddy home after Little League, and then Francine would be getting off work at the bank. Louisa promised to stop by there soon to say hello, and come again, and bring Annie's children to visit — when hell froze over — and reminded the old woman that no, her mother wouldn't be out for the summer. Rose lived in Florida now, didn't she recall?

"Of course. Of course. With that nice man Bernie. I met him at the wed—"

"No, no. They're only friends." Lord, Mrs. Rivera would be spreading tales of Louisa's mother's fall from grace all over town, along with her directions for snackerdoodles, or whatever the meticulously copied recipe was called.

The absurd concoction had fifteen ingredients. Louisa thought she had two or three of them in the pantry: butter, sugar and water. She left the recipe in the car when she got to the supermarket. Her days of catering to any man's taste were over, by god. Not that she ever cooked much but breakfast for Howard — egg whites only, over easy — but she always ordered his favorite takeouts when they didn't eat out, and kept his favorite biscotti and meringue cookies in a jar. She'd dressed the way he liked, wore her hair the length he liked — before she cut it off when she got to Barbados. No more. She was not going to start sweating over a cookie sheet for a complete stranger, not even if he was nice to old ladies and little children. Besides, Rico was the one who'd done her the favor, and he cheated on his wife.

She bought a roll of slice-and-bake chocolate chip cookie dough — her favorites — and three new kinds of dog biscuits.

When she got home, a pile of post-and-rail lumber was dumped next to the old fence. She turned around and went back to the supermarket for those other twelve ingredients.

Dante felt so guilty for thinking of that Waldon woman in such a salacious way, in such a place, that he stopped by the lumberyard before driving to Teddy's game. She was a stranger, and no woman deserved to be thought of so . . . so lasciviously. Well, she deserved it — no, that was a sexist thought, according to his cousin Francine — she merited it, wearing those tight shorts and skimpy tank tops. She earned it? She evoked it? Hell, a man couldn't help thinking about making love to such a prime package.

Then he stopped at the florist and ordered flowers sent to Susan because he felt so guilty he didn't think of her that way. In fact, Dante couldn't remember the last time he'd ever lusted after his own wife, even when they were married. He wrote "Good luck, Mom," on the card. And meant it.

With all of his work crews busy on other jobs before the summer season really got started, Dante decided to wait a couple of days before going to work on the fence, half to prove to himself that he wasn't any randy schoolboy anxious to sneak a peak at a pretty girl, and half so the uppity female didn't get the idea he'd come if she snapped her fingers for the hired help. It wasn't as if he had nothing else to do, anyway, with eight houses to ready for the tenants, to say nothing of his own house, Susan's house, and Aunt Vinnie's, all of which were always needing something fixed or oiled or painted. It looked as if he was going to have to do some work at his cousin Francine's place now, too, with that bastard she married moving out. And

Teddy needed a lot of batting practice. And fishing season was underway.

He stopped by Whaler's Drive after dinner, just to make sure the lumber had arrived, he told himself. The wood was there, and cripes, so was the woman, standing on her front porch in an old man's shirt and nothing else that he could see, not even sandals. He almost drove his pickup into the old oak tree himself. Then he noticed what she was doing, not that he could figure out why the crazy female would keep opening and shutting her front door. Letting the dog in or out? No, he could hear the shrill barks coming from the backyard. Such bizarre behavior couldn't be rational, so maybe she really was a drunk. Dante couldn't forget the picture-perfect bride sloshing champagne down her wedding gown, the price of which — dress and champagne — could have reduced the property tax for everyone in the village.

She stopped flapping the door when she saw him pull up the driveway. "Flies," she called out, right after a muttered word Dante never thought to hear from such a classy-looking broad. She was soused, all right. Too bad, but none of his business. He could tell her where the local AA meetings were, but that was as far as he was going. Too bad he'd already bought the wood, too.

"Checking the delivery," he offered as an excuse for his coming, and his quicker going.

No hello, how are you, nice evening, Louisa thought. The man had the manners of a mole rat. She was glad his lousy cookies burned, except that now her whole house smelled of incompetent cooking. She didn't even have a fan to direct the smoke outdoors. "Bake in a hot oven until brown at the edges." Hah! What kind of directions were those, and whoever heard of a house without a smoke detector anyway? Every apartment she'd ever lived in had them, by law.

But he'd sent over the fence wood, just as he'd said he would. Perhaps Dante Rivera really was a man of his word, few though they were, and as hard to believe. Unless, and here the breath caught in Louisa's throat — no, that was the smoke settling in her lungs — he expected her to pay for the lumber. The way he was frowning at her now, she half thought the man was going to demand the money or her life. He'd have to take her life, because her credit cards were already at their max.

Not even such a dark scowl could ruin the guy's looks though, she noted, making him resemble a swashbuckling pirate tonight instead of some wealthy English lord or devil-may-care cowboy. He'd shaved recently, too, so the cleft in his square chin was even more noticeable. All he needed was a dagger between his teeth to be the perfect cover model, and he'd make a lot more money that way too.

He wasn't going to make it off her. No jack-of-all-trades was going to jerk her around. Not after she'd been had by Howard. "I didn't order this stuff."

No hello, how are you, thanks for the fence posts. Aunt Vinnie must be loonier than Dante thought, because there wasn't an ounce of sweetness in this woman. Hands on her hips, pointed little chin jutting forward, she looked like she was ready to get in the ring with Cora Alice. Except for the pink nail polish on her bare toes. "I had it at another job."

"Oh. In that case I can pay you to put it up."

"I don't want your money."

Then what did he want? Louisa had to wonder. If this stud thought she'd trade services, he was missing a couple of hinges on his toolbox. If she were still in the office, she'd have him up on sexual harassment charges so fast his head would —

"The fence goes between the two properties so it's just as much my responsibility as yours. You can plant the flowers around it, make both yards look better."

There had to be a catch somewhere. She bit her lip, trying to find his self-serving motive.

God, there was no pleasing some women, Dante thought. He'd been divorced too long to remember. "So do you want the fence fixed or not?"

"I think so. That is, yes. Yes, thank you. If you don't think the renters will just wreck it."

He looked even fiercer. "They won't." Not after he threatened to cancel their lease. There was no way they could find another house for the summer, not in June.

Louisa wasn't so sure the party crowd would be intimidated by a handyman.

"And what about the noise?" Dante cocked his head, listening to the dog's yammering.

"We're working on that. But they don't help, slamming car doors all night, shouting to one another outside. They were at it 'til three in the morning this past weekend." Annie and her brood had slept through it all, the merrymaking and the barking, but Louisa'd lain in bed half the night, wide-awake with her dismal thoughts and strangers' laughter.

"It was a holiday."

"It was Memorial Day. Do you mean to tell me those people were honoring the war dead by drinking German beer?"

Who was she to criticize what a bunch of rich kids drank? As a matter of fact, and a matter of fact-finding, so he could tell Aunt Vinnie once and for all that her swan was nothing but an ugly duckling under her fine feathers, Dante took a step closer, to smell Louisa's breath.

No drink he ever heard of smelled like that. All right, he conceded, the female wasn't three sheets to the wind, but she sure was nuttier than Aunt Vinnie's Christmas fruitcake. He could have kicked himself for not following his own instincts. He'd known what a headache Louisa Waldon was going to be the minute he'd spotted her here in the Harbor, but he'd gone and gotten involved. The woman was trouble with a capital T, and he could usually smell trouble a mile off. He just never knew it smelled like a burned cookie.

Chapter Eight

The handyman did not return to dig the holes. The renters did not come out for the weekend. Howard did not call.

Louisa took three romance novels out of the paperback exchange at the library, where no one could see what she was reading. None of the half-naked heroes on the covers could hold a candle to the blue-eyed, fence-building Fabio. Of course, that was just an objective, disinterested observation. She stayed up reading all night Friday, Saturday and Sunday, weeping at the happy endings, because she didn't have one.

And she ate all the perfectly baked chocolate chips for dummies cookies.

The man who did arrive on Monday morning wasn't a flowing-maned Viking, a knight come to carry her off on a white horse, or a Scottish laird getting down on kilt-clad knee, damn it. The guy who pulled his fancy black car into the driveway at ten o'clock was bald, middle-aged, wore a lot of gold jewelry, and had come to steal her dog!

"Ms. Louisa Waldon?" he read off a scrap of paper.

"Yes." Louisa put down her trowel and wiped her hands on her jeans.

"My name is Avery, Carl Avery, and I got your name from" — he consulted the paper again — "Jeanette at the animal shelter."

"Yes?"

"According to her, you adopted a dog from the shelter a few weeks ago."

The dog was barking from the backyard, so Louisa could hardly deny it. "That's right."

"Actually, it was wrong. You see, it's my dog."

"No, that can't be. My dog wasn't a stray. He was put up for adoption by a neighbor of the previous owner."

"Kerry blue terrier, about this high?" Avery held his hand out, heavy gold ring flashing.

"Yes, but Galahad belonged to an old lady."

"Silver Crown's Mental Image belonged to me. I left him with my aunt while I was abroad. I did not give him to her."

"You named a dog Silver Crown's Mental Image?"

"His official name. We called him Midge."

"I like Galahad better."

Mr. Avery consulted his watch. "I really have to be back in Riverdale this afternoon for an important meeting, Ms. Waldon."

"Don't let me keep you, then, Mr. Avery. I assure you the dog is in good hands. He gets to run on the beach, sleep on the bed, and visit with the Yorkie on the next block. He couldn't be happier."

"You misunderstand, miss. I did not sit in traffic for four hours to inquire into Midge's well-being. I came to take him back."

Take back her dog? He might as well take back her left lung. "I am afraid you do not understand, mister. I adopted the dog from the pound, where he was in a cage because he'd been abandoned. His owner died. No one wanted him. He is mine."

"He was not abandoned, I tell you. I was in Cannes. That's in France, you know," he said with a sneer.

Louisa was tempted to plant her trowel somewhere other than in the dirt. "I am aware of Cannes's location. I just wasn't aware that they had no phones there. Didn't you ever call your aunt to find out how the dog was — or how she was?"

"Of course I did. When I got no answer I figured she was out at mah-jongg or bingo. When I did not hear anything from her, I assumed all was well."

"For a month? That's how long Jeanette said she was in the nursing home, for Pete's sake!"

"My secretary's home phone number was right in her address book. She should have had someone call me."

"She was dying! How could she find your secretary's name?" By now Louisa was shouting. "And the neighbor said she left messages on your machine."

"Which I didn't receive, naturally, until I got home," he snapped back at her. "That's how I found out where my dog had been taken. Now could we get on with it?"

"Get on with it? Get on with what? You're not going to steal my dog, and that's the end of it."

"I have papers that prove he's mine." He took a step closer to Louisa, a threatening step.

She would not back away. "And I have a license that proves he's mine."

"Listen, lady, I'll go to the police if I have to. I'll call my lawyer and sue you for all you're worth." He looked around at the sagging porch and missing roof shingles. "Though it'll hardly be worth the effort."

"And I'll go to the Humane Society and charge you with cruelty to animals. Neglect and . . . and neglect. You couldn't even take care of your old aunt. How could anyone trust you with a dog?"

Mr. Avery's face was all red by now, and his hands were clenched in fists. "Why, you —"

"Is there a problem here, folks?" Dante Rivera asked in a pleasant enough voice, but his eyes were narrowed, and he held a heavy shovel crosswise, loosely, as though ready for action. He needed a shave again, and his denim shirt had rips and stains and sweat on it — and Louisa had never seen a more welcome sight. Now that the cavalry had arrived, she felt her knees go weak as she took a step toward his side, away from the blustering, belligerent baldy . . . with bad taste in jewelry.

Dante hadn't meant to get involved. In fact, he swore to himself that he wouldn't. When he first drove up and saw Louisa with a man, he figured it was the missing bridegroom. There was no way in hell he was going to get in the middle of that confrontation, so he went around the side to the garage for the shovel and a sledgehammer. When he came back, the pair was still too intent on their argument to notice his presence, so he started moving some of the wood around to make sure he couldn't hear the conversation. Bad enough he had to witness the showdown. Frankly, he thought a looker like Louisa Waldon could do a lot better than a middle-aged clown.

As the voices grew louder, though, the words he could pick out made less sense. Something about nursing homes and old ladies and dogs. And the old guy kept crowding Louisa. The girl had grit, Dante had to concede her that, standing up to a man at least twice her weight. Too bad she didn't have brains to go with that stiff backbone. The man was getting more ticked off with every word she shouted, and he looked like he was going to explode soon.

Ex-fiancé or not, this was none of Dante's business. No way, nohow. That's why he picked up the shovel instead of the sledgehammer when the scumbag raised his fist.

Carl Avery was obviously glad to see another male. A rational being at last, his half-smile seemed to say, one who could clear up the matter in a second, and shut this dumb blonde up. He held out his manicured hand. Dante ignored it, him, and the urge to commit mayhem on anyone who threatened this woman. Who threatened any woman, he amended to himself.

"He wants to take my dog," Louisa blurted before Avery could say a word. "He left Galahad for months, letting him practically starve in the streets, and now he wants him back."

"All this is about a mutt? He's not your fiancé?"

"Howard? Of course not," Louisa replied at the same time Avery said, "Heaven forbid." Avery then gave a fake cough. "The animal in question is not quite a mutt, either. Silver Crown's Mental Image is one win away from grand champion. Here's the pedigree, the bill of sale, and the AKC registration, in my name, Carl Avery."

"I have the dog license, in mine," Louisa countered.

Dante glanced at the papers the windbag handed him. "I'm no legal expert, but it looks like you both have a good claim to the dog. Why don't you ask him?" He nodded for Louisa to go get the mongrel.

She came back with Galahad on a leash, but at Dante's nod, she let go of the lead.

The dog immediately flew to Dante's side, barking joyously. "Not a fair test," Dante admitted. "I just gave him some of my buttered roll. He most likely wants the rest. You both call him."

Louisa called out first: "Here, Gally, come, lovey. There's my sweet doggie. Good boy."

Mr. Avery scowled at the sappy endearments and the dog's immediate lunge for Louisa's side, where Galahad cavorted at her feet, yipping and carrying on as if he hadn't seen her in ages, instead of minutes. "Enough of this bull." He made a clucking sound, then said, "Midge, here. Stand."

Galahad was at his side in a flash, posing there as if he were cast in bronze. Avery looked over at Dante, not Louisa, flashing a smug grin, besides a heavy gold link necklace.

"So?" Louisa asked. "So what if you've got him trained to be a bookend? Where's the love and affection? He's not even wagging his tail."

"Of course not. He's a show dog. Midge lives for the adulation of the crowds, the excitement of the ring, the approval of the judges."

"That's what he has to live for, not your company? What about when he's too old for blue ribbons, do you put him out to pasture, or just trade him in, like an old car?"

Avery started to get red in the face again, with sweat beading on his forehead. "I assure you, once Midge has all his championship points, he will have a long and rewarding future outside of the show ring."

"He's not in the ring now, mister, so let him sit down, for heaven's sake."

Galahad bounded over to Louisa as soon as the man raised his hand, pointed and said, "Off." She scratched behind his ears, the spot he liked best. "He's mine."

Avery was making loud, grunting noises about lawyers and courts. Louisa turned to Dante.

"Look, I don't know what's legal in this situation," he said. "The guy's owned the dog longer than you have, certainly paid more for him than you did —"

"I should have known you'd take his side. Men always stick together, don't they?"

"— But possession is ninth-tenths of the law," Dante continued, as if she hadn't interrupted. "And you did adopt him in good faith."

"That's crap," Avery yelled. "If you buy stolen property you're not allowed to keep it, no matter how much you paid, or how good your intentions."

"But the dog wasn't stolen merchandise."

"And I didn't steal him!" Louisa was getting more and more upset, seeing the only good thing she had slipping out of her hands.

What a damnable situation, Dante was thinking, figuring he could run the guy off for now, but Avery looked just mean enough to take Louisa and her dog to court, if he didn't come back some night and kidnap the mutt. For all Dante knew, he'd be within his rights. "I think we should call my friend Richie, the lawyer, and find out if there are statutes for these things. Unless you want to call yours, Louisa."

Call Howard or one of the partners at her former job? About a dog? She'd rather jump off the roof, which she might anyway, if they took her dog away.

Avery, meanwhile, was studying the dog. "What did you do to him?"

Louisa bent down to pet Galahad where he lay panting, his head on her sneakers. "I had to have him clipped, because he was filthy with mats and had sores from flea bites."

Avery winced at the mention of fleas on his dog, but brushed that aside. "His coat will grow back by the fall show season. But he looks logy, out of condition."

"No, that's just the chocolate chip cookies. They didn't agree with his stomach."

Dante looked at Louisa as if she were crazy. Actually, she thought, he usually looked at her as if she belonged in a padded cell. Some defender he'd turned out to be! Mr. Avery, though, was gaping at Louisa as if she'd sprouted horns and a tail.

"You gave him chocolate? Were you trying to kill my dog?"

"He's not your dog, and how was I to know chocolate was bad for a dog?"

"Everyone knows that!"

"No, they don't. The books I read never mentioned chocolate, and the directions on the cookie dough sure as the devil never said 'Warning, this product may be hazardous to your dog.' "

Dante was shaking his head, and Louisa could feel tears welling up in her eyes, darn it. Had she really almost killed her own dog? The Solomon in work boots seemed to think so. "I suppose now you're going to say I'm an unfit mother and don't deserve to keep him. I bet you're thinking I'm not capable of loving him, caring for him, that he'd be better off with . . . with his prior owner. That I can't keep any relationship going."

"Huh?" Avery couldn't follow her reasoning, but Dante was all too afraid he could. He'd been around too many emotional women not to realize that once the gates to the loony bin were open, all the inmates started crawling out. Like the runaway groom.

"Now that you mention it," the interloper was saying, patting his meaty thigh so the dog got up and padded over, "you don't know the first thing about dogs, do you? You don't know what to feed him, how to school him. You don't even have a proper run." Sunlight glinted off the diamond ring as he waved his hand around the yard. "You won't stand a chance in court. Give it up now, lady, and save us all a mountain of trouble." He picked up Galahad's leash.

Louisa was searching in her blue jeans pocket for a tissue.

"You know," Dante said, wishing with all his heart that he'd gone fishing today, "instead of picking on Miss Waldon here, you ought to be thanking her for rescuing him.

If it wasn't for her going to that shelter on just that day, the dog might have been put down, no matter what claim you have. She saved his life."

"Yeah, yeah. And next you're going to say I should pay her back for expenses."

Louisa found a wadded tissue that had gone through the dryer. She couldn't blow her nose, but she could wipe it. "I wouldn't take your money if I was starving." She was so mad at herself for losing her composure — again — and in front of the hired worker, that she could spit. Instead she had to sniffle again. "Not even for the outrageous prices they charge for grooming a dog." She sniffled once more. "Or for getting him fixed."

"Fixed?" The leash might have been a snake, Avery dropped it so fast. "You had my champion show dog neutered?"

He was gone before the now-useless pedigree hit the ground.

Chapter Nine

Dante reached for the dropped papers. It was that or reach for his privates, just to check. He knew neutering was the responsible way to go, cutting down on the number of unwanted dogs, but it was one hell of a thing to do to a man. Or a dog. He wouldn't be surprised if the Waldon woman got a lot of satisfaction out of emasculating the only male she could get her hands on, too. That escaped bridegroom had turned her into a regular man-hater, he guessed, unless she'd been one all along, like his ex-wife. Dante supposed he should introduce her to Susan and Cora Alice, but what a waste of those long legs and rounded breasts and tiny waist and — He patted the dog this time instead of readjusting an entirely inappropriate reaction. To Louisa Waldon, for chrissake.

"Poor mutt," he started, then corrected himself. "Poor pedigreed pooch. You were going to be a champion, and then a lucky stud. Now you're nothing but a lapdog."

"But he will be loved, and . . . and cared for the best way I know how. I'll read more books, and talk to his vet." No matter how much it cost. "At least he will never be lost and alone again."

She sniffled, and the dog immediately went to her side, wagging his tail and leaning against her. At least the animal didn't seem to know what he was missing, wriggling and reveling in the hugs and kisses Louisa bestowed on him. Dante stomped down a twinge of jealousy at the sight of all that obvious affection between the two. He swore to himself that he wouldn't curl around Louisa Waldon's legs unless . . . Well, maybe if she asked nicely.

Maybe he ought to get himself a dog. No, he had enough people to worry about. Like now, the damned woman was pale and trembly in reaction to that pig's threats, and the dog was getting soggy. Dante couldn't stand a woman's tears. He jerked his head toward the stack of fence posts. "You'll need gloves," was all he said.

He was giving her a chance to regain her composure, Louisa knew, and wipe her face. So he wasn't such an insensitive clod after all. And he had come to her aid, more or less. Even if he hadn't supported her claim to Galahad his presence had been protection, which she should not have needed, of course. But he'd been there, and he would still be there after she blew her nose and found her gardening gloves, the ones with the rubber palms and the roses on the backs.

"Thank you," she said, when she went back out, trying to encompass the dog, the fence, the rout of that awful Avery person.

Dante looked at the silly gloves that would give her blisters in ten minutes and shook his head. Not his problem. He nodded for her to start rolling the chicken wire he'd been pulling off the rotten posts. "Four thousand dollars," he muttered.

Louisa let go of the wire fencing so fast it uncurled and snapped back, tearing a hole in her last pair of everyday jeans, the ones she'd delegated as work pants. "Four thousand dollars? I don't have that kind of money! You said you would help fix the fence for free because it was between the houses and you had the lumber and —"

"That's what he paid for the dog. From the bill of sale he showed me."

"Oh." She started rolling the chicken wire again, keeping a better grip on it so he wouldn't think she was a total incompetent. "Can you imagine spending that much money on a dog?"

"No. Or for a wedding dress."

Everyone knew that too? Did they have

nothing else to talk about in this place but her affairs? Damn. Whatever warm feelings Louisa might have been harboring for the gorgeous workman took a sudden chill. "That is none of your —" she began, only to remember that she needed the fence for her dog — *her dog* — and so she needed Mr. Small Town, Small Mind Rivera. Besides, he was a pleasure to watch, even if she had to peek out of the corner of her eye so he wouldn't see her looking. Any man that good-looking had to be conceited enough without adding her admiration.

He was pulling the old posts up now, while she stacked the rotted cross rails in the renters' driveway for his helper Rico to pick up later. Her back was aching already, but Dante was lifting and tossing the uprights as if they were those bamboo garden stakes she'd bought to support her new tomato plants. His denim shirt hid the muscles he obviously possessed, and Louisa found herself wishing he'd take it off so she could see the suntanned, rippled skin of her imagination. Most likely he had too much chest hair, she tried to convince herself, or a beer belly hanging over his belt. His blue jeans were well worn, but without stains and rips like hers. They fit well enough not to show his butt when he bent over. What kind of handyman was that, anyway? If she'd been paying the guy, Louisa would have felt cheated. On the other hand — the one without the blister — with his thick black hair, Dante Rivera would have a hairy butt too. He had to if there was any justice in the world. No man could be that perfect except a paperback cover model. So what if Aunt Vinnie's nephew had the brains — and the manners — of a flat, glossy piece of cardboard? He was putting up her fence, so she'd put up with his snide comments. Besides, she wasn't interested in any man, no way, nohow, and certainly not any sweaty, red-faced, gasping low-life laborer.

He wasn't sweaty or red-faced or breathing hard, though. She was, damn it. No matter. She wasn't about to quit and let the ape think she was some weak, whiny female. She kept quiet, concentrating on not whimpering, wincing or wobbling when she brought the next post over to him.

Dante liked the way she worked, despite himself. Louisa Waldon didn't fret about her ripped jeans, and she didn't chatter to fill the silence, she just kept doing her job. He couldn't stand a woman who yammered. His cousin Francine never shut up, and his ex-wife had always filled every second with conversation, whether he was interested in her day's minutiae or not. Most times not, but that was past history. He wouldn't be thinking of Susan at all, except for thinking of her having his baby. Maybe she would change her mind, or maybe she wouldn't conceive. And maybe, if he finished this lousy fence, the Waldon woman would stay on her own side of it and stop complaining about her neighbors. He worked faster.

She kept up with him despite her slight build, moving the rotted rails, putting the new wood right where he needed it. Half the work crews he had couldn't follow directions as well. None of them were half as pretty.

She'd been stunning as a bride, right off the cover of one of those wedding magazines at first, but he liked her looks better now. With a streak of dirt on her cheek instead of makeup, she seemed more like a flesh-and-blood woman than a skinny, sexless, lifeless mannequin. With all that fussy hair lopped off, she looked younger, more innocent than the tough career woman he knew her to be. Light blond hair hung straight to just below her ears now, held off her face by a single blue doodad. She

111

didn't keep fussing with it, either, to his surprise. Dante would have thought a near-professional beauty like Louisa Waldon carried a mirror in her back pocket — if one could have fit in those tight blue jeans.

He'd been disappointed at first that she had on long pants today, so he couldn't see those slender, shapely legs, but the striped tank top made up for the lack. He had no trouble picturing what was under those stripes, with no bra to get in the way with seams and elastic and wires. Louisa's breasts didn't need the constraints or the construction. Firm and high, they would be a perfect handful, not soft and melony.

He missed the post he was pounding and almost crushed his own ankle.

Oh, no. He was going to replace the lady's fence, not replace her missing groom. No way was he going to lust after a stuck-up, spoiled snob. By the end of summer, maybe earlier, she'd get tired of playing at country girl and go back to the city where she belonged. Besides, he reminded himself, she didn't like men. Which suited him fine. Now if only she would stop bending over to pick up the wooden posts, he'd get his mind back on the rails, instead of on her rear.

She went inside and came back with cans of iced green tea — it figured — and a hammer and nails. She'd wiped her face, but left a cobweb in her hair. He didn't tell her. She might get hysterical, like his cousin. She might get more hysterical if he offered to pull it out. Drinking his tea, he couldn't help notice that she looked pale and limp, as if someone had washed the starch out of her. He gestured toward the hammer. "I'll come back tomorrow with the heavy-duty staple gun to put up the chicken wire. It will be tighter that way, and less apt to come off."

"Thank you, but the wire is on my side, for my dog. It's my responsibility."

"Don't worry. I won't charge you." His tone was harsher than he'd intended. Did she dislike men — or him — so much she didn't want one around, even to do the dirty work? Hell, his ex-wife's girlfriend called him to unclog the drains. It wasn't as if he wanted to give up another day to finish the frigging fence, either, now that he thought about it, whether Louisa wore a bikini or a burnoose. He didn't leave jobs unfinished, though, and he didn't leave helpless women in the lurch, especially not favorites of his aunt's. "I am being neighborly, that's all."

"I appreciate that, but Galahad —"

"It's not as if the dog is going to run away before we get the yard enclosed. He hasn't left your property the whole time we've been working." He slapped his thigh and the blue-gray terrier trotted over to sniff his hand. "You wouldn't run away from such a good home, would you, champ? You've got no reason to go visiting the ladies now."

What about squirrels, though? Or deer? Without the fence Louisa would have to walk the dog late at night, with no streetlamps, nobody home on either side next door, and a couple of acres of woods across the street. She bit her lip. She couldn't admit to being afraid of the dark, not to Mr. Musclehead. He'd already had enough laughs at her expense. And he'd tell everyone in the town, besides. "I'll just tack it up temporarily. Okay?"

Dante shrugged. "Suit yourself. It's your fence and your dog. And your blisters."

Louisa'd taken off her gloves to drink. Now she tucked her sore hands in the dog's coat. "I'll be fine. Thank you. Again."

Dante bent down to gather up his tools. Then he looked up at her. Big mistake. She looked like a waif, all big green eyes and a cobweb in her hair. Damn. Besides, he'd promised Aunt Vinnie he'd make sure Louisa was all right. "I, ah, have to go watch my nephew's Little League game. I could come back afterward if you want, to get the job started."

The sun came out in her face. "Would you? That would be wonderful. I can make cookies."

He doubted that, after the other day. "Maybe a beer."

A beer. Of course. One didn't offer cookies and milk to a grown man, a man who drove a battered red pickup truck. Louisa rubbed her face against Galahad to hide her embarrassment. At least she had a couple of cans left from her brother-in-law's visit. "There is some in the fridge."

Dante remembered the drunken bride. He'd bet there was beer in the house, and wine and a full liquor cabinet, too. He determined to have one bottle and get out. Not that this one couldn't do with a little loosening up, but Louisa Waldon sober was pain in the neck enough. "Fine. Later, then."

She smiled. Dante couldn't remember if he'd ever seen her smile before. Talk about pain. It was as if the female barely recalled how to curve her lips upward. She was watching him gather his tools, alone except for the dog. The smile faded, leaving her looking sad and vulnerable. Oh, hell. "You could come to the ball game, I guess. It's just at Heroes' Field at the end of the village. They're playing the kids from Montauk."

"Oh, no. I don't know anything about baseball."

"Neither do the kids. That's not the point. Half the town comes to watch."

She took a step back. Half the town, who knew all about her aborted wedding, right down to the color of the bridesmaids' dresses? "No, thank you. I don't know any of them, or their children."

"You know Aunt Vinnie. She never misses one of Teddy's games. Francine will be there when she gets off work."

Louisa shook her head. The hair clip fell out and a blond lock fell across her right eye. She brushed it back with a quick motion, then twisted the hair in her fingers, a nervous habit she had outgrown in high school, or so she'd thought. Her fingers touched something sticky, which she tried to wipe on her jeans. "No, I couldn't. Too much to do, you know." She waved her hand vaguely in the direction of the run-down cottage behind her, as if she was going to reshingle it before supper.

Dante didn't want to think she was too snooty to mingle with the common folk. Somehow he didn't want to think she disliked him too much to spend the five-minute drive with him, either. That didn't leave a whole lot of other choices. Guessing, he nodded toward the posts and rails. "You know, fences work both ways."

"I don't understand."

"They keep people out. They keep people in."

Louisa couldn't pretend not to understand. He thought she was building walls around herself, just because she didn't want to go to some idiotic children's game — with him! Of all the conceit. And all the gall of him to be questioning her motives. He was a handyman, for heaven's sake, a hot-looking hole-digger, not her shrink. "No, no. It's for the dog. I promised the lady at the pound. Really. And to keep the renters from running over my flowers, of course."

He raised one dark eyebrow, obviously disbelieving her protests.

She was not afraid to face the locals. She was not! She simply saw no reason to make herself the object of gossip, or pity, any more than she had to. "I am, uh, waiting

117

for an important phone call."

"The errant bridegroom? It's been what? A month? If he hasn't called by now, lady, he's not going to."

"Howard? Of course not." She'd stopped listening for his voice weeks ago, eager for the opportunity to hang up on him. "If you must know, I am waiting to hear about a job."

"In the city?"

"No, here. At the library. They need someone to help computerize the card catalog."

That had to be a comedown for a personnel manager at a big law firm, and for minimum wage, besides. His aunt would know if Ms. Waldon actually needed the money, or was playing at Lady Bountiful doing volunteer work. Meantime, he said, "Mrs. Terwilliger at the library will leave a message."

"She would if I had an answering machine. I haven't had time to buy one yet." She lied; she didn't have the money to buy one yet. "And no, my E-mail is not hooked up yet either."

"We could stop at the library on the way home from the game."

"We could, if I wanted to watch little boys run in circles, and their parents shout themselves hoarse in the bleachers."

"See? You do understand softball. Come on, it'll be fun."

"I can only suppose that females rarely refuse you anything, Mr. Rivera, but this time you shall just have to accept a no. No, I will not go to your nephew's ball game, and that is final."

He handed her the hair clip from the ground, spiderweb and all. "Then I guess he won."

"You mean I won?"

"No, him."

Louisa was confused. "Your nephew? Mr. Avery about the dog?"

"The fiancé. Howard." Dante walked toward his truck. "He won."

Chapter Ten

"Howard? What game was he playing?"

Dante called back over his shoulder as he got in his truck. "You're supposed to be so smart. You figure it out."

She hadn't figured it out in all the weeks since the wreckage of a wedding. How could she have loved a man who could be so heartless, or understood him so little? For that matter, how could he have stopped loving her so suddenly, unless he never had? Maybe he had another woman, someone more domestic, more like his mother, more . . . What, damn it? What more had Howard wanted that Louisa hadn't been?

She just did not know. Now she felt like the losing contestant on some quiz show where no one had told her the rules. What blasted game? Cards? Dice? "Jeopardy!"? Oh, yeah. Give the wrong answer and you were in Purgatory, or Paumonok Harbor.

Life wasn't a game, and she was no loser. Was that what the tool guy meant, that she was letting Howard's defection destroy her life? Well, who gave Mr. Dante Rivera a degree in psychology? He was the neighbor house's caretaker, not Louisa's, by god. She was taking good enough care of herself, thank you. She was doing fine, in fact, Louisa told herself. She had a roof over her head, even though it leaked around the chimney, a possible job, a car and a dog. Her sister was a phone call away and her mother had offered to lend her money in emergencies. Her medical insurance was paid through the end of the year by the law firm, and her car insurance had gone in with Howard's in March. She wasn't in debt and she wasn't starving. So there.

Howard may have cost her a fortune, and her job, her home, her friends and her self-respect, but she was managing. She was even learning to cook and garden. That ought to be enough for the post-digger posing as Plato. Dante Rivera could just keep his deep thoughts for the deep holes the fence needed. Louisa did not appreciate his cryptic comments or his company. He was a fixer-upper, and she was not broken.

Unless she was hiding out in the old beach cottage, afraid of the dark, afraid to face new people. Unless she was reading her romance novels and playing computer solitaire and poisoning her dog with chocolate instead of getting on with her life. Unless she was growing too broken-hearted-bitter to enjoy an afternoon in the sun, watching children play. Then he was dead right. She was a loser. Howard had won.

Not that creep. He wasn't worth her lost savings; he certainly wasn't worth her tears. No way was Howard worth the rest of her life. She snapped her fingers. Click, that part of her was gone. Finished. Kaput. Except for the sticky spiderweb.

After she nearly scalded her hand, trying to sterilize it clean, she called Jeanette at the animal shelter.

"Yeah, I was wondering when you'd call. We got in a litter of Maltese pups confiscated from a puppy mill. You know, little white lapdogs, long hair. One of them ought to suit you fine."

"Galahad suits me fine. Mr. Avery decided not to pursue his claims of ownership."

Jeanette whistled, over the background barking. "You stood up to that blowhard? I'm impressed. I couldn't do it. Didn't want to give him your number, but figured I had to, with all the papers he had. You go, girl!"

Louisa basked in the praise, not admitting her courage had come from a stud at her back and the victory had come from the suddenly studless dog at her feet. "I only wanted to know about chocolate."

"I couldn't make it through the day without it."

Once she was sure she wasn't killing her new best friend, not such a big dog with so little chocolate, Louisa decided to go to the ball field after all. Those cookies needed to be walked off — her hips, not the dog's — and she could appear to be simply exercising her dog if no one welcomed her. As for Mrs. Terwilliger, the librarian had said to call back at the end of the week.

So what did one wear to a Little League game? Louisa didn't want to look too well-dressed, so no one could accuse her of putting on airs. That eliminated her work trousers and pant suits and dresses, which was most of her wardrobe, besides a few T-shirts and shorts, most of which now had paint and rust on them. She couldn't go in what she was wearing, though, or she might insult her new neighbors with stains and sweat, as if they were not worth a shower. No way was she putting her last good, pricey designer jeans on wooden bleachers either, or her silk blouses, linen shorts and rayon sundresses that were her trousseau. Finally, from the back of her bottom drawer, she pulled out a Hawaiian print shirt she'd bought for Howard to surprise him on their honeymoon. It had bright blue orchids and yellow parrots and green leaves. He would have hated it. Louisa loved it. It was long enough to cover the tear in her work jeans, besides. She rummaged in the hall closet to unearth an old baseball cap someone had left there ages ago. The Yankees. Good, at least they were still playing in New York.

"Come on, Galahad, let's go play ball. You know, buy me some peanuts and Cracker Jacks." He didn't get up. "Peanuts and popcorn and hot dogs, right?" She wondered if they had anything like that at Little League games. She took a few of the chocolate chip cookies with her, just in case. The dog barked.

"That's root for the home team, silly. Not woof."

The cretin must be right. Half the town had to be at the game, and the opposition town too. Both bleachers were crowded and Louisa didn't know where to sit. Then Aunt Vinnie waved to her and called out: "Over here, Annie."

Annie was Louisa's sister, but she went in that direction anyway, stopping often so everyone could pet Galahad, who was in his element, thinking all these people had come to see him strut, as usual. Gally was a perfect gentleman, unlike the clod who'd invited her to see the game and was nowhere in sight.

Aunt Vinnie patted the seat beside her and introduced Louisa to a chunky brunette on her other side. "This is my Francine. You played together when you were little."

"No, that was my sister Annie. She's older. I'm Louisa."

"Of course you are. I went to your wedding, didn't I? A shame. Francine is divorced too."

"But I'm not —"

Francine shook Louisa's hand. "Don't worry about it. You just skipped the middle innings."

"Oh, I didn't think I was that late."

"Not the ball game. The so-called wedded bliss that comes between the courtship and the court case. Some of us weren't that lucky. Anyway, I'm glad to meet you. Dante's been telling us about you."

Louisa made sure Galahad couldn't fall

through the bleacher seats, instead of commenting on the obvious. Everyone in this town talked about everyone else.

"He didn't think you'd come, being so busy fixing up your house, which is really ambitious of you. Not that there is anything wrong with being ambitious, of course," she hurried to add.

"Francine wants to go back to school to get a teaching degree," Aunt Vinnie put in, feeding Galahad a grape. If chocolate wasn't going to kill him, Louisa guessed a grape wouldn't either.

"Oh, Ma, you know I just talk about it. It'll never happen." Francine pointed out to the grassy area. "There's my Teddy. He plays in the field."

Louisa thought all the kids were playing in the field, but she followed Francine's finger toward a skinny little boy whose Paumonok Pirates black uniform was about two sizes too big. His socks were falling around his ankles and his helmet hid his eyes, his hair and his expression. No matter. He was practically skipping in place he was so excited. Or else he had to pee.

Francine shouted, "Yeah, Teddy!"

He hopped some more, but never took his gaze off home plate, where a boy who looked at least three years older was coming up to bat. "That kid's a ringer," Louisa said. "It's not fair."

Francine smiled. "Welcome to the world of sports. I'm glad you came."

The parents on the other bleacher started yelling for RJ. Over the noise, Louisa asked, "Uh, where is your cousin? I thought he would be here."

Francine nodded toward the bench where the extra Pirates waited their turn. "He's the batting coach. He watches to see what the other team does, what our boys can do better. He has an analytical mind, you know."

Louisa did know that. She hadn't known about the coaching, naturally. She knew very little about the man, in fact, except that he looked even better in his black T-shirt with the pirate on it. Either he was a good citizen, coaching other people's kids, or he was one of those men who never outgrew boyhood games. He turned his back to speak with a young woman in a halter top and shorts. Or else he'd found a new way of impressing the girls.

He looked over and smiled. Louisa told herself it was a good thing she was not easily impressed. She waved with the hand not holding Galahad's leash, then turned back to the game. That's what she came for, wasn't it?

RJ missed the first ball thrown toward him by a tall, red-haired Pirate — they all seemed taller than Teddy, she saw now — with freckles. The Paumonok side clapped, especially a red-haired woman sitting in front of them holding a red-haired baby. He missed the second pitch and the cheering grew louder. Galahad barked. Aunt Vinnie fed him another grape. The baby cried, Francine shouted, "Heads up, Teddy," and Louisa checked the scoreboard. The Pirates were losing. "Go, Pirates," she yelled. "Three points are nothing."

"Runs, Louisa. They're runs in baseball."

"Of course. I knew that," she said, grinning at Francine, who laughed and handed her a bag of potato chips. Louisa took a handful, fed one to the dog, and handed the bag back.

The ball didn't come close to the plate and everyone moaned. The next pitch was over the catcher's head. The red-haired woman looked like she was going to cry along with the baby.

Louisa found herself holding her breath. "Three strikes you're out, right?"

Francine didn't answer, too intent on

watching the pitcher, the batter, and her son in the field at the same time she was cramming potato chips in her mouth. She passed the bag to Louisa without looking.

The pitcher threw, the batter swung, the ball went soaring out — toward Teddy. "Oh no," Francine groaned. Aunt Vinnie covered her eyes. The Paumonok crowd was silent. Teddy looked up, ran forward, ran sideward, ran back, his mitt out in front of him. The ball went over his head.

Another boy ran after the ball and threw it back before RJ could go around all the bases, just most of them.

"He stinks," Francine said, sinking back against the bleacher, letting the potato chips fall.

"He does not!" Louisa wasn't quite sure why, but she felt both Teddy and his mother needed encouragement. "He's just smaller than the others. He couldn't have caught that ball unless he stood on a ladder. He'll get the next one."

He dropped the next ball that came his way.

Louisa cheered louder. Teddy was the littlest kid on either side, his team had lost ten out of twelve games, Aunt Vinnie said, and they were losing this one by four points — no, runs — now. He was out in that field by himself, alone, vulnerable, maybe scared of being hit, maybe worried that people would laugh at him, or his friends would not want him on their team anymore. Oh, how Louisa wanted him to catch a ball, hit a home run, steal a base, anything not to lose. She understood losing. Teddy was too young for that pain.

No more balls came his way, thank goodness, and the Montaukers were finally out. "What a relief!"

"Yeah, but now Teddy gets to come up to bat."

More torture? If Louisa ever had a kid she'd never let him play competitive sports. Maybe chess. At least then no one else was depending on you. How did mothers survive this? Most likely by junk food. Louisa found the cookies in her pocket and passed them around. Galahad ate the crumbs, plus a teething biscuit he stole from the red-haired baby when the pitcher's mother wasn't looking.

Dante was giving the boy some last-minute pointers. Louisa hoped he was a better coach than he was a counselor. Nagging at her to come to a ball game for fun? Hah! She was a nervous wreck, and getting fat besides.

She and Francine stood to cheer when

Teddy stepped into the batter's cage. Dante said something to him that had the boy turn to look at them. They both grinned. The handyman showed a dimple. The boy showed a missing space where one of his teeth should have been. Then he turned to face the pitcher and Dante stepped back behind the fenced-in area.

The opposing pitcher had braces that glittered in the sunlight like armor. Teddy seemed even younger, smaller, weaker. How could his own uncle leave him out there, defenseless? Louisa was right from the first: Rivera was a louse.

She stood up and shouted along with Francine. "Go, Teddy. You can do it! Come on, Pirates! Hit it!"

They were both almost hoarse by the time he struck out.

Francine sighed and ate the last of the grapes while the rest of the team went down in order. "Maybe he'll do better at soccer."

"Nonsense. Your son is a wonderful baseball player!"

Even the pitcher's mother looked at Louisa like she was crazy.

Aunt Vinnie said, "You are just as nice as your mother, Annie. But Teddy struck out, and he missed all his plays in the field."

"Yes, but he looked marvelous doing it."

Francine grinned. "I knew I was going to like you. Dante said I would."

"He did? That is, why would he — ?"

Then he was there, with Teddy, who was eating an ice cream sandwich. "Coach takes us for pizza if we win. I like ice cream better," the boy said after Dante introduced him to Louisa. He broke off a piece for the dog, after politely asking Louisa if it was all right, after his uncle squeezed his shoulder.

"I'm sorry your team lost," Louisa told him, "but you played a good game."

"No, I didn't," he said, swiping at the ice cream dripping down his chin, "but that's okay." He grinned up at her, showing the same dimple his uncle had. "All the other guys were jealous."

"Of your batting?" Louisa asked, three strikes of doubt in her voice.

"Nah. Because I had the hottest babe in the stands cheering for me."

Chapter Eleven

God, she was incredible when she smiled. Dante thought Louisa looked about as old as Teddy in the too-big shirt and crooked Yankees cap, at a distance. Up close she looked like a temptress and a tease and too good to be true. Which she was, of course, standing out in her brightly colored shirt like a rainbow trout in a guppy tank. She didn't fit in here, although Francine had seemed pleased with her company. His cousin was now berating Teddy to mind his manners and his aunt was asking no one in particular, What Babe?

"I hated that movie. Couldn't eat bacon after it, either. And Babe Ruth's been dead forever. And if Christina Hapgood's baby didn't match the rest of her redheaded brood I'd swear she was carrying on with Nate, down at the fuel company."

"He meant a pretty girl, Ma."

"Teddy's too young to know about girls. It's that computer stuff, I swear. What do you think, Louisa?"

She gave the dog the last cookie. "I, uh,

think it's getting late and I better get home to fix Galahad's fence."

"I'll give you a ride," Francine offered before Dante could. He was happy his cousin might have found a friend. Lord knew she could use one. And he didn't need one more minute in Ms. Waldon's company, so why was he disappointed?

Aunt Vinnie, who couldn't remember her way home sometimes, remembered her own plans for Louisa and Dante. "No, Francine. I need you to help make labels for the strawberry jam for the church bazaar."

"That's not for a month."

"You can't keep putting things off, like going back to school."

"Ma!"

"Don't 'ma' me. Dante can drive Annie home while you and Teddy help me with the labels. That will keep the boy from looking at those dirty pictures on his computer."

"Grandma!"

"That's Louisa, Aunt Vinnie, and I'm fine walking home, really. It's good exercise."

"I'll drive you," Dante said. It was a statement, not a question. Louisa would have resented the man's high-handed attitude, but she needed his help to finish the fence. A bossy man who could fix things was a lot

134

more tolerable than one who couldn't. Besides, her feet hurt.

"Thank you." She said good-bye to Francine and Teddy, who invited her to the next and last game. Aunt Vinnie promised her a jar of jam the next time she came to visit. Then Louisa followed the caretaker-cum-coach to his decrepit truck. At least none of her New York acquaintances could see her now, in a pickup instead of Howard's Porsche, with a country lumpkin instead of her successful lawyer.

She had to wait until Dante cleared the passenger seat of cups and napkins and cardboard trays. "Teddy and I stopped for a snack."

Howard never let her have a breath mint in his car.

Dante threw a bag of garbage into the back of the truck, but he tossed half an uneaten hamburger to Galahad, who leaped into the cab before Louisa to scrounge for french fries, then sat on her lap, his head out the window. As she struggled to get the seat belt around her and not the dog, she said, "I wonder if an afternoon like this can make up for his lost days in the show ring."

"Champ looks happy enough."

Louisa wasn't sure. To her Galahad

looked confused, as if he was waiting for the blue ribbon, or to be put back in his crate until the next show. "I'll bet he never went to a ball game before. Or had a whole Little League team share their ice pops with him."

"I'll bet you never did either. Go to a kids' ball game, that is. Little boys must have been offering you their treasures since you were six."

She made a face, remembering Denis Bromley offering her a pet frog in kindergarten.

Dante saw her scowl and thought she was still worried about the dog. "Who knows, maybe Champ is happier being a real dog."

"But who can say what's real for a dog? Hunting with his pack, herding a flock, defending his territory, or parading around a ring? He's been bred from lines of show dogs. It's all he's ever known."

"You know what they say about old dogs learning new tricks. People can change. So can dogs."

Dante was watching the road, as all the cars tried to leave the parking lot at once. Louisa wasn't sure if he was speaking of the dog or of her, who was as much out of her element as the terrier. Nah, the guy was a handyman. What did he know about metaphors?

He was waving to all the SUVs and vans as they pulled out. All the kids — and their mothers, particularly their mothers — waved back and smiled and yelled good-byes.

He must know everyone in the whole town, she thought, and wondered what that would be like, walking down a street and recognizing someone. That almost never happened in Manhattan, so people stopped looking at each other. Well, now she knew a few more people, and a ball team.

"You looked like you were having fun," he said when they were clear of the ball field.

Louisa had to ask herself about that. Watching inept children destroy their psyches in inane games of skill and chance? She was surprised when the answer was: "Yes, I did enjoy it. Thank you."

He laughed. "Don't thank me. The kids were the ones who put on the show."

"But I liked Francine, and spending time with Aunt Vinnie and getting to know your nephew, too."

"Francine talks too much but she has a good heart."

"That was obvious. But I meant thank you for inviting me, for encouraging me to go. You were right."

They were stopped at the light on Main Street and he reached over to pet the dog, in her lap. "I usually am."

"If your head gets any bigger you'll bump it on the truck's roof." But she smiled. He chuckled, and it was a nice sound.

"So what was I right about this time?"

"That I was hiding, I suppose."

"You were nursing your wounds, like an injured bear. It was time to come out of your den."

"I would have, eventually."

"And missed a sunny spring afternoon and kids having fun. Life's too short to let chances like that go by. But now I am sounding like an old graybeard. And you were right, too. It was none of my business what you do, or don't do."

Louisa stared out the window, wondering how this stranger, this backwoods bumpkin, got so wise, or so easy to talk to. Maybe she had spent too much time alone, after all. She stared out the window, almost speaking to herself. "I was afraid to go out."

"Good girl. At least you recognized it."

"I'm no girl." But his words felt good, as if someone really understood.

"Pardon. My mistake. You are an ancient crone. So what were you afraid of? Meeting Harold in the street?"

"That's Howard. No, I was afraid everyone would laugh at me, I guess. Or give me those 'poor dear' looks, wondering what was wrong with me that my fiancé did a flit."

"That's just pride. Didn't anyone ever tell you that vanity is a sin?"

"Wrong church, I suppose. My mother always said people will think what they want, no matter what, that bad thoughts were their problem, not mine. The premise is easier than the practice."

"Your mother is a wise woman. Look what she'd be missing if she worried about what people said about her and Bernie."

Talk about sin, he knew about her mother and her rest-home Romeo? "I forgot, you must have met them at the . . . ah, party." When Louisa was too traumatized to speak to the guests. "Bernie is good for my mother. She's happier than she's been in years, and I am glad for her." Mortified that her own mother was shacking up with a septuagenarian, but glad.

"Even if people talk?"

"Like she says, talk can't really hurt her, and now she is not so alone." The dog made up for some of Louisa's own loneliness, but his conversational skills were somewhat lacking. Then again, he never disagreed with her or told her to be quiet when he was watching the business news on TV. She rubbed the spot behind Gally's collar that he liked scratched, and was rewarded with his shiver of pleasure. Thank goodness some males were easily satisfied. "Pride is poor company, I am finding."

The very virile one behind the wheel made a snorting sound. "You don't have to tell me about that."

Louisa would never have put Dante Rivera and loneliness in the same sentence. She knew he was divorced, but she also knew there were maybe ten women looking for every unattached man. Maybe twenty, if he was as attractive-looking as this one. And she'd seen how every female between sixteen and sixty smiled at him as if he were a free sample at the bakery counter. No, she did not think he suffered from lack of confidence or lack of companionship. Oh, yeah, a man with his own business — looking after other people's houses was a business, wasn't it? — his own truck, such as it was, and a respectable family in town, was going to have to look real hard for a dinner date. Sure. Louisa bet women brought him casseroles and cakes all the time.

"Oh, Mr. Rivera," Louisa could imagine them saying, "thank you for fixing my trellis. Do you think you could look at my shower? It seems to be dripping." Hell, hadn't she been thinking of ordering a pizza to go with his beer? And those cookies . . .

Even if he couldn't change a lightbulb, the man was bound to have a harem of women waiting on him or on his phone call. He liked kids and dogs. What more could a female want in a man? She doubted they'd let him coach the kids if he was a drunk or a druggie. He had dimples, for Pete's sake! And a strong chin, even white teeth, and thick black hair. Chances were the women in the town, or the entire county, were lined up thirty-deep to become the next Mrs. Rivera, or the next mistress.

Louisa decided she'd save her pizza money and eat a frozen dinner. Alone. She was not interested in joining the queue, not at all. The playboy could have his beer and go spend the night with whichever willing bedmate was first in line.

Alone, Dante Rivera? Hah.

Louisa must have made a similar snorting noise to his, for Dante looked over at her. "What, you think a woman has exclusive rights to injured pride and hurt feelings?"

"Of course not. Male pride is one of those forces of nature women are taught not to fight, like heavy surf and undertows. I just cannot imagine you feeling embarrassed or ashamed by a divorce, or being shunned by other women. Not even Paumonok Harbor could be so backward as to find a broken marriage scandalous or offensive to their moral precepts."

"You haven't heard about my divorce then."

She sat up straighter, or as straight as she could with the dog in her lap. "I do not gossip about my neighbors. I find that offensive."

"And Aunt Vinnie wouldn't have told you."

"There's that, naturally."

He stopped at a crosswalk to let a black Lab tug an attractive young brunette toward the opposite corner. She waved and called, "Hi, Dan, see you Saturday?"

"Right."

Louisa's dog was much better trained, she told herself, and far handsomer.

"There's a beach cleanup on Saturday. Ingrid and her husband organize it."

Ingrid had a husband? "Nice-looking dog."

"Hmm."

A few blocks went by and they were almost at Louisa's house before she finally asked, "Well?"

"Well, what?"

"Well, aren't you going to tell me what happened to make your divorce so gossip-worthy? I know that's being nosy, but you did bring it up yourself. Besides, after the hints you've dropped, I am imagining the most outrageous possibilities. I'm sure Francine will tell me the next time I see her."

"That's not gossiping?"

Louisa thought about her own sister. "Not if it's your cousin. Then it's family concern."

"I'm surprised she didn't tell you the minute you sat next to her." He exhaled audibly. "My wife left me."

He must have been an ogre for a woman to walk out on him. Louisa wondered what he'd done, and inched a little closer to the door.

"For another woman." He looked over at her instead of the road. "If you laugh, I'll drive you and the mutt back to the ball field and leave you there."

"I wouldn't laugh," she said, choking to cover the telltale sound. "And there is nothing so terrible about that. It happens."

"Not in Paumonok Harbor, it doesn't. You cannot imagine what it was like to walk into the Blue Fin for a beer."

"Like facing the caterer and the photographer and the justice of the peace at my wedding?"

"They didn't fall off their bar stools laughing, did they? Or impugn your manhood? Your attraction for the opposite sex, that is. Gads, I break out in a sweat just remembering those first weeks."

"You lived through it."

"A better man, as Aunt Vinnie would say. One who understands invisible wounds."

"Did you love her? Besides having your pride shattered?" Louisa gasped. "I am sorry. I have no right to ask such personal questions."

"It's all right. I think the way Susan left was worse than the loss itself. We were friends, though. I thought so, anyway, before her lawyers started putting their hands in my pockets. In fact, she said that's why she was moving out. She liked me too well to keep cheating on me."

"Keep cheating?"

"That's what I asked, too. Anyway, she likes me well enough to want me to father her children. Hers and Cora Alice's. Artificially," he quickly added.

The poor man! Louisa rethought her decision about the pizza. He'd lost his wife, maybe his house and his life savings, along with the respect of his peers. The least she could do was offer him a hot meal. Pizza counted as that, didn't it?

"So do you think you and Hobart can ever be friends? After all, he didn't marry you and then leave you with bills and a baby like Francine's husband."

"Now that I look back on the relationship, I don't think Howard and I were ever friends. We were a couple and then a habit, following the expected paths until he took a detour. So I guess I was lucky. But no, I wouldn't want to be friends with such a misguided maggot."

"That's understandable enough."

He pulled into the renters' driveway, past the old oak tree that was starting to leaf out, despite all the missing limbs. "Are you sure you need that fence up tonight?"

Dante asked. "Champ doesn't look like he's going to run off."

The dog had lain down, his rear end on Louisa's lap, his head on Dante's thigh. He didn't stir, not even when the truck stopped.

"I suppose not. But tomorrow . . ."

"I'll be here."

Louisa opened her door to get down, pushing the dog off her lap. Galahad whined and crawled more onto Dante's side of the truck. Embarrassed, she said, "I guess he likes going for rides."

Dante stroked the terrier's ears. "Guys like trucks, huh, Champ?"

Louisa didn't want to reach over to grab Champ — Galahad's — collar, not when the collar was resting against a man's stomach. Which reminded her: "I did promise you a beer, though. And I was going to order in a pizza."

The dog wagged his tail as if he understood the word "pizza" and was ready for the crusts, despite everything he'd eaten this afternoon.

"I have a lot to do."

"But now you don't have to help me with the fence."

"I can use the time to catch up on some of my other chores."

Louisa was not going to beg. "All right, then. I'll see you tomorrow. When, so I am not out walking the dog?"

He heard the disappointment in her voice, and knew how much he'd hated eating alone until he became used to it. He was going to have to accept, despite his vow not to get any more involved with this female. Instead he said, "I really can't stay."

He really couldn't. Not after the dog puked on him.

Chapter Twelve

He wasn't coming. Oh lord, he wasn't coming.

Louisa was having a nightmare. Not the kind that makes no sense unless you pay someone to make up an interpretation, or the anxiety-wrought dreams of being late for an appointment you didn't have, or missing an English Regent when you'd been out of high school for ten years, or being lost in a traffic circle. This was the half-awake kind of nightmare that end-lessly repeated the worst times of your life until you were wide-awake, heart pounding, mouth dry, tangled in the sheets.

He wasn't coming. He was never coming, and everyone was pointing at her, laughing. She couldn't do it. She couldn't go on by herself. He had to come!

Oddly enough, the man she was waiting for, almost praying for in her dream, was not Howard. He was Dante Rivera, and he had a leather carpenter's apron on, with tools hanging all over it. Louisa sat up suddenly, eyes wide open. She didn't need any divinator to tell her what that image was about. Good grief, Dante Rivera.

Then she heard it, the pop-pop-pop of a staple gun. No wonder she had dreamed of him. He had come, as promised! Louisa had meant to be up hours before Dante said he'd arrive, with coffee brewing and eggs and toast ready to cook. She'd been up half the night with the dog, though, out in the yard with her flashlight, wondering if there was a 911 number for dogs. The stars were out, brighter than she'd ever seen them in the city, and somehow she was not half as fearful as she'd been, outside at night. Maybe she was too worried about her dog to think of prowlers and perverts and predators, oh, my, lurking in the brush.

Now Galahad was fast asleep at the foot of Louisa's bed. He hadn't even barked at the noise, but he was whuffling in his sleep, not moaning anymore.

"Some watchdog you are," Louisa grumbled as she threw on jeans and a T-shirt, telling herself that she deserved the rotten night, for being such a bad dog owner. She might not have known about chocolate, but cookies and ice cream and potato chips and hamburger? That could make anyone sick. Louisa felt queasy just thinking about it, and what else Gally might have picked up from under the bleachers. Then she thought about her dog being sick in Dante's truck, on Dante's leg. She felt worse. Nightmare worse. Cup of hemlock worse. Crawl back into bed — no, crawl under the bed — worse, and never come out.

But he came back. What, was he running for sainthood, or mayor? He wasn't interested in her, Louisa knew. He'd have accepted her invitation yesterday otherwise. Or else he would have suggested another night for pizza and beer if he truly was busy. As a matter of fact, Louisa did not think he liked her at all, most of the time. He was nice enough and helpful, but with a sense of distance and dread, as if he was only being friendly for Aunt Vinnie's sake. That was fine. Louisa was not interested in him either, except as a handyman, of course, and as a masterpiece of masculinity.

Louisa couldn't afford a photocopy, much less a masterpiece. But she could look. This morning Dante had on khaki cutoffs and a tan T-shirt with the picture of a fish on it. No tool belt or apron, just firm, muscular legs, a flat stomach, and a broad chest. His dark hair was tousled by the morning breeze, and he was laughing.

There were worse ways to start the day, Louisa thought as she put on the coffeemaker, the extra one from Howard's apartment that he'd decided was hers. He'd kept the better one, of course.

From the kitchen window, she could see that Dante had come with the proper tools and Rico, who had a wife and a girlfriend, according to Aunt Vinnie. She supposed that meant the two men had a lot to laugh about. They were talking in Spanish, which surprised her. Not that Rico spoke his native tongue, of course, but that Dante was so fluent. He was a wizard with the power staple gun, too, keeping to a steady rhythm while Rico held the chicken wire against the new fence posts. Louisa and her bent nails could never have done such a good job, nor so fast. The mesh was going to be strung before the coffee was ready.

She wondered if she could hire them to fix the roof. Aunt Vinnie had said Dante looked after a lot of houses, but maybe he had a little time. Louisa could not pay him what the rich summer people paid, of course, but if she got the part-time job at the library . . . Who was she kidding? She'd never be able to pay a professional. As soon as she was back on line she was going to start selling her jewelry, just to buy gas and groceries. Most of her severance package from work had gone to pay off the catering hall, and she had foolishly, confidently signed a letter of resignation. Now she couldn't get unemployment benefits, especially when her old company would likely take her back. She would go back to work where Howard still worked, where they'd thrown her a retirement/wedding shower, when pigs flew. She'd starve first, damn it. And while she was cursing, she damned herself for seven kinds of idiot for not taking Howard's "severance" check. Pride might be poor company, but it made a mighty thin soup too.

She barely had enough extra money on hand to tip Dante and Rico for the job they were doing today. Granted they would put their hours on the bill for the next-door owner, but putting up the chicken wire on the new fence ought to be her expense. Her mother had agreed to pay for whatever materials Louisa needed to fix the cottage, but they hadn't talked about hiring people other than plumbers and electricians. Louisa had thought she could do the rest of the repairs, but the roof? She'd have to ask when her mother and Bernie got back from Arizona, where they'd gone to visit his relatives.

Meantime, she could offer the workmen breakfast. Dante drank his coffee black. Rico preferred tea. Both had breakfasted hours ago and turned down her scrambled eggs. Could you reheat the leftovers in the microwave? Louisa did not know, but she'd try. She would not feed them to the dog. "It's dog chow for you from now on, Champ. That is, Galahad."

Dante went back to his truck — "No problem. I just hosed the whole thing off" — to fetch something. Louisa noted that his pickup was older than Rico's, who was supporting two women, and wondered briefly if Dante was still supporting his former wife.

"This was in the back closet," he said, handing her an answering machine. "I got a new one with the portable phone attached. I think this still works, but I couldn't find the directions. You plug the phone jack in —"

Did he think she was an imbecile? Bad enough she had to accept charity, but she could hardly turn down his gift, not when she needed it so badly. "I can figure it out. Thanks. Now my mother and sister can nag at me when I'm not home."

"And you can screen your calls when

you are, in case you don't want to talk to Humbert when he calls."

"Howard is not going to call. He would have found out where I was by now. He knows my sister's number."

"He's a fool."

Louisa thought so too, but it was nice to have Dante Rivera agree with her. Louisa forgave him for thinking she couldn't work an answering machine, and watched him go, with regret. Her roof still leaked. She did say she'd go to the beach cleanup, though, so maybe she'd ask him about it then.

She left Galahad out in the newly secured yard and went inside to plug in the answering machine, which she had absolutely no idea how to install or operate. Howard always did those things, damn his black heart. His boring black heart.

By pushing enough buttons, she got her dial tone back and could try to create a message. She pushed "incoming" and heard "You have no new messages." So she pushed "outgoing."

"Hello. This is Susan. Neither Dante nor I can come to the phone. Please leave a message after the beep."

Louisa felt like a voyeur. Which did not stop her from pushing "outgoing" again.

So that was Dante's wife, who had left him for greener pastures, or smoother skin. Susan's voice was soft, slow and sultry. If someone could be said to have bedroom eyes, she had a bedroom voice, without sounding like she was a dial-a-dirty-talk operator.

Louisa played it again, trying to picture the woman who had left Dante Rivera. She couldn't.

She pushed the "record" button and left her own message. No, her speech was too prissy. She paused too long before starting her second try, recording seconds of breathing. Galahad barked to come in through her third attempt, and midway through the fourth Louisa decided she should not sound like a single woman living alone. She spoke louder the next time, trying to instill confidence in her voice. "Hello. This is Louisa. Neither Galahad nor I can come to the phone. Please leave a message after the beep."

There. Another job well-done. Proud that she'd already had a successful day, and before lunch, she decided to walk the five blocks into town to the library. Mrs. Terwilliger had no news about the part-time tech job. "The library board hasn't decided yet, dear. Mr. Halstrom's daughter had a baby and Miss Milligan's sister is visiting so they postponed the meeting. Oh, and it was nice of you to cheer for the Minell boy at the ball game."

"Francine's son Teddy? You heard about that?"

"Of course. My niece played canasta with Lawrence Banks's mother last night. Theodore needs all the encouragement he can get, what with his mother working and that father not paying much attention."

Louisa was surprised the librarian did not comment on her ride home with the handyman. Nothing seemed to get past anyone in Paumonok Harbor.

Meantime, her free Internet connection disc had arrived from the county library system. Louisa had to sign all kinds of papers, that she understood her rights and responsibilities. She signed them without reading the small print, figuring the county could track her Web activities if they had nothing else to do, since she had no intentions of sending or receiving porn, spam, or chain letters. What she wanted was to connect to the outside world, and see what a nice set of pearls could bring on eBay.

"C'mon, Champ. Let's go home and get wired."

When she got there, the light on her new

answering machine was flashing. Her sister's internist had just divorced his receptionist/wife. Was Louisa interested?

Not in the position nor the physician.

Her mother thought Louisa should start a new business: coaching people for job interviews. With her experience in hiring, and people desperate for work, Louisa would be a natural. And Bernie would lend her start-up money.

Exploit the unemployed? No, thanks.

Jeanette from the animal shelter had the best idea of the day. Now that she had such a well-trained dog, the message said, Louisa might be interested in the course for therapy dogs and volunteers being held in Riverhead. Once Louisa and Galahad had been certified, they could go into hospitals and nursing homes, or work with troubled kids. Now that sounded a lot better than hunting for a job or a husband. Gally would be a natural at it, too, since he was used to crowds and being handled. As long as there were no squirrels, he'd do fine, and Louisa thought she might too, helping people, if she could afford the course. She'd call tomorrow for more details. Today she was going to return to cyberspace.

The library system had assigned her a

screen name. Louisa Waldon had trans-lated by some arcane formula into lwaldo. As in where was Waldo? That was fitting, Louisa thought, for someone lost in the back of beyond. Nevertheless, lwaldo was online in minutes, and Louisa couldn't help thinking that Mr. Plug It In Here couldn't have managed the job so handily. She wondered if Dante Rivera were computer-literate at all, or stuck in the last century with his hammer and saw. No matter, she was connected.

She went through her computer's files and sent everyone her new E-mail address. Everyone except Howard, his family and friends, that is. She wrote to old college roommates and one high school pal, and the women she'd had lunch with at work, figuring she'd find out soon enough who were her real friends. If she decided to go back to the city, she would need the net-work. If she stayed out here, she would need the contact with intelligent life.

No one must be online right then, be-cause she only got one reply, and that one was an undeliverable E-mail notice. She checked out eBay, and quickly realized she had to know more about pearls before she could go any further. A quick search found about a million Internet sites and more information than she could possibly sift through. She could take the blasted pearls Howard had given her to a jeweler for an appraisal in half the time. She didn't want the pearls, and didn't want to wear clothes that required pearls.

Then she looked up therapy dogs. There were whole organizations for them, tests the dog and the handler had to pass, doctoral theses on the principles behind the method, and case studies that could warm a curmudgeon's heart.

"We can do this," Louisa told the dog at her feet, who drooled on her bare toes. "You'll be great. You've already helped me a lot, haven't you?"

Galahad thumped his tail and dropped a tennis ball in her lap. Now if he could only send an E-mail, Louisa wouldn't feel so abandoned.

Chapter Thirteen

After a late lunch, Louisa decided to transplant some of her marigold seedlings instead of tackling the storage shed and the old lawn mower again. According to the gardening books and the seed packet, the baby plants were ready for their permanent homes. Louisa was not ready for the lawn.

She was carefully separating the seedlings' roots for the front yard when a car pulled up next door at the old Mahoney place. Paumonok Realty was written on the side of the BMW, and a woman in a short-skirted pink suit got out. She was in her well-preserved thirties, Louisa guessed, and worked hard on making sure she stayed that way forever. Jogging, dieting, facials, a little highlighting in her auburn hair, a bunch of makeup, and a lot of shopping, Louisa bet. She knew the type from Manhattan, but was surprised to see a day spa doll here. Not that any woman should let herself go, Louisa thought, thankful she'd remembered to put on the sunscreen this morning, but this real estate lady was wearing heels. Granted they made her long legs and rear end look more shapely, but they were as out of keeping with a morning in a little seaside village as an ocean liner would be, tied up at the sagging fishing dock.

The woman walked around the Mahoney place, carefully picking her way through the weeds. She ended up on Louisa's side of the property, so Louisa stood and said, "Hi. Is the Mahoney place for sale, then? I heard they were ill, but hoped they'd come out for the summer."

The woman feigned surprise that Louisa was there — she couldn't have missed her in the front yard — and smiled. "I'm not sure, but I have a client who might be willing to make them an offer too good to refuse."

It was that voice, the one from the answering machine. Slow, soft, sultry. "Mrs. Rivera?"

"Why, yes. How did you know?"

Louisa did not want to confess that she recognized the voice from listening to an old public message that seemed private for being stowed away for years. Talk about being out of the closet . . .

Dante's ex-wife laughed before Louisa could speak. "Of course, from the sign on

161

the car. Everyone knows everything about everyone in this town, don't they?"

Louisa had no idea who ran the real estate office in town, but she had a good idea that Mrs. Rivera had come to Whaler's Drive to find out about her. Louisa stood taller, although she'd be inches shorter than Susan, even without the other woman's high heels, and she kept herself from fussing with her hair. Susan's auburn curls — Louisa would give anything for curls — were swept up on top of her head and held with a turquoise barrette. Louisa's straight, short hair was held off her face with a paper clip, which was all she'd found that morning in a hurry. Susan's nails were so perfectly polished Louisa could not tell if they were real or not. Her own blistered hands and ragged nails were thankfully hidden in the garden gloves.

Louisa could not imagine this woman with the rough-edged Rivera. Oh, they'd make a handsome pair, if the handyman were cleaned up and dressed better, but they seemed to inhabit two different worlds. Day and night, chalk and cheese, badminton and bowling. Definitely an odd couple. Then again, Louisa could not imagine Susan Rivera flouting convention to live with another woman, or wanting to be a mother, for that matter. Perhaps her partner wanted to be the full-time, stay-at-home mom, so Susan got the nine-month job. Life was full of puzzles, and Louisa had learned in the personnel business not to judge applicants by appearances. The best-dressed could be dolts, and the slobs . . . Well, the slobs were usually unsuitable for work at the law firm, except in the mail room. She had also learned not to be fooled by insincere smiles. Susan Rivera was showing perfectly even, most likely bonded teeth, as many as a piranha.

"I am Louisa Waldon," she said, politely if unnecessarily. "Recently taking up residence in my family's summer home."

"Of course you are." Susan's glance took in Louisa wearing more dirt than clothes, then the old house with its sagging roof, age-darkened shingles, and warped screen door. At least the windows and doors were freshly painted, and Louisa had found a wicker rocking chair for the porch at a yard sale. With a can of spray paint and some string where the caning was coming undone, it was almost as good as new. She hoped to find a table to match, and cushions, perhaps an old urn to hold the flowers she was counting on to bloom eventually.

Susan finished her survey without curling her lip, which would have made wrinkles. "You've done, ah, wonders with the old place. Are you considering putting it up for sale?" She started to reach into her jacket pocket for a business card.

"No. Actually, I am thinking of staying on here after the summer." Actually, Louisa had been thinking how much she'd hate going back to Manhattan to look for a stressful, demanding job and an ugly, expensive apartment. She'd hate having them even worse, living in a shoe box, working in a crate, dealing with cardboard people. "I'm finding myself enjoying the peace and quiet, the simple pleasures like walking on the beach and planting flowers." She held up her trowel, which should have meant "Good-bye, I'm busy" to anyone with the tact of a termite.

Susan laughed. "What, you're thinking of staying year-round, when you haven't even lived through a summer here? Wait until you see all the traffic, hear all the noise. Your pretty, private beach will be wall to wall with blankets and umbrellas, and you won't be able to smell the sea for the suntan oil. You won't hear it, either, not over the boom boxes. And that's to say nothing of the winters. You're from the city, right? You'll hate it here. Autumn lasts a week, then everything turns gray. The weather turns cold and dreary, with wind that goes through every crack of an old house. Keeping an ancient place like this warm will cost a fortune."

"It has a fireplace. I had the chimney cleaned."

"Good, so you'll add to the air pollution. All the heat escapes up a chimney, unless the fireplace is enclosed. Everyone knows that."

Louisa hadn't.

"But that's just the weather," Susan went on, proving she was not a member of the local Chamber of Commerce. "You're used to New York City, you'll be bored to tears here, with nothing to do. No museums or galleries, no shows or concerts. Half the shops and restaurants are boarded over. Even the local movie theater shuts down."

Since Louisa hadn't been out to dinner or to a movie in a month, she didn't think she'd mind. Concerts in the city were too crowded and Broadway shows too touristy. The museums would still be in Manhattan for her to visit by train. "There's always TV, and books. I understand the library has a lecture series."

"The Fauna of Long Island. Pirates on

Paumonok. Gravestone rubbings. Feh."

"Feh" must be a Long Island Lady expletive. Louisa thought she'd have to try it the next time she was tempted to use the f-word. "There is a course in Riverhead on dog handling for —"

Susan did not let her finish. "And where will you get your hair done? Janie Vogel's back parlor? Incidentally, I love your haircut. No one can get that dramatic flair but a true artiste. Let me tell you, no designer hairdresser would be caught dead in outer bumfuck."

Shouldn't that have been bumfeh? Louisa made note of Janie Vogel's name, because the artiste in her needed someone to straighten out the back of her hair, where she had lopped off about ten inches of demanding, curl-defying locks. Which reminded her that she could sell her wavesetters, curling wands and blow-dryers. Maybe she'd have a yard sale, if she found enough other stuff in the attic.

Susan tapped one pointed toe, as if she were impatient that Louisa was not already packing her bags. "What I am saying is that there is no social life for a person like you."

Like her? What, was Louisa some new ethnic group, outcast religion, or social demographic? Were rejected brides in a class of their own? Hell, if Paumonok Harbor could accept a lesbian divorcee, they could handle another single woman. "I am not really worried about making friends. I met a few nice people already."

Susan brushed that aside with one of her elegantly elongated nails. "I am not speaking of friends. I am speaking of men."

Which was odd, unless Susan was trying to ascertain Louisa's own sexual orientation. Did she think one broken engagement would turn Louisa against the entire male population? Well, it might have, but that did not mean Louisa was open to other suggestions. "I am not really interested right now."

"In anything," was left unspoken.

"But you will be and there are no decent men around here, men of your, ah, caliber, shall we say."

We shouldn't be saying anything.

Susan didn't wait for Louisa's reply, though. "Half of the locals didn't finish high school, much less college. The jerks have no ambition or they would have left here. They drink too much and smoke too many controlled substances."

Was that why she left Dante? Louisa wondered. Was the other woman just an excuse to get away from a bad, dead-end marriage? But then why would Susan want to have Dante's child? It made no sense, nor did this conversation. "I'm not sure why you are telling me this. I can't sell the house, even if you convince me to leave, you know. It actually belongs to my mother."

"Oh, I know that. It's a matter of record. I am just thinking about you. It's the small town in me, I suppose, minding everyone else's business. You've already had a rough deal, and Dante took you home from the ball game."

Ah, here was the answer, Louisa thought, to the question that had been gnawing at her: Why the feh was Mrs. Rivera here? Susan might not want her husband, it seemed, but she did not want anyone else to have him either. Louisa wasn't being warned away from Paumonok Harbor. She was being discouraged from Dante. "He has been very helpful."

"Of course he has. That's what he does, who he is, but it doesn't mean anything. I don't want you to be hurt. I've tried to interest him in every female I can find, and he is always nice, but that's all."

Could Louisa be that wrong? "Excuse me, but you want him to find a new girlfriend?"

168

"I gave up, but do you think I want to feel guilty for the rest of my life? I know it's my fault, but he swears he'll never marry again. He'd have been snared by some gold digger years ago, otherwise."

Gold digger? For the post-hole digger? "He has money?"

"Don't tell me you didn't hear that, not in this town."

"I try not to listen to gossip," Louisa said automatically, running on autopilot as her brain was in shock.

"They don't have anything else to talk about, in this town."

"He has money?"

"Other than some of the summer people, he's the richest man in town."

His truck, his clothes, his work . . . "I thought you got the real estate business in the divorce?"

"But you don't listen to gossip? You should have paid more attention. He let me have the realty company, but he kept the houses, except for the one I live in, of course."

Houses? "He owns the one next door?"

"And a bunch more. My agent's share of the rental fees alone makes me more than comfortable. When he fixes one up to sell, I get a lovely commission."

"You mean that's what he does, buys old houses and renovates them for profit?"

"Well, it's more like a hobby to do some of the work himself. He made his money by inventing some kind of computer code or something I never understood, right out of Princeton. Instead of taking his money all in stock in the new business, he took cash. Thank goodness, for he might have lost it all, like so many others. He said he did not like California or the technical work, so came home when his parents were ailing. He invested his money here in land and houses. He hasn't left since, the clod. I wanted to move closer to Manhattan, or have a pied-à-terre at least, but he wanted to be close to his family."

Princeton, computers, money? Oh boy. "So he doesn't need to work?"

"I told you, he doesn't call it work, but pleasure. It's like his boat or his golfing, his charities, just something he does for fun."

Oh boy, big time. Louisa had screwed up before, but this was a major miscalculation. What was that about not judging those job applicants by appearances? God, she'd been about to offer Rich Man Rivera a tip for stapling up her fence! She was baking him effing cookies when he might own the bakery in town! Louisa was ready

170

to die of embarrassment, right after she murdered him. The bastard must have been laughing at her the whole time, knowing she took him for a handyman. Handy? She'd hand him a piece of her mind, if she ever spoke to him again.

Susan was going on, oblivious to Louisa's dismay and disgust and detestation of her former husband. "So you'd better forget about any plans you had for Dante. Of course he's usually open to a quick tumble, if that rows your boat. The man has no heart to give, and I will not take responsibility for that. He never even wanted to be married to me, not really."

Now that Louisa could understand.

"Anyway, that's what I meant, about finding a man. If you were counting on Dante, you are making a mistake, and I had to warn you. And there simply is no other choice in Paumonok Harbor."

"Of course there is. I am not a snob." But she was, Louisa realized, the worst kind of snob, looking down on people who deserved her respect. Half of them were better people than she was — and sometimes better off.

To prove her broad-minded nature, and to prove Susan Rivera wrong, she accepted a date with the ironmonger.

Chapter Fourteen

She didn't really want to go out with the welder. He worked at Cal's Collision, for heaven's sake, and had a hoop through one eyebrow. Being broad-minded was one thing. Alvin MacDonald was another. Of course, she acknowledged from her newly won wisdom, he might have a PhD in behavioral sciences from Oxford, with inherited millions in a trust fund. Or he might have a regular appearance on America's Most Wanted. What he definitely had was tattoos.

Oh, man, did he have tattoos. Up one thick, rope-muscled forearm and down the other, past biceps bigger than Louisa's thighs, across his massive neck, and on his broad fingers. Snakes and dragons and scorpions and a few skeletons mixed with hearts and flowers.

"Want to see the rest?" he asked with a rakish raised eyebrow, not the one with the hoop, which was likely too traumatized to twitch.

Caught staring, Louisa could not compound her rudeness by refusing his offer to go to the Albatross with him Saturday night. "They're having a live band."

"A live band, wow." He was being friendly; she would not be judgmental. Nor would she let anyone in this rumor-ridden town accuse her of chasing after its own personal land baron. She did not want any man whatsoever, so she might as well show them that she did not want this man as much as she didn't want that man. Which made sense to Louisa, anyway. So she said yes.

It was all that damned Dante's fault. If she hadn't been so boggled by his bank account, she might have had enough wits left to make up an excuse for Alvin. No, she was having company for the weekend. No, she was invited to a friend's art show opening in East Hampton. No, she was too stupid to be allowed out of the house. Any of them would have done as a thoroughly believable alibi.

Actually, it was all Howard's fault, along with famine in Africa, global warming, and the price of gas. If not for her former fiancé, Louisa would not have been anywhere near Cal's Collision, or Tattoo Al. For that matter, she would not have been in Paumonok Harbor, entertaining the locals.

After Dante's wife left, Louisa had considered digging a hole deep enough to bury herself in. Her trowel was too small; her dog was too liable to dig her up again. Then the mail truck came. The postal delivery person, Ralph, tossed a packet of catalogs and credit card applications into her mailbox and drove off, despite the fact that Louisa was sitting two feet away from the thing. Among the junk mail and bank statements forwarded from her New York City address was a yellow slip stating that she had a registered package waiting at the post office. Ralph could have brought it and had her sign right here, rather than having to fill out the yellow form. That would be too easy and efficient for the U.S. Postal Service, though, which might be why they lost more money every year. To say nothing of packages.

Curious, Louisa drove to the post office behind the school and signed for her mail, a shoe box–sized carton that had come all the way from Austria, via her City apartment. She instantly knew what it had to be, and almost tossed the whole box, unopened, in the trash barrel next to the stamp machine.

Then she remembered how much money she had paid for the darned thing, and how much money she could make back at the

Internet auction sites. She slit the sealing tape with her car key and pulled off the wrapping, then opened the carton. By now two old men were standing nearby watching, bay clammers, from the hip-waders and the smell. One of them whistled when she pulled out a hand-painted, metal, scale model of Howard's beloved red classic Porsche. She'd ordered the painstakingly reproduced replica from a small factory in Ziftsweig, Austria, as a wedding present. She'd been disappointed that it hadn't arrived in time, before she became distraught that Howard hadn't arrived at all.

The old men were admiring the detail, right down to the leather seats. Louisa's asking price was going up. Then she noticed the personalization that she'd paid extra for. The tiny license plate in front read "Porsche," but the one in the back said "Howard." No one was going to want the little car but the little schmuck himself.

She tried to pull off the rear license plate.

"Don't do that, lady. You'll wreck it."

Which was her intention. Then she had a better idea. She'd give it to Howard after all, to prove to herself that she was not going to be eaten alive by regret and rancor, that she was moving on with her life. She might never forgive Howard, and she'd certainly never respect him again, but she did not need to hate him. He was nothing to her anymore, nothing but a piece of misguided metal that didn't fit in her mailbox. She'd send the car to him, an apology for inadvertently causing the destruction of his, an acknowledgment that he'd made the right decision, if at the wrong time. Then she'd be done, once and for all, done with the memories and the misery.

Of course she had to make a few changes to the car first.

She asked the old fishermen if they knew anyone who could replace the license plate she'd mangled. They'd directed her to the auto body shop that did the finest detailing on the whole East End.

Which is how Louisa ended up at Cal's Collision, ogling Alvin's arms.

"Man, I'd give my eyetooth for one of those babies," Alvin, who turned out to be Calvin's son, said when he saw the model. "The real thing, that is."

"I think I know where you can get one, cheap. It's in a lot of pieces, though."

Alvin waved one grease-blackened hand at the junkyard that was his work space.

"The more pieces the better."

"I'll ask about the wreck, then, when I hear from Howard. I'm sure he'll call when he receives the model. But you can make the changes I want, can't you?"

Now Alvin silently pointed out the garage door at his own car, which had so much customizing that Louisa couldn't recognize the make or model. The gold-colored two-door had a dragon for a hood ornament and flames painted on the chassis. The front grill was in the shape of a medieval shield, and the rear-mounted tire had a painting of a knight and his sword. Ah, a classicist.

"And I design my own tattoos, too."

Louisa was now confident he could fix the miniature car, once he understood what Louisa wanted for the new license plates. Alvin had a lot of trouble with the front one.

"If he's a golfer, shouldn't it be spelled PUTTS?"

Howard had balls to match the scale model, but they weren't white with dimples. "No, it's a term of endearment," she told Alvin, who was obviously not from New York City. "Spelled P-U-T-Z."

The rear license plate was easy, even for Alvin: "Love, Louisa." She might forget about the gutless groom, but now he'd never forget her.

So it was Howard's fault she was wearing her $500 Gian Todaro sandals and her $300 silk blouse to a two-bit gin joint. She knew she was in trouble when they pulled into the parking lot and had to walk past a gauntlet of smokers outside the front door. Shaved heads and chains — and those were the women — made her glad she was with Alvin. He'd turned out to be a weight lifter, a semiprofessional car racer, and a volunteer ambulance driver, besides being a visual artist . . . and an auto body man. Alas, he had no graduate degree. "Putts" was most likely the longest word he could spell. His hands had not come clean, either.

The Albatross was no more inviting inside. The band was live, but they had to be deaf, from the volume of the noise. Louisa had to shout her order twice, at the crowded bar. The dance floor was too small for three couples, much less the five who were already there. The place was filled with noise and dirt, sweat and cheap perfume . . . and a poolroom. Alvin tugged her in that direction.

"Sorry, I don't play."

"C'mon, I'll show you."

He put his beefy arms around her to demonstrate the proper form. Louisa accidentally drew the cue stick back and up so it poked him in the chin. "I'll watch, thanks."

He played for beers and shots, and kept winning. Which meant he kept drinking. Louisa sipped her spritzer, then switched to plain seltzer and lime. She talked to an improbable redhead who worked in the butcher department at the supermarket, who knew more about meat than anyone Louisa had ever known. She turned down a dance with a man with a braided beard, and another with as many neck chains as Alvin had tattoos.

Louisa tapped her so-called date on the shoulder. "Hey, Alvin, it's getting late and I have a lot to do tomorrow. How about going home?"

"Later, baby. One more game."

The redhead yawned. "They'll go on 'til the place shuts down. It's the same every Saturday night. 'Less there's a fight and the cops close it early."

That was another new experience to look forward to.

Louisa went back into the other room, looking for a telephone to call a taxi. Out of order, the sign read. Everyone had cell phones anyway, a very pregnant teenager told her. Louisa didn't; she couldn't afford one anymore.

She passed the ladies' room and kept going. She couldn't drink seltzer all night without needing to pee, though, so she turned back and went in. The room was filthy and foul and smelled of vomit and worse, with water and paper towels all over the floor. She'd been in cleaner Porta Pottis at street fairs.

She opened one stall. She'd die of uremic poisoning first.

The Board of Health was obviously sitting down on the job, but not in this john. The second stall wasn't as revolting, so Louisa carefully laid toilet paper strips over the seat, wishing she'd learned to piss standing up. Myra at work had sworn it was possible, but Louisa never wanted to practice at home. Now she struggled to make sure no inch of her bare skin or good clothes touched any surface. Her mother would have been proud. When she was done, Louisa turned to flush the toilet, but there was no way in hell she was going to touch that side lever. Chances were, the rusty sink had only cold water and no soap, so she raised her foot to do it. That's when the Fates sent her a message about the direction her life was taking. Louisa's hand-sewn sandal, her honeymoon splurge, fell into the toilet.

She stared down into those murky, miasmic depths, her soul crying, "Do over. Do over." There was no imbecility-rewind button handy, of course, nor a hanger, a broom, or anything.

Nothing. She needed Alvin's cue stick. He wouldn't give it up. She grabbed one from the redhead's date, saying, "Don't even ask." She went back to the cesspool of a rest room, where no self-respecting rat would rest.

As she fished her sandal out of the toilet, Louisa asked herself three questions: Would she wear that shoe again, knowing where it had been? Would she carry it out in her hand? And what the hell was she doing here?

She put the sandal on the floor and hopped out, using the cue stick as a cane.

"We are going home, Alvin. Now."

Since she'd picked his weighty key chain up from the side of the pool table where he'd put it, Alvin had no choice.

"How about if I drive?" she asked when they reached his car. "I think you've had too much to drink."

"What are you, my mother? No woman

drives my wheels. But, hey, maybe I'll let you this time, if you treat me nice."

Alvin's ideas of nice didn't match Louisa's. Her silk blouse was torn in the tussle, but Alvin's eyebrow was bleeding, from where Louisa had pulled out the ring, without opening the hoop. She thought of using the pepper spray from her pocketbook, but Alvin seemed subdued, even contrite, and he still had Howard's toy car.

While he was still mopping at his eye, variously swearing at her and swearing he only meant to grab a kiss and a feel, Louisa tossed his keys into the overgrown grass at the side of the parking lot. Now the dickhead, the bloody dickhead, couldn't kill himself or someone else.

Louisa stomped off down the street. She would have stomped, that is, if she had two shoes. Now she stomped and hobbled, stomped and hobbled, out of the parking lot and onto the road back to town. She'd call a cab from the gas station. Unless the taxis stopped working this late at night. She'd worry about that problem when she got there.

The more immediate problem was that she'd forgotten how far away from the gas station they were. Alvin had driven so fast it seemed like a few blocks. She'd also forgotten that there were few street lights in Paumonok Harbor except on Main Street.

No cell phone, no flashlight, no shoe.

No tears, she told herself. She was an adult, an independent, intelligent woman, who had just bested a weight lifter with licentious intent. She was not afraid of the dark. Or drive-by demons. She had her pepper spray in her hand now and enough adrenaline pumping through her body to see her through six more skirmishes. Why, she could save the cab fare and walk all the way home.

And then she'd never, ever leave the house again.

Chapter Fifteen

Dante was on his way home after minding Teddy so Francine could go to a baby shower for one of the girls at work. Fran deserved a night out without having to pay a sitter, and Dante enjoyed his nephew's company. Against his better judgment, but at Teddy's urging, he'd been going to invite Louisa Waldon to come watch the Harry Potter video with them. She might have seen the movie, but there was no magic like watching wizardry with a wide-eyed kid. They were going to ask her at the beach cleanup that morning, but she hadn't come. Dante supposed her enthusiasm for joining the community began and ended at the ball game. Teddy was disappointed. Dante was not surprised, but he was surprisingly disappointed too.

Well, he'd been disappointed before, by better-looking, better-built and brainier females. Now he wouldn't have to chance his expectations being underwhelmed by this particular nutcase again. Not that Louisa was a typical bitchy or buffle-headed blonde, but she had enough baggage for a world cruise.

Dante could finally wash his hands of her once and for all, before things got complicated, like Teddy growing fonder of her.

He might have regrets — or he might have eaten too much sausage and peppers for lunch after the cleanup — but Dante's conscience was clear. Louisa had her fence, her peace and quiet, and her privacy. He'd given the troublesome renters their deposit money back, so they were out of her short, silky, straight hair. It was late for a summer rental at top price, but Dante was confident his ex could find a sedate couple or a nice family for the cottage. If not, he could afford the loss of income. The loss was worth it, to cut down on the complaints.

Louisa had her job too, such as it was. Dante had put in a good word for Ms. Waldon with Bob, president of the library board, yesterday during their golf game. The position was part-time, temporary, and paid peanuts, but it was hers if she still wanted it.

The case was closed, the book was shut, the game was over. No score, a couple of errors. So why the devil was he still thinking about a woman who gave him indigestion?

Dante shook his head as if to clear it of wayward thoughts. Then he shook it again, staring out at the dark night. He hit the brakes, thinking he'd seen something moving at the side of the road, and you never knew when a deer could jump out in front of your truck.

Cripes, as Teddy would say. That was no deer. Speak of the devil, there was Louisa Waldon, as if Dante had conjured her out of moonbeams. The she-witch was tottering down the grass verge, in the dark, in the middle of the frigging night. She must be soused again, Dante thought, feeling a pang that wasn't heartburn this time. What a waste. And what a good thing Teddy hadn't seen her like this. Damn, he'd recommended her to the library board!

Drunk or not, Dante couldn't leave her out on the road. Not many cars passed, and heaven knew who was driving the ones that did. Besides, the worst she could do was throw up in his truck. Why not? Her dog already had.

He inched his truck closer, then realized she was not weaving from side to side as he'd thought; she was limping, with one shoe on and the other missing, but traveling in as straight a line as possible under the odd conditions. If she wasn't DUI,

Dumb Under the Influence, then Dante didn't want to know what the hell she was doing out here, alone. He wasn't going to like it, he was sure of that.

Sighing, he pulled the truck alongside her and leaned toward the open passenger-side window. "Lost, little girl?"

Louisa stopped lurching and lowered her hand, the one with the can of pepper spray. Her voice was more lethal. "You!"

Dante might be guilty of a lot of crimes, but no one could blame him for this . . . whatever it was. "Me. Rivera's Taxi and Limousine Service."

She started to move again, but Dante kept pace, with the truck. "Would it help if I apologize for the sins of all mankind, now and in the future?"

She didn't even look over her shoulder. "No. I do not want to hear anything you have to say."

Then her snit really was personal? Dante dredged his mind without coming up with a plausible explanation for how he could have stolen her shoe and left her in the dark, while he was watching Harry Potter. The woman had the mind of an addled octopus, going eight places at once and getting nowhere. "Couldn't we discuss the situation on the way home?"

She kept going. "I am on my way home, in case you haven't noticed."

"But it will take an hour at this rate of speed."

"An hour?"

He heard the dismay in her voice and couldn't resist adding, "Or two."

She stumbled, but recovered and limped along faster.

Dante was beginning to enjoy himself. She didn't seem drunk and she didn't appear damaged, only temporarily deranged. He smiled at her retreating figure, then pulled alongside her again. "You know, there might be snakes sleeping in the grass where you're walking. There are definitely ticks. And spiders. Maybe fleas."

She leaped onto the pavement inches from his front fender, then winced when she stepped on a pebble. "Go away."

Dante had no intention of leaving, but he said, "Not until you tell me why."

She turned and faced him, glowering into the glare from his headlights. "You're rich."

He must have missed an exit ramp to the conversation. "Yeah, and you have one shoe. So?"

"You own a hundred houses."

"Not even fifty. I'd have to print out a

list to get an accurate —"

"And you're smart."

Not smart enough to figure out what the deuce she was nattering on about. "That's a hanging offense these days? I didn't realize that being successful was against your principles. It is the American way and all that, you know. Or are you some kind of Marxist? I doubt you made a habit of sharing all your income with the masses, unless they were masses of caterers and florists and five-man bands."

"This isn't about that damned wedding. Will you forget about it already? I have."

He didn't bother replying to that absurdity. No woman forgot her wedding, even if it never came off. Especially if it never came off. "Okay, so I have money and brains. Does that mean you can't ride in my truck?"

She pounded on his hood. "You didn't tell me!"

"Oh, I should have introduced myself with my bank book in one hand and a master's degree in the other?"

"You have a master's degree?"

"Two, actually, but one is honorary. That's not the point. You would have heard all that garbage soon enough if you'd visited Aunt Vinnie more. The only reason she didn't fill your head with my credentials was she forgot you didn't hear her boasting at the — you know, the party you forgot. Anyway, why won't you get in the truck? It's the same one you rode in last week."

"I thought you were a handyman then!"

"I fixed your fence, didn't I?"

"You let me make a fool of myself."

"Let you? Lady, you didn't need my help. You were in a rant about the renters, about the dog and the fence. You believed what you wanted to, that all men were pond scum, beneath your notice. So you saw a dumb slob breaking his ass to fix someone else's house. How was I supposed to know no one handed you my résumé? God knows they don't talk about anything else around here."

Louisa threw her remaining sandal at his windshield. She didn't want its match back, anyway. "You could have driven a nicer car so I had a hint!"

"To carry lumber and tools and iced fish boxes? My car is in the garage. Besides, you don't have a great track record with fancy automobiles, do you?"

Now both her feet were being jabbed by pebbles, and who knew how many rusty nails, broken beer bottles, or slugs crossing the road. "As you are very well aware, I do not have a good record at anything. I cannot fix my house by myself, cannot find a job, and now I cannot even go out on a real date."

Dante pretended to look in the shadows. This was the most fun he'd had in years, and he intended to enjoy every minute of it. "I hate to say this, Juliet, but I don't see Romeo around."

"Stop making fun of me!"

"I'm not, I swear," he said, glad she couldn't see his grin. Spitting-mad and shoeless, Princess Louisa was almost as comical as old man Mullins mooning the St. Patrick's Day parade.

Louisa sat on the front bumper of the truck, resting her feet. "I left him to walk home too," she said over her shoulder.

"Ah, the revenge of the deserted. Howdy Doody took French leave, so you kiss off the next man to buy you dinner?"

"No, I left the next man who thought he could paw at me in a seedy parking lot."

Suddenly Dante wasn't finding her story half as amusing. "Who was it?"

"Why, so you can get together with him and laugh at me, at how the mighty are fallen? That's what your wife would do."

Tilt. The woman's mind worked like a pinball machine. Boing, boing, boing, bells and whistles and lights, and the ball never going in a straight line. "My ex-wife. What the hell

191

does my ex-wife have to do with anything?"

"I met her and I didn't want to be like her."

"What, gay? Susan says you don't get to choose, you just get to accept yourself."

"Not gay. A snob."

"Let me get this straight. You did not want to seem snooty, so you went out with some lowlife who mauled you?"

She stood and started walking again. "I went out with a very talented, artistically inclined gentleman."

"Who didn't take no for an answer?"

"Who didn't ask."

Dante used a word he tried not to, on account of his nephew and his aunt, then he turned the truck off and got out, leaving the headlights on in case another car came down the road. He walked beside her, in the cone of light, trying not to think of her poor feet. If he thought of them, he might just have to pick up the fleawit like he would Teddy and sling her in the truck. Without asking. "Listen, Louie, I am not going to let you walk home by yourself, and we both know it. So how about getting in the truck? You can yell at me the whole way home if you want."

"Would you let me drive?"

He tried to sniff her breath for alcohol

fumes. He smelled shampoo and perfume and the honeysuckle starting to bloom in the scrub brush. A man could get drunk on those, but Dante thought she was sober, unless she drank odorless vodka. "Sure. Can you drive a stick shift?"

"No. I was just checking anyway."

"But you'll get in the truck?"

They were almost out of the headlights' arc. Louisa looked ahead and saw nothing but emptiness. She sighed and turned back.

Dante released the breath he was holding and then held the door for her. By the interior light he could see stains on the silky shirt she was wearing. This time he didn't worry about Teddy hearing the words he used. "That isn't blood, is it?"

Louisa looked down and sighed again, a $300 sigh this time. She'd have to throw the blouse away too. "Yeah, but not mine."

Dante got in and started up the truck but waited a minute. "Want to tell me what happened to your shirt and your shoes?"

"No. The sad story of my sandals will go to the grave with me. I might live down the wedding, if I live to be eighty, but the sandals? Never. And the blouse merely suffered collateral damage."

"Want to tell me about your date?"

"Hah!"

"What about my former wife? Trust me, there's nothing you could tell me about her that would surprise me. Did she arrange a blind date for you?"

"Hardly. She told me I didn't belong in Paumonok Harbor. In polite terms, of course."

"Susan is always polite, even when she is twisting the knife in your back."

"Yes, well, I figured that if she could be accepted in a conservative little town, with all her, um . . ."

"Quirks? Susan is tolerated because I'm rich. Everyone knows I'll stop donating to the local charities, pull my money out of the bank, and resign from their committees if she is not shown respect. She might be marching on Gay Pride Day, but she was once my wife, and might be the mother of my, ah, test tube someday."

"That's very loyal of you. Very droit du seigneur, but loyal. Anyway, I wanted to show Susan — no, I wanted to show myself — that she was wrong. I can make a life in Paumonok Harbor."

Hell, Dante thought, for once in her life his ex-wife might have been right. Louisa Waldon couldn't make it five miles from her house without losing her shoes.

Chapter Sixteen

Dante put the truck in gear then said, "I'll find out who he is, you know."

He being her late, lamented date, of course. "How, by following a trail of blood from the Albatross? The better question is why you'd want to make the effort? What is it to you, anyway?"

Dante did not want to examine the answers to those last questions too closely. He had no legal or moral responsibility to this disaster-prone dame. He did not want any, or the woman, for that matter, except in the way any red-blooded male would want the slim, shapely, green-eyed blonde. And yet . . . there was a niggling feeling in the back of his mind that he had to look after Louisa Waldon. Lord knew, someone had to. He had sworn not to take on any more injured doves, yet here she was, in his truck, rubbing her wounded wings.

Feet. She was massaging her sore feet. Instead of being aggravated the way he should be, Dante was amused, relieved, glad to have her so close, and wishing he could rub her toes. Worse, to his thinking, was the fact that the idea of some prick laying his hands on her almost made him turn the truck around and drive back to the —

"Did you say the Albatross? Damn, Louie, that's no place for a lady!"

"My name is Louisa, and thanks. I know all about the Albatross. Now."

"Fish-packers go there, and transient crews from the commercial boats. Everyone who's been thrown out of the Blue Fin or the Breakaway hangs out in that dive." His blood turned cold to think of the prickly but delicate rose in that field of poisonous weeds. "You could have been murdered, or worse."

"I met some very nice people there. A charming woman who knows more about beef than you know about baseball, and a lovely young girl, much too young to be legally drinking, but old enough to escort various male acquaintances — at least I hope she knew them — to the men's room for ten minutes at a time. I am sure she will make a fine mother someday, perhaps next month. Oh, yes, there was the pleasant barmaid who had lesions on her hands, an interesting gentleman with more ear studs than teeth, and a friendly lady in the corner by herself, most likely left alone because her wig could not hide his Adam's apple. She thought my blouse was divine."

"At least there were no knife fights or flying bottles."

"No, I left before the real entertainment started. Stanley and the Split Eardrums was treat enough."

"I am sure there are neighborhoods in Manhattan where you wouldn't walk by yourself in the dark."

"There are neighborhoods in the city where I wouldn't walk by myself in broad daylight. I just didn't know there were any like that in Paumonok Harbor."

"Hey, I'm the biggest booster the Harbor has, but even I acknowledge it's not the All-American, apple pie model of a small town. We've got our share of rotten apples in the bushel, like everyplace else."

"I'll remember that, the next time I decide to go slumming." She leaned her head back against the seat, letting the motion of the car steady her heart rate. "At least I felt safer on the empty street than I did inside the place."

He looked over at her. "We don't have a high crime rate. Mostly kids breaking into houses to raid the liquor cabinets. Drunk driving, bar fights, vandalism and domestic quarrels. That kind of thing."

"Good, now I can sleep better knowing I won't be murdered in my bed. I don't have any liquor."

"Good. That is, you won't be attacked at a bar, either, if you pick your dates more carefully."

"What, doctors and lawyers never slip drugs in their dates' drinks? Accountants don't think a free meal entitles them to a free lay? Get real, professor. And save the lecture for some other innocent twit. I have learned my lesson."

"You? For a sophisticated chick from the big city, you sure are naive at times."

"And for a young man, you sure are prosy at times."

Dante was pleased she thought he was young. Prosy? Well, she deserved a lecture for going out with — "Who the hell took you there anyway?"

"You see? Prosy. Pushy. Patriarchal. You'll make a good father however the baby is conceived, but you sure aren't mine."

He was almost ten years older than she was, he figured. Not old enough to be her father, certainly. Too old for anything else? He refused to think about it. There was not going to be anything else, period.

When the silence had gone on for a few more blocks, Louisa said, "I'm sorry. I shouldn't have snapped at you. I've had a lousy night but you've been a lifesaver, again. It's not your fault that you are over-protective and authoritarian. I guess you had to be for a long time, the head of the family and all that. Or maybe it was just bred into you. You know, blue eyes, pride, and thinking you know what's best for everyone."

That stung, so Dante replied, "And I guess you can't help making bad choices now that you are out on your own. I suppose Hagrid made all the decisions for you."

"Howard?" Louisa sat up straight again. "He did not! I . . ."

. . . did what Howard wanted. Louisa had accepted all Howard's choices, because that was easier than arguing, and he was better company when he had his way. So they ate when and where he wanted, vacationed where he selected, and saw the movies he chose. He was paying for all of it, she always figured, so he had the right. He never paid for her hair or clothes, though, and she still listened to his opinions, catered to his tastes. She was pleasing her partner. She called it compromise, not caving in. What could be wrong with that?

Nothing, unless she'd given up her own ideas, subjugated her own likes and dislikes, until she was a mere extension of Howard, a reflection, a big nothing of her own.

Had she really been a spineless jellyfish, all for a faithless, feckless mama's boy? Feh, as Susan would say. Yeah, she had been. Maybe she'd wrecked his car on purpose, exerting her personhood, subconsciously destroying the relationship that was swallowing her alive.

And maybe she was just drained from the events of the evening, introspective and maudlin because she had screwed up again. She shouldn't be so angst-ridden, not when she was safe and secure. When she was gnashing her teeth together to keep Alvin's tongue out of her mouth, that was the time she should have been questioning her past and her personality. Now she should just sit back and enjoy her victory. She'd won, by god, expressed her wishes in as forceful a way she knew, barring a gun license. She had made a bully bleed and back down. Good triumphed over evil, or over Alvin, anyway. So what if she needed a ride home? She, Louisa Waldon, had fought her own battle.

And she, Louisa Waldon, was cared about by a handsome, intelligent, desirable someone. He might have stopped for a stray dog on the street, too, but he cared about Louisa, despite himself. She could almost see Dante fighting to deny it, but she knew he did. And she felt better for it.

When the old truck pulled up behind her, Louisa had never been so happy to see anyone in her life, even though Dante was a deceiver and a dastard. She couldn't tell him of her relief and her joy, of course, and she was mortified that he, man about town — man who practically owned the town — had found her in another ridiculous situation. Still, she almost flew into his truck, into his lap, like her dog when someone set off an early firecracker. Here was light and safety and going home. Here was comfort and time to breathe.

Here was Dante Rivera, whose heart would be as battered as his old truck, if he had a heart.

"It's okay to like me, you know," she told him now, a few blocks from her house.

"It is?"

"Yes. You see, I don't want anything from you. I wouldn't take it if you offered, so you don't have to worry about being entangled with me and my rotten roof and misguided life choices. I am on my own and I like it that way, learning my own lessons as I go, like how to caulk the bathtub so it doesn't leak down into the kitchen. And how not to let anyone else do my thinking for me. I won't listen to your wife, and not to small-town gossip, either."

"So I have your permission to like you?"

"Well, you already do it, so you might as well admit it."

"How did you arrive at that conclusion?"

"Well, you are grinning, for one thing, showing both dimples at once. You are jealous of my date, and you haven't drummed your fingers on the steering wheel for the last ten minutes. Oh, and you've driven past my block twice."

"Okay."

"Okay, you like me?"

"Yeah, I can manage that, as long as you don't start calling twice a day and showing up everywhere and expecting me to care about your relatives and your migraines and your wrinkles."

"I don't have wrinkles!"

"You will."

She wouldn't mention moisturizers and sunblocks. Or his former wife's foray to the plastic surgeon, which he must have paid for. "Okay. I will restrain from prostrating myself at your feet. There, now we can be friends."

He waited. And waited some more. Finally he asked, more a complaint than a question, "Well, aren't you going to say you like me too? It's only fair, after you made me say so."

"Can't you tell?" She smiled.

He rubbed his chin in mock deliberation. "Well, you haven't thrown anything at me lately, and you're not twisting your hair into knots. Oh, and you've never called me Howard by mistake. Or Galahad."

She laughed and said, "I'm working on liking you, Danny boy, I'm working on it. It takes a little effort, but I'll keep trying."

When they pulled into Whaler's Drive, the whole street was bright with the glow from Louisa's house. "What, were you throwing a party?" Dante asked as he turned at the old oak into her driveway, behind her car.

"No, I just don't like coming home to a dark house. And I thought the dog wouldn't feel so lonely."

"With a light on in every single room?"

She shrugged. "The TV is on for him too."

"Speaking of the beast, that's some watchdog you've got. I haven't heard a peep out of Champ."

"No, he only barks when I'm home, it seems. I think he is alerting me, not guarding the house. He's had so many homes, the poor baby, that maybe he doesn't feel possessive about this one yet. I think he's still confused about his name. Silver Crown's Mental Image, Midge, Galahad, Champ. He doesn't know who he is."

"He might be confused about his sex, too."

Louisa ignored him and opened the car door, her keys in her hand. Dante opened his. "Oh, you needn't see me to the door."

"Aunt Vinnie would have my head if I didn't."

Louisa walked carefully across the grass in case she missed cleaning up after the dog. She opened the front door and Champ bounded out, barking and leaping at her, wagging himself silly, as if she'd been gone for days instead of hours.

"At least he knows his owner," Dante said, looking on at the reunion. Finally acknowledging that someone else was there, the terrier came toward Dante. He lifted his leg on a bush first, as if to establish that he was top dog, and Dante was merely one of the pack.

"I'm not in the contest, Champ. She's all yours."

Louisa was uncertain what to do next. Should she invite Dante in, offer him coffee? Or say good night and offer her hand to shake?

She rubbed her feet, which were now cold and wet from the dewy grass, against each other. "Well, thank you."

Dante was not taking the hint to leave. "So have you forgiven me for having money and property?"

"I'm happy for you, of course. It's not that I wanted you to be poor. No one should be."

"And we're friends, now, right?"

Louisa wondered what he was getting at. "Yes?"

"Then how about telling me what happened to your shoe?"

Louisa smiled, and that's when Dante kissed her. He bent his head, slowly lowering his lips toward hers. He didn't ask permission, but the question in his eyes meant Louisa could have said no.

Sure she could have. Right after she flew to Alpha Centauri. She was mesmerized, paralyzed, energized. She was so ready she raised her face closer, sooner, yes. Oh, yes, without thinking. If she stopped to think, she'd kiss the dog instead. There was no time for thoughts, and hours 'til their lips met.

He was smiling too. Oh, Lord, he was smiling, so sweetly, so knowingly. His lips were smooth and warm and firm and sent sparks down her spine. No, those were his hands, rubbing electricity through her silk blouse. She was already melting when the tip of his tongue parted her lips and touched her teeth, her tongue, her soul. He tasted of . . . popcorn? No matter, now she was smoldering, every breath they shared fanning the fire. God, he kissed even better than he looked. And he looked . . . stunned.

Dante dropped his arms, which had somehow found themselves under her blouse. "Damn."

"Damn?" Louisa was shattered. No, she was already in shards from the kiss. Now his horrified look splintered her self-esteem. "You . . . you didn't like it?"

He was halfway back to his truck. "I liked it. Too frigging much."

Chapter Seventeen

Dante almost ran back to his truck. He didn't care what he stepped in. He was knee-deep in trouble already.

He did not want a woman. He especially did not want a woman on the rebound, out of loneliness or gratitude or sheer proximity. He mightn't be the only fish in Louisa Waldon's sea, but he was the one almost in her net, so he ran.

He did not want a woman, damn it. Dante was content with his life, and he'd worked hard to get it just the way he liked it. He had his friends, his boat, his golf clubs, plenty of rewarding, satisfying work. He didn't want a woman with more issues than *National Geographic*, one who'd share her bed with her babied dog, her bitter memories. Hell, Humpty Dumpty Howard would be watching the humping.

But, oh, how he wanted Louisa Waldon in his bed, in his arms, all around him, part of him.

He wouldn't do it. He thought of Aunt Vinnie matchmaking, his cousin Francine wanting to be Louisa's friend, his ex-wife asking his intentions. His intentions were strictly dishonorable, and a good cowboy didn't dirty his own ranch, not when he wanted to keep living there.

So he jumped on his trusty steed and rode into the sunset. He shoved the truck into reverse, anyway, and drove back into the night, as chilled as if it were October, instead of June.

Louisa was glad he left. At least she convinced herself she was glad he left during a hot shower, scrubbing the last of Alvin and the Albatross away. Who knew what might have happened if Dante had stayed? She might have invited him in, and they'd have sat on the couch, which sagged so they'd be touching. He might have stroked her, out of pity and consolation, and she might have let him, because his hands felt so good, which he would take as an invitation, as he'd done with that kiss. And then they might have gone upstairs so the dog wouldn't see, and she'd have to worry if he had protection. (Was she supposed to buy them now that she was not an almost-married, one-man woman?) Which meant she would have lost the mood, remembering Howard and the horrors of dating. But he wouldn't have lost it, not a hot number like Dante. And he would have proceeded anyway, and she'd have let him, because he was nice and that's what he wanted, and she hoped to enjoy herself. But she wouldn't, not after the foreplay, and she'd be bored or seasick, like she was with Howard, or bumping her head on the bed frame. And he'd be disappointed there were no fireworks, so she'd never see him again anyway, which would be worse after they'd been intimate. And she'd have to change the sheets.

So it was a good thing he was gone. And stayed gone.

Louisa was too busy for a fling, anyway.

She got the job at the library, a phone call from Francine, flowers from Alvin, and a new pair of sandals.

Francine wanted to know if she could drive Aunt Vinnie to Teddy's last game. "I can't get out of a meeting that day, and Dante has to drive a bunch of other kids. He said you wouldn't mind. Okay? Oh, and how about lunch on Tuesday? There's a special at the Triangle, and I have a discount coupon."

Alvin brought a hanging basket of geraniums, fancy pink ones with purple centers. She liked them a lot better than she would have a bouquet of flowers to toss out in a week. Alvin helped her screw a hook into the porch roof so she forgave him, a little.

"I had too much to drink," he said by way of an apology. "You know how it is."

Louisa was noncommittal, admiring the plant. She'd never assaulted anyone, even in her one, one-day depth of drunkenness.

"I thought you were fried, too. You know, the shoes." He picked up a brown grocery bag from the porch steps and dumped out her Gian Todaros.

"You found my sandals?" Louisa was busy wondering if a combination of ammonia, vinegar and bleach would kill the germs, corrode the leather or explode. She did not stop to wonder how Alvin had located both shoes.

"I was kind of hoping they might convince you to go out with me again. You know, to celebrate having them back."

Celebrate cesspool sandals? The look of horror on Louisa's face made Alvin quickly add, "Not to the Albatross, but to a movie."

"Thank you, but I'm sorry. I've already seen it."

"How could you when you don't even know what's play— Oh, I get it. Well, I can't blame you, I guess. Dante said the flowers might do the trick, but I didn't really believe him."

"Dante?"

"You know, Mr. Rivera."

"What, he holds a mortgage on your garage and threatened to have you evicted if you didn't come apologize?"

"I was going to come apologize anyway, I swear! The plant was his idea, is all."

There was a connection Louisa was not making, like a short circuit somewhere. "How . . . ?"

"Oh, he came back to the Albatross to tell me you were home safe." Alvin had the grace to blush for not thinking of how she'd get back, he'd been so mad at her for tossing his keys. "He drove me home too, once we found the keys and locked the car up. It took an hour, but he said you'd been trying to save my life, so I'm not mad anymore."

"That's nice of you."

Alvin was not big on sarcasm. "Anyway, I went in to tell Pete to look after my wheels, and he handed me your shoe. Then Dante said he knew where the other one was. That took another hour. Cleaning up his truck took another one. I couldn't get up in time to drive my mother to church Sunday morning."

Alvin went to church? "I'm sorry about that. What happened to Dante's truck?"

"You don't want to know, but he said your dog did it too. Anyway, I guess we're even now, and you still want me to put that pet name on your Porsche model?"

"Even, and yes, I still want that, ah, endearment on the little license. Oh, but I need to apologize about your brow-ring." She reached toward the Band-Aid over his eye.

"That's all right. I was tired of it anyway. I'm thinking of having a tattoo put there, to hide the mark. What do you think?"

"I think that might be lovely." As long as he didn't write "putz" there.

She didn't wear the sandals. She left them on the porch to air — for a week — and bought rubber flip-flops at the corner souvenir store instead. Bright orange, with big plastic flowers on them, they were the cheapest pair of footwear Louisa had ever owned, and she adored them. She loved how they actually made a sound like their name. Only a soul that soared would dare to put on orange onomatopoeias. She was flying. She had a job and a friend, Francine, not Alvin, and someone to impress, Teddy, not his uncle.

She wore her new sandals to the last ball

game, with a yellow linen sundress. What was she saving her fancy trousseau for, anyway? She tucked a sprig of honeysuckle in the clip that kept her hair off her face, and felt like Cinderella going to the ball in glass slippers. Or Dorothy in her ruby ones. Anything could happen to a girl in special shoes.

She picked up Dante's aunt — Teddy's grandmother, that is — and cheered herself hoarse. With Francine not there, Louisa felt she had to encourage Teddy and his team twice as loudly. It must have worked, for they played better. Teddy bunted and got to first base. The team lost anyway, and now they were out of the play-offs.

"Thank heaven," Aunt Vinnie whispered as they watched Teddy and his friends shake hands with all the winners. Louisa thought she'd miss the games, miss watching the children just being children, and watching their coaches being kind, caring, and heart-stoppingly handsome.

Then Teddy was rushing over to pet Champ, declaring Galahad a sissy name for such a primo pet. Teddy was thrilled with his personal rooting section and his success, despite the loss. He was even more excited that the coaches were taking them out for pizza, ice cream, and miniature golf afterward, because it was the end of the season and they'd played hard and been good sportsmen. The other team was still jumping up and down and pounding on each other in the middle of the field, which Louisa thought was somewhat insensitive of the victorious little buggers.

Teddy was reenacting his magic bunt when Dante came to fetch him.

"A word with you, Mr. Rivera, if you have a minute," Louisa said, nodding politely.

"Uh-oh, Uncle Dan. You're in trouble," Teddy said, running back to his friends. "I can tell. We'll wait in the truck."

"What?" Dante wanted to know. "You wanted flowers and an apology from me, too? It was only a kiss."

Only a kiss? Louisa was about to add that to the items she wished to discuss, but then she remembered her companion. Thank goodness Aunt Vinnie was talking to a man in a Dodgers jersey, telling about going to Brooklyn for a game, last year. Even Louisa knew the Dodgers were in Detroit now.

She climbed down the bleachers with care until she stood on the lowest step, which put her at Dante's eye level. It would have, that is, except that his eyes were on her legs in the short yellow dress. He was smiling appreciatively. Only a kiss, hah! "That is not what I wished to speak about."

He raised his eyes, and one dark eyebrow. "Yes?"

"Did you speak to someone at the library? Mrs. Terwilliger said someone made a personal recommendation that swayed the board to decide in my favor."

"I told one of the board members that I thought you'd be a good worker. Was I wrong?"

"Of course not. I intend to be the best computer data enterer they've ever had."

"They've never had one."

Louisa ignored that. "Did you send Alvin to my house?"

"He was going to apologize eventually. He might have gone a little sooner."

"Did you threaten him?"

"I might have, if he hadn't looked so pitiful on his hands and knees in the grass."

"Looking for his keys or my shoe?"

"Wishing he were dead, I believe."

"What about Francine? Did you tell her to invite me for lunch?"

"I told her you might be busy after this week."

"And Rico?"

Dante didn't bother to feign ignorance. "I didn't need him at the other jobs, so I told him to look at your roof. I'm paying him by the week, so he doesn't care where he works. So what's your point, Louie? The kids are waiting for their pizza."

"The point is I thought we were friends."

"And I did my friend a couple of little favors."

"No, you took over. Friends don't try to manage each other's lives. That was part of our agreement. You were to stop treating me as a helpless female or a little sister."

"Alvin convinced me you weren't helpless. And I never kissed my sister like that."

Louisa looked over her shoulder to make sure no one heard him. "You know what I mean."

"But I don't remember agreeing to anything like that."

"Well, remember it from now on. I do not want your interference."

He nodded and turned to head for his truck, then turned back to face Louisa. "Then I suppose you don't want to hear about the job I found for you."

"I already have a job. One I found for myself."

"This one is part-time too, so you can

216

keep the library position. Unlike the library, this job actually pays. Real money."

Louisa was interested despite herself. "How real?"

"Personal assistant to a retired celebrity writing his memoirs? It's only for the summer, but I'd say it will cover the cost of your new roof, at least."

Louisa was looking down the gift horse's throat, her eyes narrowed. "What would I have to do?"

"Help him with the computer stuff he hates, organize his papers, but mostly keep people from bothering him when he's writing."

"No, ah, hanky-panky?"

"I'd say Wesley Bradford could find all the hankies and pankies he wanted, if he's not too old to care. He does like looking at pretty women."

"Wesley Bradford, the famous art critic?"

Dante nodded. "He's mostly been lecturing these last few years, and consulting at museums. He's been spending summers here for years, at the big house on the hill overlooking the bay. He always brings a secretary-companion, usually a graduate student or a budding artist. Always brilliant, always gorgeous."

"But he'll hire me?"

Dante grinned. "His aide broke her leg last week so he's desperate. He'd stay on his own but he had a stroke this winter. The doctors don't want him overdoing it."

"I wouldn't have to cook or clean, would I?"

"Mr. Bradford has a live-in cook-housekeeper, Marta, Rico's girlfriend."

While Louisa was thinking, she absently said, "You shouldn't encourage Rico in that affair. He's a married man."

"What, I should interfere in someone else's life? Me?"

Louisa shook her head. "So what's the catch with the job?"

"Does there have to be a catch?"

"There always is. Offers that sound too good to be true usually are."

"Hm, let me think. Well, you will have to drive his Mercedes. And attend all those boring cocktail parties and gallery openings with him. Oh, and he likes someone to sit on the beach while he swims, in case he gets a cramp or caught in an undertow."

"And I can still work at the library?"

"He has a physical therapist who comes three days a week. You could coordinate with him."

Louisa shook her head. "So what's the catch?"

"It's only 'til fall. Mr. Bradford goes south for the winter, but you might have enough weeks in to qualify for unemployment."

"I can really have the job?"

"If you want it."

Louisa jumped off the bleacher step, into Dante's arms. "I want it!" She kissed his cheek. "I want it, you incredible man!"

"So I am not an interfering, managing, condescending clod anymore?"

"Of course you are, but you're a wonderful clod!"

Chapter Eighteen

Despite Dante's assurances, Louisa knew she had to pass an interview with Mr. Bradford. No one hired a secretary-assistant sight unseen. She dressed with care in one of her charcoal gray business suits, silk blouse, and heels.

"How the devil are you going to get down to the beach in that getup?" was Mr. Bradford's first question. His next was, "What do you think of this?"

He thrust a sheaf of misaligned, written-over and crossed-out, coffee-stained, printed papers at her, then went back to his computer while she read. Louisa hoped this wasn't some kind of test, like having her critique Hemingway or something. Mr. Bradford was in his mid-seventies, she guessed, with gray hair that had gone past thinning to one step from bald, but he had a thick white mustache. He wore heavy bifocals, a hearing aid in one ear, and kept a cane propped against his desk. Otherwise, he appeared to be in good shape, except for a slight tremor in his left hand. No wonder there were so many smudges on his manuscript. So far he seemed impatient but not impolite. She read as slowly as she dared and hoped for the best.

"So what do you think?" he asked when she placed the pages, now neatly aligned at least, on his desk.

"Honestly?"

"If I didn't want an honest opinion, I'd stick with my own. One day I think it's brilliant, the next day it's crap."

"Well, I haven't read enough to say, but I do know it can be improved. You do not seem to understand the purposes of commas, and, here, this sentence is about a paragraph long. That makes it too hard to read, so whatever brilliance might be expressed is lost. And here" — she found the page she wanted — "when you talk about that artist D'Allessandrio, you spelled his name three different ways."

He waved his hand. "I always had editors to fix that garbage."

"Yes, but you aren't clear about whether you liked him or not. Readers are going to want to know. This next section makes no sense, because you didn't name the woman you met at that showing, you only use pronouns. That's not just grammar, and no one but you can fix it. I can point out the

221

parts that I think need your attention, though, and I can make the changes in the computer so you'll have a clean copy to read."

"When can you start? Oh, and where's the dog? Dante said you took him everywhere. I might have seen him or his sire at Westminster. That's the worst thing about traveling around so much: I don't get to own a dog. Always had one as a boy. Good companions, eh?"

"The best. I'll bring him Monday afternoon."

"Just make sure he doesn't break his leg like my last companion. Or you either, young lady. I need you. And wear shorts. I like legs. If all I can do is look, I might as well have something good to look at."

Louisa's sister was thrilled to hear about the new job.

"No, not the musty old library."

Louisa liked the library job. It was boring and repetitive, but peaceful in her little cubby behind the check-out desk. Everyone who tiptoed by smiled at her and welcomed her to the job and the Harbor.

Annie was going on: "You'll never meet anyone there but musty old ladies who read romance books."

"What's wrong with romance novels? I've been reading them."

"Who cares?" Annie yelled into the phone. "It's Wesley Bradford, you jerk. He's famous!"

"And he's very nice, too. He lets me bring the dog and —"

"He's rich. I think he owns a place in Hilton Head, and I know he has a penthouse in the city. He travels all the time, and goes to every charity event you can name."

"How do you know all that? He's an art critic, not a movie star."

"But he's on TV a bunch, not that I watch PBS all that much, and he had a piece in one of the magazines. I remember, because it mentioned how he always summers in Paumonok Harbor. They said he got a huge advance for his biography."

"Well, he seems to be working hard to earn it."

"Just think, Lou, if you play your cards right, you could end up being a wealthy widow before you know it."

"Annie! What a thing to say, when I just started working for the man. Even if ours weren't a strictly professional relationship, which it is, I think it's dreadful of you to wish Mr. Bradford an early death."

"What's wrong with wishing my sister a trust fund? You deserve it after what that bastard Howard did."

"I am over Howard, Annie. Forget about him. He's dead and buried."

"You killed him? I know Jeff said he knew someone who knew a man . . ."

"Figuratively, Annie. He's out of my life."

"Oh, then what about that nephew of Aunt Vinnie's? Are you making any progress there?"

"Yeah, we no longer hiss and snarl at each other like dogs and cats."

"I told Mama nothing could come of that. He's way too popular with the women. But Wesley Bradford, now —"

"Thanks for the vote of confidence, Annie. Give my love to Jeff and the kids. Bye."

Her mother was not happy Louisa had a nice, well paying job. "Now you'll stay in that place forever. There's nothing for you there, sweetheart. It's fine when you can sit by the water, go to bingo at the church and play canasta. But there's nothing else."

Mrs. Waldon had just described her life in Florida, except for Bernie. "There's lots more, Mama. I am making friends and I signed up for a dog training program.

They have concerts year-round, I hear, and a community theater group."

"Tscha. That's not what I meant and you know it."

Louisa knew exactly what her mother meant. She'd been hearing the g-word since she was sixteen, it seemed. "But now I can fix the roof before it falls in. You did say you'd pay for the materials, right?"

"Yes, but I don't want you up on any ladders, Louisa. You'll fall and break your neck and then I'll never have more grand-children." The g-word wriggled into every conversation somehow.

"When are you coming back to New York to see the ones you already have, Ma?"

"Don't be fresh. You be careful."

Louisa wasn't up on the ladder; Rico was. Dante let her pay his salary, when he didn't need him, and Rico liked working overtime, except on Marta's day off. He needed the money, he said, to send to his wife and family. And for Marta's day off.

Louisa didn't think Dante was letting her pay his workman's full wages, but she was okay with that, because she could re-turn the favor, if not with money, then with her time. At lunch with Francine, at which they decided that all men were worthless, and women were better off without them, Louisa realized that a lot of cast-off women were in worse shape than she was. Francine's husband was always late with his child support payments, trying to screw her out of half the house they owned before Francine left him, and sticking her with bills and back taxes from before they separated. Fred was mean, besides being unfaithful, cheap, and stupid.

The cashier job Francine had at the bank didn't pay enough for her to afford college. Without the education, she'd never get a better job. She'd moved home so her mother could watch Teddy after school, but she was afraid someone was going to have to watch her mother soon. Now Francine had to worry about both her mother and Teddy, her bills, her ex-husband coming around, her future, and turning into a fat, frumpy, soon-to-be middle-aged matron.

So Louisa made Francine skip dessert, offered to redo her makeup, and went with her to Janie Vogel's for a new hairdo, with streaks. She drove Aunt Vinnie to the senior citizens' center, and picked Tommy up after the rec program day camp a couple of times a week, when Dante was busy. Mr. Bradford paid the boy to swim in the pool with him, counting laps, while

Louisa worked inside on that day's pages.

Louisa decided that her employer's worries about swimming alone had more to do with fearing another stroke than with drowning. He was a superb swimmer, with more stamina than Louisa had. She worried about his health though, once she saw what they served at the Friday night gallery openings, the Saturday benefit lawn parties, and the Sunday charity brunches. There were also polo matches, pancake breakfasts and patio barbeques — and it wasn't even July yet. Louisa was putting on pounds, but she was saving on grocery money. And she was getting to wear her expensive honeymoon wardrobe.

She and Marta made sure Mr. Bradford ate healthy foods at home, at least. He grumbled about the greenery, but he seemed pleased that Louisa cared about him. And his book was going much quicker now that someone else was helping with the editing. He also did not lose so much work to the voracious computer during his constant rewrites, once Louisa set up automatic saves and a better filing system, with backups on discs.

"We're a good team, Louisa," he said one night when she drove him home from Guild Hall in East Hampton, where there had been wine and cheese afterward. "Are you sure you won't move in here?"

Louisa wasn't quite certain what he was offering, but she was sure of her answer. "Positive. I love having a house of my own, watching the old place come back to life." Her seedlings were starting to bloom, and Louisa still went to yard sales for bright new Navajo rugs and cobalt blue glasses and pottery bowls — and anything else cheap that took her fancy. When she drove Mr. Bradford to some function in the evening, she left Champ at the big house with Marta, so she had the dog for company on the way home. Between the new automatic timer lights on her house, the dog, and the nice couple with two young children who moved in for summer next door, she wasn't half as afraid of coming back to Whaler's Drive in the dark.

She was coming back to life, too.

"Don't you meet any eligible men at all those parties you're always off to?" her sister wanted to know. "Everyone goes to the Hamptons for the summer social life. You're right in the middle of it, and all you talk about is your old man and your dog."

They were better company than the men she was meeting. Louisa could have been a telephone operator, so many of them asked for her number, but she felt no desire to go out with any one of them. She was busy with Mr. Bradford and the library, and cherished her time alone when she had it. She had her gardens and her books and the beach to walk on in the early mornings before anyone else was there. Besides, the party bachelors reminded her of Howard.

They were polished and poised and groomed like Champ for a dog show. They posed and strutted as if they were in the judging circle too. The men who could afford the benefit tickets or who were on the invitation lists were all successful and talented, self-assured . . . and cell-phone superficial. Louisa assumed they were all looking for Ms. Right, but they wouldn't mind sleeping with a different Ms. Left every week. They left her cold and indifferent, and unable to tell one stockbroker turned Yoga instructor from the other.

Why would she go out for a drink with Sam Sociable when, since she was driving, she never finished the glass of wine in her hand? What would she talk about with Handsome Harry, after she heard his golf handicap? As for Douglas the Dentist — Yuck. Not even her mother could expect her to go out with a dentist.

She stuck close to Mr. Bradford, for her

sake and for his, having decided that part of her job was ensuring that no one offered him a cigarette or more than two drinks, his physician-set limit. If people chose to think she was the older gentleman's sweet, solicitous young plaything, well, let them. At least the men stopped looking at her like a canapé.

Dante Rivera was at some of the same parties, always surrounded by lovely women in designer labels. Louisa and he smiled, exchanged a few polite words like "roof," "rain" and "new renters," then went back to their companions. That was as it should be, Louisa told herself. She was working. He was working the room.

She saw Dante at the social events; she saw Alvin at the garage.

"Yeah, your model is ready. I was going to bring it by, but you're never home." Alvin sounded almost accusatory, as if she'd betrayed the common man by taking up with summer people.

"I have a job now, helping Mr. Bradford with his memoirs. Up on the hill. And I drive him around places."

Alvin went into the front room of the body shop and brought back the replica Porsche. "Yeah, well I'm busy too. Going to AA meetings."

"That's great, Alvin. I'm really happy for you. And I like the new tattoo. So how much do I owe you for the car?"

"Nothing. It was fun, didn't take no time at all, and I kind of owe you. I wouldn't be going to meetings if it wasn't for you."

"Of course you would. You'd have realized sooner or later that your health, mental as well as physical, was suffering."

"And I could have wrecked my car."

"That too." After admiring Alvin's meticulous handiwork, she tucked the little red Porsche, with everything spelled right, back in its box. "Are you sure I can't pay you something?"

"The Fourth's next week. You could go watch the fireworks with me. It'll be no fun hanging out on the beach with the guys, not if I'm not drinking. We always get a keg, build a fire pit for burgers and ribs. Someone brings a CD player. You know."

"I'm sorry, but Mr. Bradford's having a party that night. He says up on the hill is the best place to watch the show, over-looking the bay."

Alvin went back to polishing the Jaguar he was working on. "Sure."

Louisa took two steps toward her car, then came back and touched his shoulder, between the grease spots on his T-shirt.

"Why don't you come, Alvin? Mr. Bradford said I could invite anyone I want. Francine Minell is bringing her mother and her son and a bunch of his friends, and Rico is going to help Marta build a fire afterward, for marshmallows. The two girls who reshelf books at the library are coming, and Janie Vogel, who cuts hair. Between the two of us, I bet Mr. Bradford and I invite half the town. It'll be fun, without all the beer."

Alvin said he'd think about it, the distance from his apartment over the garage to the house on Osprey Hill being measured in far more than miles. Louisa left, thinking about who else to invite to the estate for the Fourth.

How could she not ask the man who had found her the job there?

Chapter Nineteen

Dante was thinking about going up to Osprey Hill for the Fourth. He went every year. With the fireworks barge anchored right in the bay below, the light show was spectacular from there. On a clear night you could see the displays from Devon to Montauk and across to Connecticut.

Then he thought about not going. Louisa Waldon was bound to be there. Hell, there were enough fireworks every time he saw that woman.

He was seeing her more than he wanted, out and about, looking gorgeous on Mr. Bradford's arm. And he was seeing more of her than he wanted, in the skimpy little dresses she wore with no backs, nearly no fronts, hardly any skirts to speak of. No one spoke of anything else. Wesley Bradford's secretary was a stunner. She was also almost unapproachable, which made her even more appealing to the pricks at the parties.

Dante heard all the whispers about her, saw the speculation in the eyes of the free-dinner Don Juans. He had put a stop to that fast enough, saying that she was a connection of his family's, that his was the introduction that led to his friend hiring her. His.

Dante was not exactly making a personal claim, it was understood. He hardly spent more than a minute or two in her company. It was more as though he were putting a posted sign and a fence around the woman. Louisa Waldon was off-limits, out of bounds, not fair game for the wolf pack on the prowl. She was not any fille du jour to be passed around with the hors d'oeuvres. If she'd gone flitting around the rooms, flirting through the rented tents or flouncing across the backyards of the affairs, that would have opened the field, but she didn't, to Dante's surprise. She stayed at Mr. Bradford's side, listening to him and his admirers without putting herself first into the conversation. Every other woman Dante knew had to be the center of attention, the world revolving around her. When asked an opinion, Louisa gave thoughtful answers, not hesitating to contradict her employer, but always showing respect. Dante, in turn, respected her for that.

The older man loved it. He loved the girl, he told Dante when he called to invite him to the Fourth of July party. According to Mr. Bradford, Louisa was beautiful and brilliant and the best assistant he'd ever had. She was twice as competent as that last twit he'd had, the one who'd broken her leg at the beginning of the summer.

Louie?

Mr. Bradford also said she was bossy.

Yup, Louie.

The older man liked that about her. He was eating better, feeling stronger, working harder, thanks to Louisa's pushy ways. And his book was going to be a best-seller, with her help. In fact, Mr. Bradford told Dante, he was going to stay right here until the book was finished, then ask her to go south with him for the winter. She could handle the editorial revisions and the proofreading stuff he hated. Then, next year, she could go on the book tour with him.

She might even marry the old coot eventually, Dante considered. Why not? They seemed to admire each other, and Mr. Bradford needed a secretary and Louisa needed security. A match made in heaven — he kept the sarcasm to himself — with the honeymoon in Viagra Falls. Out loud, he said, "I'm glad things worked out so well. That sounds like a great opportunity for her. She'll be grateful."

So would Dante, to see her gone. So what if he'd keep looking for her short blond hair and long tanned legs at every party? He'd be better off, and better able to enjoy himself with whatever woman was at his side.

If Louisa left, he would not have to wonder about her staying. He'd told himself to wait, to keep as far away from the coming train wreck as he could. Maybe whatever oddball attraction he felt for the female would not last until fall, but would start drooping like the summer flowers. God knew he wasn't drooping yet, when he thought of her and that kiss they'd shared. Electric kiss or not, he had to know if she was a keeper, or if Paumonok Harbor was going to toss her back to the city, too small and small-minded to be content in the little town when the fancy tourists were gone. If she was leaving soon, why should he get involved now, enough to miss her later? He didn't have to wonder anymore.

He did wonder why she hadn't invited him to the party, though. They were supposed to be friends. Aunt Vinnie and Francine and Susan had calls from her, why not him? Maybe she knew that Mr. Bradford had extended the invite, but that rationale did not sit well with Dante either.

He did not like thinking of Louisa and her boss as a domestic couple, chatting over who called whom, exchanging little details, sharing their everyday lives. Mr. Bradford was supposed to be sharing his memoirs with Louie, nothing else. And she! She was already sharing her time and her dog and views of her bikini-clad body with her boss.

Good god, were they sharing more, already? Dante felt his stomach clench at the thought. Damn, they could be sharing the same blanket at the fireworks, the same burned marshmallow on the same frigging stick. He wouldn't go.

"Darling, you are not paying attention."

"What?"

"I said, you are not paying attention. We're supposed to be looking at this house together, remember?"

"Oh, yeah." The house, more a fishing shack, was down a low dirt road near the bay and might be for sale, cheap. Dante had wanted his ex-wife's opinion on its re-sale value before he bought the place, fixed it up, and put it back on the market. "It's going to need a lot of money poured into it."

Susan consulted her notes. "I don't think you'll ever make a profit, not even if you tear the cottage down and start over. It's private, but there's not enough land to build the castles people seem to want these days, and the power lines are too close. Besides, one good northeaster will flood the road, and a hurricane will wipe the whole place out. That's why the price is so low."

Dante thought he might buy the house anyway, see if he could get permits to put it up on stilts. He could let Rico fix it up on his own time, instead of paying rent somewhere else. Then Rico might be able to bring his wife up from Colombia, which would make Louisa happy, if not Marta. If there was a hurricane before then, well, all of Paumonok Harbor was in peril, so close to the bay, with the ocean itself a few miles across the low-lying strip of land that led to Montauk. Montauk would be an island, but half of Paumonok Harbor would be underwater, which was why they evacuated the waterfront when a big storm was predicted. The little shack had been here since the hurricane of '38, though, so Dante wasn't worried. He was worried about Francine and Aunt Vinnie missing their new friend, when Louisa went traipsing off on her merry globe-trotting way. Teddy would miss her too, and Champ. Maybe he'd get the boy a dog of his own, or a kitten, with fur as soft as Louisa's —

"Dante!"

"I was, um, thinking how low an offer I could make."

"Yes, well, if you can pay attention," Susan said, "I have something else I wanted to speak with you about." Dante turned the car back toward town and the real estate office.

"No."

"I haven't asked you a question."

"You will, and the answer is no. No, I am not going back to that clinic and no, I am not donating money to the East End Gay Organization. No, I am not cutting you a bigger percent than any of the other realtors get, and no, I am not writing you back into my will."

"I'm pregnant."

"No shit." He hit the brakes, then leaned over and brushed her cheek with his lips. "I mean, congratulations. That's what you wanted, isn't it?"

"It is. Cora Alice and I are thrilled. We're thinking of names and choosing a decor for the nursery and —"

"Isn't it a little early?"

"You think we should wait for the am-niocentesis to find out if it's a boy or a girl?

I thought a jungle theme could work either way."

"No, isn't it too early to tell if, you know, if it took?"

Susan patted her hair back into place and waggled her long ornate fingernails for him to start driving again. "A woman knows these things. Can't you see the glow?"

He hadn't looked at her. Now he studied the familiar face and decided that she'd been going to the day spa at Gurney's in Montauk. "Nice," was his noncommittal reply.

"And I've been sick to my stomach all the time."

He slammed on the brakes again. "Not in my car, you won't."

"If you keep driving like that I am certain to. Besides, we're in my car, remember? I wouldn't be caught dead in that truck of yours."

"There's nothing wrong with my —"

"But let us not argue. About that. I wanted to talk about the paper you were supposed to sign."

"No, I was supposed to come in a bottle. I did my job. Adequately, it seems." Something in his chest started to expand. He had made a baby!

"Do not, and please pardon the phrase, get cocky. Any college boy could have done it. The agreement your lawyer had was to protect all of us. We make no claims on you, and you make no claims on the child."

"My son. Or my daughter."

Susan checked her lipstick in the visor mirror. "Only in the slightest, biological sense. Cora Alice intends to adopt him or her, so the baby will be ours, hers and mine. Not yours in any way, shape or form. Although your green eyes might be nice."

"What name goes on the birth certificate?"

"Why, mine, of course. The state won't recognize Cora Alice as my marriage partner, but we are lobbying Albany."

"Your name: Susan. B for Bethingame. Rivera."

"That doesn't mean anything."

"Maybe not to you, but it means a hell of a lot to me. And it will mean something to the kid when he goes to school with my name on his lunch box. 'How come that strange man has the same name as mine, Mommy?' " Dante mimicked. "So he'll know I am his father anyway, unless you move out of town. Damn it, Susan, I am not stealing your baby. I just want to be part of his or her life, to make sure the kid has a male role model, to be there for my child if he or she ever needs me."

"You didn't used to be this difficult, darling."

"You didn't used to be carrying my baby. Maybe the only baby I will ever father."

"I'll discuss it with Cora Alice. We can talk about it at Mr. Bradford's party. You will be there to watch the fireworks, won't you?"

"I'm not sure. I might skip this year."

She frowned, then remembered not to make lines on her forehead. "You're not refusing because Cora Alice is going to be there with me, are you? I thought you were over that silly embarrassment ages ago. The rest of the town is."

The rest of the town thought she and her lover were aliens from outer space. "Not at all. One of my old computer partners asked me to come watch the Macy's celebration from his penthouse on the East Side of Manhattan. They put on a lot bigger show."

Dante parked behind Susan's office and walked around to open her door out of habit, and because she'd sit there talking for an hour if he didn't. When he handed her the keys she said, "You know, that's the first time I ever heard you admit something about Manhattan was better than Paumonok Harbor."

"I've never been blind to the drawbacks of a small town. You're the one who was blind to its good points. I always wondered why you stayed if you hated it so much, and why you're staying now, when the city would suit your lifestyle better. And keep the baby safe from my influence."

"I stayed, darling, because you and the Harbor have made me a very rich woman." She patted his cheek. "And I am staying now because this is the ideal place to raise a child. But do think about that agreement, Dante. I'd really feel better if you signed it."

"What will you do if I don't? Give the baby back? Sorry, you and Junior are stuck with me."

He thought about it as he got in his own pickup truck. He was going to be a father. Another Rivera would carry on his name. This should be one of the proudest days of his life, a champagne moment, a time of wonder mixed in with fears and uncertainties. Would his child be born healthy? Would he be a good father? Would the baby love him?

Would Susan and Cora Alice even let him hold his own infant? Dante didn't know. Instead of the joy other men got to feel, he felt hollow, as if someone had stolen something from him.

His ex-wife was having a baby without him and Louisa would most likely be leaving town. Sure, he felt like celebrating Independence Day. Sure, he did.

Chapter Twenty

How hard could it be to give a dog a bath? Certainly not hard enough to demand the prices that the groomer in Sag Harbor was charging. Champ — she had given up on Galahad permanently when Mr. Bradford declared it Hamptons pretentious — stank, though. He'd been rolling in something on the beach, and smelled like junkyard dog at low tide. She couldn't bring him to the party this way, not even if she tied the red, white and blue bandana around his neck.

She'd seen a fake sheepskin mattress while she was at the pet place making inquiries, with a tag that said dogs should not lie on the bare floor; their joints suffered. A bed or a bath? The choice was easy. After all, she had a garden hose in the backyard, an old plastic baby pool from the garage, doggie shampoo that cost more than her own, and the most obedient, well-trained dog in the county. She gathered a stack of those yellowed towels from the attic, the ones that were stamped in indelible ink with her and her sister's names from when they went to swimming lessons. Then she wrapped her St. Jerome's honeymoon sarong, or pareo, around her, trying to figure where to put the knot in the fringed fabric rectangle. It didn't matter what it looked like because no one would see her, just that she have her arms free. She figured she'd be getting wet whatever she had on, no matter how cooperative Champ was, so was ready to jump into the shower afterward.

No one told Champ he was supposed to cooperate. He was used to warm baths in a dog sink, with a shower nozzle, with a choke collar clipped to an overhead bar, with a professional groomer at the other end of the water. He was not going to stay in any low-rimmed, slippery, tippy kiddy pool. He was not going to let Louisa douse him with a cold blast or get soap in his eyes and water in his ears.

He started whimpering, then whined, then wriggled, then made every effort to head back to the dog shelter where he merely faced euthanasia, not drowning. Of course Louisa had taken his collar off to wash him better, so she had nothing to grab on to except wet, wild dog. Her wrap was slipping and her hair was sopping and her patience was wearing as thin as the check she wished she'd written for the dog groomer.

"Stop that! How are you going to qualify as a canine companion if you smell?"

She should have remembered that dogs didn't care what they smelled like. Champ only cared about getting out of the plastic wading pool. He did it with a final leap, tipping the whole thing over on Louisa, of course, not that she could get much wetter. She hiked the sarong's knot up on her chest, and picked up one of the towels.

Now that he was out of the water, Champ was ecstatically exuberant. He raced around the backyard, with Louisa behind him, trying to dry him off before she let him in the house. "It might be dog food for both of us next month, but you are going to the Puppy Palace," she threatened, panting. Champ turned and grabbed the towel, now playing tug-of-war instead of tag. Louisa had to laugh, shaking the other end of the towel when he growled in mock ferocity. "You are a silly dog."

Then Champ snatched the towel out of her hand and pranced with it to the fence, where he started to bury it in the loose dirt of Louisa's latest gardening effort. "Oh, no."

Dirt was flying, in the air, in the yard, in

the fur of her briefly clean dog. "No! Stop that!"

He didn't, so Louisa ran toward him, waving another towel temptingly in front of his nose. He leaped up for it, leaving muddy streaks on her wrap. She backed away, still holding the towel, leading him back toward the garden hose with its spray handle. "And stop jumping. You know the instructor said that was bad."

The instructor had also said that Louisa had to speak with more authority in her voice, so she yelled: "No! Stop that, you beast! Get off me!"

Champ made one last jump for the towel, but got the corner of her sarong instead, and pulled. Which was when, of course, Dante Rivera charged through the gate to her backyard.

He still had not decided about the party and thought he'd ask her. Did she want him there or would his presence make her uncomfortable? Hell, if it was half as uncomfortable as she made him, she'd tell him to move to Kalamazoo. Louisa always spoke her mind, mare's nest that it was. They were friends, though. She'd said so. So he should ask.

He knew she wasn't working this afternoon. Mr. Bradford was with his physical therapist and the library was closed today. Friends should know their friends' schedules, shouldn't they? He could say he'd come to check on the progress of the roof.

Her car was in the driveway, the house's front door was open, which was a sure sign that she was losing some of her New York City paranoia. He put his hands in his pockets to look more nonchalant . . . and so he wouldn't grab her and beg her not to leave, but stay and have his babies.

No way! He just wanted to know about the fireworks, that was all, not her feelings or fertility. Louisa Waldon would drive him crazy in a week. Just look at what she was doing to him without even trying, turning him into a tongue-tied teenager asking a girl to the prom, and just as horny.

Besides, he'd promised to let her go her own way, plot her own course, sail her own ship.

Unless she was sinking.

"No! Stop that, you beast! Get off me!"

One minute he was slouching by the front door. The next he was in the backyard, gasping. Gasping? He had no air going to his lungs, no blood going to his brain, and only one thought in his head: "Cripes, Louie, you're killing me."

Startled, Louisa let go of the last corner

of her erstwhile covering, the corner that the dog had in his mouth. He took off with it. Now she stood, wearing nothing but muddy pawprints. She could feel the heated blush start at her toes and climb to her cheeks — and Dante was watching! She yelped and dove for the pile of towels.

Her mother sent them to swimming lessons with these minuscule scraps? How was Louisa to cover — to recover — her modesty with something the size of a washcloth? She picked up another and tried to hold the pair in strategic positions.

"The least you could do," she said, trying futilely to maintain her dignity and her decency, both long gone anyway, "is turn your back."

He managed to shut his mouth enough to speak. "What do you think, I'm crazy?"

"A gentleman would." Louisa looked longingly at her muddied sarong, halfway across the yard by now.

"Only if he had one foot in the grave."

She started to inch backward toward the back door — and tripped over the kiddy pool. The towels went flying in a heap of arms and legs and barking dog, who was ready to play this new game. Dante was ready too, altogether too obviously. He stopped grinning and gawking and gasping enough to come offer her a hand.

Just where he was going to put that hand was going to remain a matter of conjecture.

"Laugh at me, will you? Gawk?" Louisa picked up the garden hose and turned the spray on both of the miserable, mangy curs. The dog ran off. Dante took off his T-shirt. Now it was Louisa's turn to gasp. And to ogle.

She knew he was well-built, but she never imagined . . . That is, she'd imagined, but the reality was . . . more. More smooth, flat, tanned planes, covered in the center by short, soft-looking dark hair. More muscles, glistening with the sheen of water. More width to the broad shoulders. "More," she murmured.

"More? You want my pants, too?" He reached for his waistband.

Louisa shrieked. "What are you doing?"

"Trying to cover you up before we both land in the suds, literally and figuratively. Not that it's not a prettier view than sunset on the bay. All the tourists should come here, instead of the overlook." He held his damp T-shirt out, and this time he did turn his back, slightly, while she wiggled into it.

The hem came down just far enough, if she tugged on it, didn't move fast, and didn't expand her chest by breathing. She tried not to think of what her chest must look like in the wet shirt. The fact that Dante was staring told her enough. Between his staring and the cold fabric, she could feel her nipples harden. God, what would he think? Whatever it was, was likely the truth. If the Chamber of Commerce put him with his bare chest on their posters, there'd be a constant traffic jam on Main Street. There'd be a heat wave in the winter. There'd be —

She would not lust after Dante Rivera. She would not. She'd seen any number of totally naked men: a small number, granted, other than Howard, who should have received her unwedding gift by now, but a number. She must have seen thousands of men, maybe, bare-chested on the beach, in the park, at construction sites. She hadn't felt her toes curl for any of them. Including Howard, which was a whole 'nother story. She stamped her bare foot to make the tingling stop. "This is absurd. I am going in now. You can tell me what you wanted later."

He'd be taking cold showers later. A lot of them. This was absurd, all right, wanting Louisa Waldon. He'd seen plenty of naked women with more to offer than the slim blonde. God, she had blond curls there too. He swallowed and nodded. "Later."

Louisa took careful steps toward the back door, holding the bottom of his shirt down in front. Of course that pulled it up in back, but Dante didn't think he should point that out. Then the ever-efficient, frugal Ms. Waldon bent over to turn off the water at the spigot.

Dante groaned.

Louisa turned. "Are you all right?"

"No. I don't think I will ever be all right again."

She came closer, inspecting him for bee stings, splinters, whatever could have wrenched such a piteous sound from him. "What's wrong?"

"You are. Everything about you is wrong. And perfect. Perfectly wrong." Two steps brought him to her side. One more had her in his arms. At last. "God, this is not what I came for," he said before lowering his lips to hers.

Louisa's arms twined around Dante's bare back, her hands touching, feeling, stroking what she had so admired. She could feel the warmth rising in him. Lord, between them there must be enough heat to steam-dry the T-shirt she wore. Between them, that wet T-shirt was the only thing keeping her from melting altogether.

His hands were busy too, under the back of the shirt, kneading, rubbing, learning the contours he'd glimpsed. He moaned again, right into her mouth.

Tingle? Hah. She couldn't remember she had toes, much less feel them. Was she even on the ground? This incredible kiss made the last one seem like Teddy's batting practice. This was a World Series home run.

Run. Home. She should. She couldn't, not with his leg between her thighs. She would die first, which she was going to do soon anyway if she didn't inhale. She pulled back, maybe a quarter of an inch. "So what" — she panted, taking a breath — "did you come here for?"

Dante wasn't thinking. He wasn't thinking, that is, past whether he could make it inside to a bed, a couch, a chair, a rug. No, the wet, muddy grass was fine. Then they could shower together. What was she asking? For that matter, why was she talking? He kissed her again, or still, because he figured this was all one kiss of glory, with pauses.

"Hm?"

Damned persistent woman. He played

her query back in his mind and answered between tongue touches. "I . . . to know . . . do you want me . . ."

"Oh, yes."

". . . to come to the party tonight."

A heartbeat or two went by. Louisa opened her eyes and looked into his, frowning. "That's why you came?"

Dante struggled for rational thought. He hadn't come yet. Maybe it was the mud. "I didn't come to seduce you in the shrubbery, if that's what you're thinking."

Louisa hadn't been thinking either. That was the problem. She disentangled herself from his arms and stepped back. "Is that what this is, a seduction?"

"You didn't seem to need any — That is, no. This was just a, um, a moment of weakness."

She took another step back, the rosy color fading from her cheeks. "So you didn't really want to make love with me?"

Dante winced. What did love have to do with it? He wanted to roll in the grass, that was all. Trust a woman to ruin perfectly good sex with linguistics. He sighed. It wasn't going to happen now, and maybe that was for the best. "No, not really. Not with you. We're friends, right? Sex only complicates things. Why ruin what we already have?"

"You're right. I don't want to screw you either." She took the shirt off over her head and stood in front of him, proud, defiant, daring him to lower his eyes from her face. "Here, put this on. Then maybe I'll believe you don't want me, if I can't see the bulge in your britches."

"I never said I didn't want you."

"Well, one of these days you are going to have to figure out just what it is that you do want, Mr. Rivera. Meanwhile, if you do not come tonight Teddy will be disappointed, as will Mr. Bradford. More importantly, the library aides, Janie who cuts hair, and Jeanette from the animal shelter will all be devastated."

"Come on, what do they care if I'm there or not? They're coming to see the fireworks, not me."

"That's what you think," Louisa said from her doorway. "They can see the pinwheels and starbursts from the beach. The Playboy of Paumonok Harbor is the real attraction."

Chapter Twenty-One

He was playing with her, wasn't he? Angry, disappointed, and relieved she hadn't done or said anything even stupider, Louisa was mostly confused. She could just add men to the list of incomprehensible elements in her life, like theology, metaphysics, thermonuclear dynamics, and tire pressure. Dante Rivera moved to the top of her list, right above Howard. She thought that jackass would have called by now, out of simple courtesy for the gift. Then again, he hadn't had the manners to cancel their wedding. And maybe he didn't like "Putz" written on his car. The truth hurt.

The truth hurt so badly, Louisa would not examine her own feelings. Instead she stepped into the shower stall and washed away her confusion. And discovered a better way of washing the dog, where he couldn't escape.

Then she went to celebrate independence.

Wesley Bradford was a happy man. He was too old to go traipsing from overpriced restaurant to overcrowded art show opening every night. He was tired of his signature bow ties and linen jackets that made him look rumpled after an hour. He was sick of the sycophantic small talk that passed for conversation at the parties he attended. Half the time he turned his hearing aid off anyway.

Tonight the party was coming to him and he was delighted, sitting on his own deck, wearing his comfortable old sweatpants, surrounded by people he liked. For once he wasn't on exhibit, one of the lions at the zoo. All the children Louisa had invited couldn't care less that he was rich and famous, only that they get enough hot dogs and ice cream and a good seat to watch the spectacle. The adults had come to see the fireworks, to relax for a change, not put on a show of their own.

If there was a show, then Louisa was the star. Mr. Bradford thought he'd never get sick of watching her move with her quick, energetic grace. He knew he'd never grow tired of that smile she flashed him every few moments, checking to see that he had everything he needed, food, drink, good company. Hell, maybe he wasn't too old for her after all.

He watched as she greeted his former

magazine editor, the editor's wife and grandchildren with as much warmth as she welcomed the gardener and his family. The Pulitzer Prize nominee got the same friendly treatment as the garage guy, except Alvin had a soda put in his hand, not a beer.

He kept watching as she herded the kids toward the pool, where she'd tossed in a bunch of floating rings and balls, for some kind of game while the barbeque grills were heating. She even got his editor's prissy granddaughter to play. Young Teddy was bursting with pride, acting as host because he got to swim here twice a week, and some woman named Jeanette volunteered to act as lifeguard. The sounds of the boys laughing and the girls squealing reminded him of his own youth, days too long gone. He'd have to tell Louisa to remind him, to put some of those memories in the book.

His autobiography was going well, now that Louisa had that organized too. She had him writing more the way he thought, rather than the pedantic style he'd been using for articles and lectures. She said that kept him distant from the readers, putting himself above them.

There was nothing pompous about

Louisa, and Mr. Bradford appreciated that.

She could be elegant and dignified when they went to black-tie affairs, but she was always Louisa, thanking the waiters, joking with the valets, trading dog stories with an ambassador's wife. She was giggling now, and Mr. Bradford was glad he had new batteries in the hearing aid. That last concert they'd attended hadn't sounded half as sweet to his ears.

She was urging the adults to try out the hula hoops she'd put on the lawn — even his former editor's country club wife. And Louisa herself, swiveling her narrow hips, was a sight to stir an old man's blood.

After supper she had them all, children and adults, tossing Frisbees, red, white and blue ones, like a patriotic gyroscope. The dog grabbed as many as he could catch, which made everyone laugh more. Alvin and Cora Alice discovered the pool table in the game room and squared off for a match, and Francine took some of the children down the steps to the beach to hunt for shells. Dante's former wife had announced her pregnancy and was being congratulated by all the women, given the chaise longue of honor on the front of the deck, and reveling in the attention.

They sang "You're a Grand Old Flag"

and "America the Beautiful," by the flag-pole at dusk, and Louisa had discovered that the gardener's son was taking trumpet lessons at school, so she had him blow taps.

There were chairs on the deck, cushions on the stone patio, blankets on the lawn. Tables were set up through the glass doors to the sunroom, with more food and drinks and tiny American flags everywhere, between the citronella candles. The children kept asking if it were time yet. It never was, Mr. Bradford recalled, never soon enough. Then it was over too fast.

He watched Louisa going from place to place, making certain everyone was warm enough, full enough, had a good view. Despite her best efforts, the local people were bunched together, the summer people in separate groups. Rico and Marta were sitting with the gardener and his wife, speaking in Spanish. The only other one who crisscrossed the yard was Dante Rivera, who was invited to share the blanket with the silly girls from the library, offered a seat next to Mr. Bradford's retired movie starlet neighbor, and handed a Cervesa by the group near the fire pit.

Louisa would be disappointed, Mr. Bradford thought, her silly, sweet idealism hoping one night could bridge centuries of differences and prejudices. At least the children were still playing together, except for the little twit sitting in her grandfather's lap. Maybe the next generation could do things better.

For now, everyone was where they wanted to be, including him. He had a cigar in his hand — unlit — and a half glass of wine left in the other, which did not tremble half as much as it had last month. Life was good, and could get better. He raised the glass in a silent, secret toast to Louisa, giving her a lot of the credit. He'd thought the book was enough, that he'd write down all his memories and be done. Now he was thinking that an old man's ramblings were well and good, but maybe he should make some new memories.

He had plans, and he'd asked Louisa to think about some of them. Fall was months away, but a man in his seventies knew better than most how quickly time could skip past. He'd told her merely to consider his offer; they'd talk more when the book was finished. Now he looked around for her in the near dark, and finally spotted her bright blond hair among the children. Dante's cousin was reassuring the squirming brats that the wait was worth it, that the marshmallows would keep until afterward.

Louisa was good with kids too, he decided. She was not as confident and casual as Francine, but treated the children the same way she did everyone she met, with respect and courtesy and interest. Young Teddy adored her, Bradford knew, wondering if that might stop her from going with him at the end of the summer. Not that one little boy in particular could hold her back, but wanting a family of her own might. She wouldn't find that with an old fogey like him. What did he want with squalling infants at his age?

Some men started families even later in life, he knew, but then they lost the young mother's undivided attention and company, so what was the point? To leave something to posterity? Mr. Bradford intended to leave his book and his money.

He watched Louisa move across the patio to the tattooed cretin's shoulder and quietly hand him another fake beer. No, Mr. Bradford might not want babies, but he could offer her everything else any rational, practical woman would value.

Then he watched her pass by Dante. Now there was real competition, Mr. Bradford thought, except that the two seemed to be avoiding each other. Dante had looks, youth, money and brains. Hell, if Wesley Bradford were a young woman, he'd fall for him, too. The charming bastard even loved kids. Of course Dante had sworn he'd never get married again, but he'd never been close to Louisa Waldon before.

Mr. Bradford intended he never get close to her now, either. When Dante started to stroll beside her, likely to find a double seat for the light show — was the deuced thing ever going to start? — Mr. Bradford called him over. The way to most men's hearts might be food; for Dante Rivera it was his beloved hometown. Mr. Bradford would give him something to think about besides his assistant. "A word, Dante, if you will."

Louisa kept going, pointedly sitting beside Susan and Cora Alice, where Dante would never go. Dante raised an eyebrow, but pulled a chair next to his host's. "Great party. I can't remember a nicer one."

Mr. Bradford did not want the talk, or the credit, to wend toward Louisa. If Dante was too blind to see the treasure under his nose, Mr. Bradford was not going to draw him a map. Dante could work on plans for the town. Bradford had plans for the woman. "Yes, but I wanted to discuss an idea I had. You know how the village has been trying to raise money for a youth center?"

Of course Dante knew. He was the treasurer of the committee, and the chief contributor. Mr. Bradford had also been generous. "We are getting closer to the goal."

The older man nodded. "So the kids can have an indoor pool for the winter, and a basketball court and a hockey ring."

"And a computer room for homework help. We've got too many kids whose parents both work, so no one's home after school. The kids need a place to go."

Mr. Bradford held up his hand. "You can stop now. I read all the literature and the statistics about working mothers and day care. But I am thinking Paumonok Harbor should have another center, one for the arts."

Dante stopped watching Louisa laughing with his ex-wife and leaned closer. "The arts?"

"You know, painting and crafts, a small theater for drama productions, music studios so kids don't have to aggravate the neighbors by playing in garages. Those things are just as important as sports to children. More important to some."

"Francine would love to have Teddy take drawing lessons. Since he's been coming here, the paintings and art books you've shown him are all he talks about. Heaven knows he's no athlete."

"I wasn't, either. I learned to swim, of course, but debating club was the closest I got to a team sport. Who's watching out for those kids? And it wouldn't have to be just for children. Senior citizens could use the facilities during the daytime, the same way they were promised the pool, so they'd vote for the bond issue. The way I envision it, anyone who can afford to pay can help subsidize it, but after-school art lessons would be free. I bet the place could make a profit in the summer, teaching bored, rich adults, the ones who don't play golf or tennis. I know a few artists who would volunteer a couple of hours, maybe give guest lectures to get it going. Those art students whose graduate school scholarships I underwrite could work part-time. We could even hook up with Southampton College or Stony Brook in a work-study program."

"I can tell you've put a lot of thought into this, and it sounds great, but where's the money going to come from? You are talking land, a building, a full staff, supplies. To say nothing of insurance, permits and the rest of the incidentals. We're having a hard enough time getting grant money from the state for the sports center."

"No, this should be done privately. I have donated to enough worthy causes to call in the return favor. Besides, I have far more money than I can use in my lifetime, with more coming in every time they rerun that art appreciation program I did for TV. I've got no one to leave it to. My only sister is in a nursing home, and both her kids are doctors. Coldhearted bastards, but rich. They'll get the art collection, after some pieces go to museums that have already asked for them. Speak of coldhearted bastards, I get letters from museums every day, asking to be remembered in my will. You should have seen the boxes full after I had the stroke. Anyway, the new book is going to earn a wad, too, they tell me. There's already talk of an auction for the movie rights."

"That's great. Congratulations."

"Unless they pick some jerk to play me, and some box office bimbo to play my first wife. Maybe they'll wait 'til I'm gone so I don't have to see it. Either way, I'm thinking of dedicating the book to the town, with the royalties and subsidiaries going to an endowment fund. I know you own some parcels of land near where they want to put the youth center, so you'd give me a good deal. You care more about the kids of this place than their parents do."

Dante was calculating square acres and side lots. "It might be doable. You'll have to give me numbers to work with."

"I'll have my accountant call you next week." He gummed the cigar, wondering if Louisa or Marta would see the smoke in the dark if he lit it. He decided to wait for the fireworks, whenever the fool things finally started, to lessen the chance.

"And I'll look at the surrounding property."

"Hmm. The Wesley Bradford Arts Institute." The older man rolled the name off his tongue slowly, like honey. "My gift to the ages."

"It would be cheaper by half if we attach it to the youth center."

Mr. Bradford nodded. "All right, I can accept that. The Wesley Bradford Arts Center Wing. But with its own independent budget, its own programs. I don't want any steroid simian deciding the art studio would be better used for wrestling practice as soon as I'm gone. Or my money paying for a new basketball hoop when they run in the red."

"That means a separate staff, too."

"I thought we could hire your cousin to run it. Not to give the classes, of course, but to act as administrator. You said she's between a rock and a hard place, yet won't take your charity. I admire that in a person."

"Francine? She's great with kids, but she's got no experience." Dante looked across the deck, to where Louisa was leaning against the railing, looking up at the stars. "I love my cousin, but Louisa Waldon would be a lot better choice for the job."

"Louisa is coming with me."

Boom!

Chapter Twenty-Two

"Louie, we've got to talk."

"No, not tonight."

All of the guests had gone home, exhausted, full, happy. Rico was in the kitchen helping Marta put things away, and Mr. Bradford was closed in his office, working out plans for his name-bearing bequest, making lists of people he could hit up for donations. Louisa had been cleaning the deck while Dante carried blankets and cushions into the pool house shed. He'd joined her on the deck, where she was leaning on the railing, looking out at the bay.

He could hear the waves on the shore, and still smell the lingering smoke from the driftwood fires along the beach, mixed in with the tide and the honeysuckle that grew on the hill. A firecracker occasionally lit up the sky, from unauthorized and illegal celebrations that would go on all night. The stars were out, and the moon cast slivers of chrome on the quiet water.

"This night is too perfect to ruin with talk."

Dante had never known a woman who didn't want to talk about events or arguments, rehashing them into oblivion, especially when she thought she was right. He knew she'd worked hard for the party and must be tired, too, but, like the puffs of smoke polluting the starry night, he wanted to clear the air. Louisa wore a baggy sweatshirt now, and looked soft and cuddlesome, which was the problem in the first place. He kept his distance, but said, "I'm not a playboy."

She sighed, knowing the perfect, pleasurable moment couldn't last, not when old Determined Dan had a bone to pick. "I know. And I should never have said what I did."

He went on as if she hadn't spoken. "I do not spend my days in pursuit of a night's pleasure. I don't use women."

"No, but you don't trust them either."

"Like you trust men?"

"All right, we're two wounded ducks bobbing on the pond of life. That doesn't mean we have to swim together. We're afloat, following separate currents."

Yeah. She was following hers into an old man's arms. "I just don't want you thinking you have to be on your guard with me every minute. I'm not going to attack you every time we find ourselves alone." And you're naked, he thought but did not say.

He could see in the moonlight that she bobbed her head. "And I won't attack you either. I'm no sex kitten looking for a tomcat. I am not interested in sex for sex's sake, or one-night stands. What happened this afternoon was a fluke, like you said, a moment of weakness in unusual circumstances. There is nothing more to be said about it. We're adults. You're an attractive man and I have been somewhat . . . deprived. That's all. Nothing happened."

"Nothing? I thought that kiss was something special."

"Nothing," she repeated with positive reinforcement, as if to convince herself. "And nothing will."

No, now that she belonged to Mr. Bradford. Dante might not approve, definitely regretted, but he would not trespass. "Right. Nothing will."

"Good."

So why were they suddenly sharing the chaise longue and saliva? Why was her sweatshirt tangled at her neck and his shirt unbuttoned? Why were his hands at his waistband? . . . No, those were her hands. His hands were everywhere else, warm and tender and touching her as if she were a priceless treasure, a magic kingdom to be explored, a fire all their own to be fanned and fed until it rose and consumed both of them. Dante could already feel its heat the length of his body. Louisa could already see the light.

The light?

"Oh, my god! That's Mr. Bradford's office. If he looks out —"

She jumped off the chaise longue so fast it tipped over, sending Dante to the wooden deck with a crash and a curse.

"Everything okay out there?" Mr. Bradford called.

"Fine. We're just cleaning up."

Dante was rubbing his shoulder. "Well, I am glad we had that little talk."

Louisa pulled her sweatshirt down and her shorts up. She pushed back the loose hair from her eyes — the bobby pin had gone missing again, of course — and righted the chair, then started to stack the cushions. "They'll get damp if left out-doors overnight. Mildew." She knew she was babbling, but couldn't help it. The man turned her to mush, and she couldn't even blame him anymore.

He carried the cushions over to the benches built along the far side of the deck. The bench seats lifted up for storage.

"I didn't know that. Whoever built this house thought of everything."

"Thanks."

"Thanks? You built the house?"

"Well, I remodeled an old place that was here since the forties. Some oil baron built it for a family compound and weekend retreat. It took years, because I was working on other projects at the time."

She brought over another pile of cushions. "You did a great job. But it must kill you to see it sitting empty all winter. I always felt bad for our little cottage when we locked the door for the last time after the summer. It's almost a crime for a beautiful place like this to have so little use."

"It's never empty. I move in when Mr. Bradford leaves."

"Oh, I thought you lived down by the docks."

"I do, on a houseboat. The kind that never leaves the harbor."

"With your money?" Louisa knew that was rude, but she couldn't believe anyone would live on a boat if he could afford anything else.

"I love the houseboat, rocking to sleep at night, all the stars for company, salt air to breathe. You can drop a line overboard and have fresh fish for dinner. It's got heat and electricity, a hot shower, kitchen, and all the comforts of home, but it's not great in the winter."

"So you stay in Mr. Bradford's house when he goes?" What, he wouldn't spend any of his money for a place of his own? Louisa always knew there had to be something wrong with him. No one could be that perfect. Dante Rivera was a miser. Or else he was nuts. "You're the caretaker?"

"Not exactly. Mr. Bradford rents it. Osprey Hill is my house."

Louisa looked up at the house, with its sweeping decks, wraparound views, hot tub, library, game room, bowling alley in the basement, two kitchens and who knew how many bedrooms. Then she peered out at the night, visualizing the swimming pool, guest house, gardens, fountain and tennis court. Yup. He was crazy. "You own this . . . and you live on a houseboat?"

The houseboat was two stories, built on a barge. It was bigger than her cottage. "I really like the water. You should come visit one day. Or night. You'll see what I mean."

"No, I could never understand. I'd never want to leave this place."

"It's only a house. I started building it when I first came back east. I built it for

Susan, but didn't have the cash to pour into it all at once, so started renting it for the summer."

Louisa almost said, "No wonder Susan left you," but then she remembered his former wife's other issues.

He went on: "Mr. Bradford loved it and offered to buy the place, but I couldn't see letting it go. So he rents it every year. That pays the taxes, the upkeep, the utilities and a really nice profit. Besides, I like him."

"And your houseboat."

He smiled, white teeth flashing in the porch light. "And my houseboat."

Louisa couldn't help herself. "What did Susan think?"

"She thought I was crazy, of course. She only wanted to live in Manhattan and couldn't understand why I'd want to sink the time and effort and money into a place out here. She never lived here, if that's your next question. We split up before it was finished."

"You two had different aims in life."

He laughed outright. "You might say that. We had nothing in common. Not even sex, it turned out. What about you and Hopalong?"

"Howard? Oh, the sex was all right. Comfortable. We were busy, and tired, so we didn't do it all that often the last couple of years. But it was nice."

"I meant your goals in life."

"Oh." At least it was too dark for him to see her blushing. "Howard wanted to make partner at the law firm. I don't know what, after that. More money, I'd guess. I never thought much past the wedding. I suppose I hoped we'd buy a house out of the city someday, but we always talked about my getting a better job, not getting pregnant. That was all right with me."

"But you like kids."

"I like some kids," she corrected him.

"You'd like your own."

She was beginning to think so, seeing other children than her sister's spoiled brats. "Maybe."

"You would." He slammed the lid on the bench storage bin, straightened and said, "Sex with us wouldn't be comfortable."

Louisa thought of the heat and the haste and the having to be closer, no matter what. He'd be black and blue from falling off the chaise longue. "No, it wouldn't be comfortable, or nice."

"Nice is boring."

Making love to Dante Rivera would never be boring. Sweet and sweaty, tumultuous and tender, raucous, rousing and life-reaffirming, but definitely not boring. "We'll never know, will we?"

"I guess not. Too bad, huh?"

She didn't answer. She went inside for her car keys and her dog.

She found the car keys and her pocketbook. She didn't find the dog. "Here, Champ," she called softly, in case Mr. Bradford had gone to sleep. "Come, boy."

Champ did not come. She went to the stairs and called, a little louder. No scrabble of claws on the hardwood floors answered her call. She went to the back, toward the kitchens, thinking he'd gone to Marta for handouts, but the lights were all out there except for the security lamp.

"Come on, baby. It's late and I'm tired." She tried the game room and the library and Mr. Bradford's office, where Champ was used to hanging out. No dog. Beginning to get upset, Louisa went back out the sliding doors to the deck, calling his name. All of his names. The longer he did not come, the louder her shouts.

Dante had gone to his truck, intending to follow Louisa back to town, just to make sure she got home safely. He heard her calling for the dog, her voice growing higher and more frantic. "Damned woman." Not damned dog, but damn the woman who wanted him to keep his distance, then drew him to her side. Either she was naked or needy; the result was the same. He got out of the truck, taking his flashlight from under the seat.

"Dante? Thank goodness you didn't go yet. I can't find Champ. I put him inside when the fireworks started, because he doesn't like the noise, and now he isn't there. The door was open all night though, so he may have gone out. Did you see him after supper?"

Dante had noticed nothing but Louisa, and Mr. Bradford's plans for her. That is, his plans for Paumonok Harbor. "No, but I bet he's hiding under one of the beds."

Louisa followed him back into the house, but she was worried. "He's never not answered my call. Except for the time a deer came in the yard, and that rottweiler someone brings out on weekends. That's why I needed the fence."

"The house is big. Maybe he didn't hear you." They started on the top floor and called down the halls, putting on lights, opening closets, checking under beds. No dog. Mr. Bradford came out of his bedroom when they reached his corridor, wiped his eyes, looked under his bed. Then he said the dog would come home when he was hungry, and went back to sleep.

"I thought he loved Champ," Louisa murmured, disappointed. "He'd help look if he did."

He'd help look, Dante thought, if he loved Louisa.

Dante knocked on the housekeeper's door. "Sorry, Marta," he called through the door, "but is Champ in there with you? We can't find him."

"The only champion I have in here is Rico, Mr. Rivera," Marta answered back with a giggle.

Dante led Louisa away before she could comment. "Come on, let's try outside. Maybe he got shut into the pool house when we were putting away the pillows."

"Oh my god! What if he fell into the pool?" She was flying out the door, not waiting for him and the flashlight.

A frightened dog might have fled anywhere. Dante flipped all the floodlight switches, so part of the property was lit up, at least: the pool and the tennis court, the long driveway, garden fountain, and the path down to the beach. The lights had been off during the party, to make the night darker for the light show. Champ wasn't in the pool house, or the pool, thank goodness, or the garden shed, the garage or the old well house. Together,

Dante and Louisa covered the entire estate and the shoreline, calling and whistling and clapping their hands. Someone down the beach yelled "Shut up," but no dog barked.

Louisa was out of breath and out of tissues, trying to keep up with Dante and mop the tears out of her eyes at the same time. "He's not here. Or he's hurt."

"Don't get yourself in a panic. No one would hurt him."

"Then why doesn't he come when we call him? You know he always does."

"Maybe he's so far away he can't hear us. I bet he got scared and went home, to your house."

"My house? That's miles away! Across town, through traffic!"

Dante didn't like the idea either, but he said, "He's a smart dog. He'll know the way."

"What, with all the cars leaving the beach when the fireworks were over? He's dark gray, no one would see him! And I never put the reflector tab on his collar, and I should have held him. I knew he was frightened and I left him alone and now he's gone."

Dante was stroking her back, letting her dampen his second shirt that day. "Come on, sweetheart. Don't blame yourself, and don't start jumping to dire conclusions. We'll find him."

"You don't understand," she cried. "You've never lost anything you loved that much."

"Yeah, Louie, I have," he answered quietly. Then he added, "I know he's your closest companion right now." He didn't say crutch. "And he loves you. He'll come home to you, you'll see."

She started for her car. "I'll go look."

"No, I'll drive back to your house. I'll call you on my cell phone when I get there."

"You do think he's lying on the side of the road somewhere! You do! That's why you don't want me to go looking. You're trying to protect me as usual."

"No, I think you should stay here calling in case he chased a deer into the woods and can't find his way back yet." He fished one of his business cards out of the truck's glove compartment. "Call me if he shows up." He kissed her forehead and drove off slowly, looking to either side of the driveway, whistling.

Now Louisa was out in the dark, on her own, terrified, imagining every possible, horrible scenario. Somehow she made another round of the grounds, cursing, praying, weeping as she ran from one circle of illumination to the next.

Her best friend was missing, and her other best friend had taken the flashlight.

Chapter Twenty-Three

What should she do? Sitting here crying was not an option. Not a good one, anyway. Louisa thought about following Dante, a comforting idea but not practical. She still had no cell phone to tell him where she was, which he found ridiculous. She hadn't found the money. Now he couldn't call her if she went anywhere else, and they might miss each other altogether. She could rouse Marta and Rico and beg them to help, but if Champ hadn't answered to her call, why should he answer to theirs? Mr. Bradford was tired and old, and paying her not to let anyone bother him, including Louisa.

She could call the town's animal control officer, but that office was closed at night, which meant going through the central emergency switchboard. The police had enough to do on the Fourth of July besides listen to her cry over her lost pet. They'd laugh. Besides, the dog warden was Jeanette, who would have driven Champ back to Mr. Bradford's if she found him on the way home. No, she might have kept him, taking him away from Louisa because she was a negligent owner, letting a dog run loose. Jeanette would give him to a better family, one who could afford to have him professionally bathed and clipped. Or she'd send him back to that dreadful Mr. Avery. Poor, poor Silver Crown's Mental Image. Poor, poor Louisa.

If anyone else leaving the party had seen Champ on the road, they'd have called. Here. Louisa ran inside to check the answering machine for messages.

Someone wanted Mr. Bradford to organize an art show in Springs; the original curator had Lyme disease. Someone else was sorry they couldn't come to the party; their hot water tank had burst.

"My dog is missing," Louisa muttered at the answering machine, "and all you can think about are your petty problems." She did write down the messages for Mr. Bradford to look at in the morning.

Why hadn't Dante called? At least five minutes had gone by. Alvin would have made the trip in half the time. Maybe it was bad news and Dante didn't want to tell her. Or he'd driven to the all-night veterinarian in Riverhead. Louisa couldn't imagine what the emergency bills would be.

Maybe Mr. Bradford would give her an advance. Otherwise she'd have to ask her mother. Louisa could hear her now: "Tscha, Louisa. It's just a dog."

No, it wasn't. Champ was her dog.

She thought of calling Dante on his cell phone to hear his progress, but he'd think she was silly. He might even be one of those law-abiding citizens who pulled over to talk on the phone. She'd only be hampering his search, or distracting him. Louisa took the portable phone from its cradle and clutched it in her hand instead, willing it to ring, rubbing it as if the cordless genie would grant her the usual three wishes.

One, let Champ be safe.

Two, let Dante find him and call her before she had heart failure. Was that one wish or two? One, Louisa decided.

Three, let Dante 1— No, now was not the time to be thinking of Dante, especially not thinking of him giving up the search and going home to his houseboat, letting the waves rock him to sleep. What did he wear to sleep in, though? She'd bet it wasn't 100 percent cotton, monogrammed pajamas from Brooks Brothers that went out to the dry cleaner, like Howard wore. Maybe silk shorts. Maybe nothing? When her mind started to drift on carnal currents, Louisa quickly called it back. Her dog was missing, not her sense of self-preservation. At least something came when she called.

She had to think of Dante searching in the streets, not searing in the sheets. Dante Rivera could do it, if anyone could. He could find Champ, that was, although Louisa had no doubt he could start a fire by rubbing his two hands together — up and down her body. No! Louisa needed to concentrate on finding her dog, not rediscovering the libido she thought she'd lost.

Dante could do it. Hadn't he beaten Alvin at pool, and Cora Alice at horseshoes? He'd built this whole house, for heaven's sake. He could do anything.

Maybe not everything, Louisa acknowledged. No man was that perfect, and Dante Rivera had plenty of faults. He was domineering and liked to organize people and things, for one. He was always laughing at her and calling her Louie, for another. And he didn't have a lot of self-control. Louisa felt a self-satisfied smile burble to her lips — her still slightly kiss-swollen lips. Mr. I'll-Make-the-Decisions Dante wasn't always in charge. Still, he was the most determined, bulldog-ish man she knew. He wouldn't let a girl down . . . or leave her dissatisfied, the treasonous thought crept into her head.

Perfect or not, he was out looking for her dog when no one else was. So why didn't he call?

At least two hours later, it seemed, when she was hoarse from calling and limp from crying and scratched from searching through the brambles at the edges of the property — she most likely had tick bites and Lyme disease herself, now, if not poison ivy again — Louisa heard a truck.

She went flying down the gravel driveway, and had to leap onto the grass when he slammed the brakes to a sudden stop.

"Damn it, Louie, I could have run you over!"

"Where were you? You didn't call and it's been days and I was so worried and —"

"It's been twenty minutes, if that."

Louisa had been peering into the truck's cab. Now she stepped back, disappointed. At least Dante had not found Champ dead on the side of the road, so she supposed she ought to be glad instead of disheartened. "You didn't find him."

"Who said so?" Dante got out and walked to the back of the truck. He dropped the tailgate and reached in.

"He's dead! Oh god, my poor dog is —"

Dante nearly threw the dog into her arms. Champ gave her chin a feeble lick and thumped his tail once against her thigh. She carried him to the front of the truck, to look him over in the headlights' beam.

"He's covered in blood!" She started rocking the dog, feeling him for injury, sobbing. "I don't know the way to the emergency vet, and what if the gas stations are closed? Howard was the one who always made sure we had enough gas in the car. What do I know about tourniquets? Poor baby, we'll fix it."

"It's not blood," Dante said in a disgusted tone.

"Not . . . ?" The dog did smell strange, now that she took a moment to sniff. So did Dante, kneeling beside her with the flashlight.

"It's barbeque sauce, and it's all over me and my truck."

Louisa dropped the dog, too late for her sweatshirt and shorts. Champ lay down with a moan. "What's wrong with him, then, and why didn't he come when I called him?"

"Guilt. And indigestion. He ate a whole

package of uncooked hotdogs, at least a pound of potato salad, maybe two dozen donuts, and I have no idea how many leftover hamburgers, all of which was in my truck, on its way to the food pantry kitchen with enough of Marta's barbeque sauce to feed every poor family in the Harbor for a month. Mr. Bradford always donates what's left after one of his parties, and I put tonight's load in my truck, on the passenger seat. Like a fool I left the passthrough window open between the passenger compartment and the truck bed. Your damned dog passed through. Then he hid back with the tools so no one would yell at him, and he'd have leisure to eat the leftover ribs."

Champ did look as contrite as a dog could look, and as woebegone. Louisa did not pet him. "You mean he was in your truck the whole time, not on his way back to my house as we thought?"

"He couldn't walk that far, not with his stomach dragging on the ground. What kind of stupid animal eats so much he can't move?"

"Look who's calling who stupid. You never looked in the truck?"

"Why should I? What would your dog be doing back there? And I was in such a

289

hurry to find him for you, I never checked the bags and boxes on the seat. The overhead light is out, or I would have noticed right away. Which isn't to say," he hurried to add, "that's as bad as not having enough gas in your car to get to the hospital, or the vet."

Louisa ignored that. "How did you find him?"

"I thought I saw something on the side of the road, so I pulled over to look. It was a raccoon, hightailing it for home. When I got back to the truck, I heard a noise. Sir Galahad, himself, groaning. At least I got him down in time, not that the truck isn't a mess."

"I'll help clean it in the morning, I promise. What do you think I should do with him now?" Champ had hardly moved.

"Pepto-Bismol. That's what Aunt Vinnie always gave her chihuahuas."

She asked him to wait with Champ outside while she looked in the medicine cabinet in Marta's kitchen.

"Why? He's not going to move." He nudged the dog onto his feet, though, and herded him slowly in the direction of the house's back door. He even held the terrier while Louisa tried to pour a spoonful down his throat — the dog's throat, not

Dante's. You'd never know it from the pink stuff dripping down both of them. When the dog shook, he got some on Louisa too, which made Dante feel a little better.

After putting the bottle away and wiping her hands, Louisa looked at the dog, then at her car, then at Dante. "Un-uh, lady," he said. "He's all yours. I'm not putting that sack of manure back in my truck, no matter how bad it is now. It can still get worse."

"I don't see how," she muttered, looking in her car trunk for rags to put down in the backseat. Champ lumbered to his feet and tried to nuzzle her leg.

"Oh, no, you don't, you bad boy. And don't think you can win me over with those big sad eyes. You're not sleeping in my bed tonight and that's that."

Dante didn't know his eyes looked sad. Oh, she meant the dog, which, according to Louisa, was too rank and ratty for her car, her carpet, and the dog's own new mattress. He cursed and picked up the fleabag. His clothes were already ruined.

"Oh, thank you!" Louisa enthused. "Truly you are the nicest, kindest, most considerate — What are you doing? That's Mr. Bradford's swimming pool!"

"No, it's mine, remember?"

"You jerk! You miserable, misogynistic maniac!" Louisa bent over the pool's edge to make sure her overloaded dog didn't just sink to the bottom.

Dante couldn't help himself. He tried, but he just couldn't resist the urge. He put his hands on the sweetest ass he'd ever seen, unfortunately attached to the biggest pain in the ass he'd ever met. Then he pushed.

Chapter Twenty-Four

Louisa got even.

She asked Dante to get some towels from the pool house. When he got back, the dog was out of the water, and so were Louisa's clothes. If that wasn't an invitation, his name wasn't — What the hell was his name, anyway? Nothing mattered but getting into that water, getting into Louisa Waldon's euphemistic pants, not the sodden ones on the tiles.

He stripped in seconds, which was about what it took for her to swim to the far end of the pool. By the time Dante had acclimated himself to the water, losing a bit of his ardor to the sudden chill, she was out of the pool, running. She picked up the dog, she picked up the towels. She kicked Dante's clothes into the pool. Then she ran for her car, while he dove for his wallet and car keys.

Poor Mr. Bradford wouldn't last a month with that woman, Dante thought on his way home. The man would have another stroke for sure. He'd have a fit tonight if he could see Dante wearing nothing but a towel and a big smile. No, Louisa needed a younger man, a stronger, healthier man. Why, Dante would be doing the old guy a service, taking Louisa off his hands. Or drowning her. The more he saw of her, the more he wanted to — take her, that is. He'd been willing to step back, but he kept stepping in quicksand. Now he didn't know which end was up or where to jump next. His body was telling him one thing, with great frequency and insistence, but his head was telling him another. He needed time to figure things out, things like his own feelings. If he satisfied one itch — which didn't look hard, considering how Louisa looked at him; lord knew everything else was hard — would he be starting a whole rash? How long was Mr. Bradford's book, anyway?

Oh, no! How could she be so stupid? Louisa wondered. Of all the idiotic things, she'd left her clothes on the side of the pool. Louisa almost turned back to Mr. Bradford's, but she was cold in the towels she had wrapped around her, her dog was wet — and Dante might still be there. What if she'd dropped something in the pool when she was stripping? Something like her panties? The pool guy would come in the morning when the filter stopped working and he'd find her pink bikinis clogging the drain. Louisa could just see him holding out his pole with her skimpies dangling at the end. He and his helper would have a good laugh. Mr. Bradford wouldn't. He'd know she wouldn't go skinny-dipping by herself. He'd think she was sex-crazed, screwing around, shameless.

Well, she might want to find out what making love with Dante Rivera was like — or having sex in the water, for that matter; Howard was anything but adventuresome — but she was definitely ashamed. How could she have more desire for a man she'd known for a month or so, than she had in all the years she'd known her own former fiancé? Maybe she and Howard had panted after each other at first, in a civilized way, of course, but that was a vague long-term memory. Now just the daisy-fresh memory of Dante's bare chest raised her heart rate.

She was absolutely not screwing around. She was not going to be just another of Dante Rivera's women. If she was ashamed now, Louisa could not imagine how she'd feel when he dumped her and moved on. Howard had bruised her heart. Dante, she feared, could rip it out of her chest, step on it, and kick it into the next county.

So she couldn't go back for the clothes. It wasn't Dante she did not trust; it was herself. If she drove back, and he were still there, maybe with his clothes still off, or clinging wetly to his warm skin, and he gave her one of those dimpled smiles . . . She turned off the car's heater. She didn't need it.

Louisa told herself she was doing okay with her life: making friends, making money, making her house cozy and clean. She did not need a man. She did not need this man. She needed a good night's sleep. If she set the alarm for 6:30 she could get to Mr. Bradford's before the workmen came.

Way before then, almost as soon as her head touched her pillow, in fact, Louisa heard a car pull up her driveway. Champ did not bark. Louisa prodded him with her toes to make sure he was breathing. He whuffled and went back to sleep.

"Some watchdog you are," Louisa grumbled, hearing the car door slam. Maybe it was next door, company coming for the weekend, people who had been stuck in traffic so long they arrived after midnight. Louisa rolled over. But what if it were Dante, returning her clothes? Maybe he was being chivalrous. Maybe he was being confident. Maybe he had reason to be hopeful. How could Louisa resist him for the umpteenth time, all on the same day? By not answering the knock on the door, that was the only way.

The problem was, the front door was open, and only the screen door was locked. Louisa was proud to be conquering some of her big city fears — and it was too hot to keep the house closed up — but anyone could come in. Francine had pointed out that a housebreaker could slit the screen in an instant, explaining why she did not bother to have a lock on her screen door, and why rich people had air conditioners. They could live in fortresses that way, but they couldn't smell the honeysuckle or wake up to birdsong. According to Aunt Vinnie, half the year-rounders never locked any of their doors, but that was too much for Louisa.

Tonight's burglar wouldn't have to fumble for his box cutter. A paw could push in the screen, Louisa had done such a poor job of replacing it in the warped door frame. Champ had gone out twice, before Louisa had nailed some crosspieces across the lower part.

She heard the knock again. At least he

was a polite thief. Louisa found the lamp switch, a robe, and her orange flip-flops. She grabbed the book she'd been reading, a heavy hardcover. She would not go unarmed to face Dante in the dark.

Her caller wasn't Dante; it was his cousin Francine, with Teddy asleep in her arms.

Louisa quickly unlatched the door and beckoned the woman in, leading her to the sofa.

"I won't be able to pick him up by next year, I bet," Francine whispered, looking down on her son by the hall light Louisa had flipped on. "He's grown so much this year alone."

And his own bed had grown too small since yesterday so he needed Louisa's couch? Louisa rubbed her eyes. "Fran, it's the middle of the night. Did your house burn down or something? I didn't hear any sirens. Is your mother all right? You want me to watch Teddy while you go to the hospital with her?"

"No," Francine said, the word catching on a sob. Louisa led her to the kitchen and filled the teapot. "Or do you want coffee?"

"T-tea."

Louisa put mugs — ones with dolphins on them from last week's yard sales — and spoons on the table. Then she put a box of tissues and a plate of chocolate chip cookies in front of her guest.

Francine took one of both and apologized for disturbing Louisa, for invading her house without so much as a phone call, for having no place else to go.

"What about Dante? He'd help, no matter what." Francine still had not told her what the problem was, but Louisa was sure of Dante's devotion to his family.

"I called an hour ago, but he's not home. I guess he went out after the party."

He went out looking for Louisa's dog. "He might be home by now. Do you want me to call?"

Francine shook her head and took another cookie. "Besides, Dante's houseboat is the first place Fred would look. Everyone knows where he keeps it."

"Fred? Teddy's father?"

Over a pot of tea — Louisa would never be able to sleep tonight — and the rest of the cookies, Francine finally explained what she was doing at Louisa's house. She'd taken Teddy up to Osprey Hill for the fireworks party, she said, rather than let his father take him on the beach with his drunken friends. Fred had taken umbrage. He'd also taken a bat to Francine's mailbox while they were gone. He'd called an hour ago admitting it, shouting that she was turning the boy against him, turning him into a rich kid wannabe. Her cousin saw more of the kid than his own father did. She was wrecking Fred's own life, he claimed, demanding all his money for a brat he never got to see. Now she was trying to get the courts to garnish his wages, costing him another lawyer's fee to fight it. She was going to make Fred's boss think he was some kind of scum, leaving his wife and son starving in the gutter. He could lose his job at the boatyard at the end of the summer, on account of her damned whining.

So he was late with a couple of payments. Francine had a job, didn't she? And living at her mother's house she wasn't paying sky-high summer rental fees, like Fred was doing. And he worked on Saturdays, fixing the tourists' yachts' engines, so he ought to get Teddy on his days off.

"Of course he did not want him this morning, when I suggested he take Teddy for new sneakers. He doesn't want to know anything about how expensive it is to raise a child. Sometimes I think he cares more about sticking up for his own rights than he does for Teddy. Fred's been late half the

Sundays when he's supposed to have him, and brings him back early whenever he feels like it, whether I'm home or not."

"You were married to this creep?"

"I know. But he wasn't this bad. He didn't use to drink so much, and he wasn't so angry all the time. He hates his job, hates the people he works for, hates being on his own. He never had to do his own laundry or anything, before."

"Fran, I have to ask, was he ever, you know, abusive?"

"Physically? No, except for the stuff he used to throw. Pillows, dishes, flowerpots. Not at me, though. But now . . ." Her voice trailed off.

"Now?"

"Now he says he's going to come get Teddy, and no one is going to stop him."

"Why didn't you call the police?"

"You don't understand. I guess no one can, unless they've been there. Fred would be even madder then, humiliated in front of the whole town. They publish the police blotter in the local paper, you know. He'd add that to his pile of complaints, and re-member it the next time he had a few drinks. And what could the police do if he hasn't done anything much but make threats, anyway? Besides, he went to school with half the cops on the local force. They're not going to hassle him over a little thing like a mailbox. They'd most likely take his side anyway, thinking no mere woman should take away a man's kid."

"Not in this day and age, surely."

"What country have you been living in, Louisa? Orders of protection aren't worth the paper they are printed on half the time."

Louisa got up and walked to the phone. "I'm calling Dante."

"No. I shouldn't have called him either. Now that I've had time to think about it, Dante would only go looking for Fred. There would be worse trouble."

"What could be worse than you being afraid to stay in your own house?"

"Dante could break Fred's arms and go to jail."

"He wouldn't." Then again, when it came to defending his family, Dante seemed capable of anything. "What about your mother? You didn't leave her home, did you?"

"She refused to leave, saying no low-life louse was going to chase her from her house. She won't let Fred in, and she won't hesitate to call the neighbors if he gets rowdy. They'll phone the police for sure, and then the cops will have to come, but I won't be there. Fred only wants Teddy, anyway. He'll know we're not there if the car is missing, and he won't cause any trouble."

"But, Fran, what about next time? I mean, you're welcome to stay here tonight. We should put your car behind the Mahoneys' house so no one can see it from the road. The house is still empty. But what then? You can't live your life in fear of some mean drunk stealing your kid."

"I know. I thought I would move, but I don't know how much longer my mother can stay on her own. But, really, Fred's not so bad when he's sober. I can talk to him tomorrow, make him understand he can't keep threatening me, and he can't ever have Teddy if he's going to be drinking and driving. He knows I can call my lawyer Monday and get the visitation rights changed if he keeps carrying on this way, so he never sees Teddy on his own. I have to believe that he loves his own son, in his own way, so he won't jeopardize that. He's not such a bad man, only frustrated with the way things have been going for him."

Louisa wasn't so sure. No one had an excuse for frightening a woman, or even mangling a mailbox.

Chapter Twenty-Five

Teddy woke up while Francine was moving the car. Champ had crawled onto the couch next to him.

"Your dog smells, Aunt Louisa."

"But he had a bath." Then she wrinkled her nose. "Oh, that. He ate too much at the barbeque."

"What are we doing here?"

"I got spooked by a noise in the woods across the street. Your mom came to keep me company."

"Why didn't you call Uncle Dan? He's not afraid of anything."

"Because your mom is plenty brave too, okay?"

His mom was in the kitchen, crying again. Louisa had left her with a dish of super fudge chunk ice cream, and the hardcover romance novel. She led Teddy up the stairs to the room she and Annie used to share. She hadn't repainted the room yet, so it still looked girly, with pink ballet slippers on the wallpaper. Her nephew had complained bitterly when he was here, but he complained of the bugs and the boredom and sharing a bedroom with his sister anyway. Louisa had felt redecorating the other rooms was more important. She moved a fluffy white stuffed cat from the pillow of one of the narrow twin beds and pulled back the pink coverlet. Luckily Teddy was too tired to notice, or care. He tucked the cat under the covers with him, whispering, "Don't tell the guys," before he rolled over and went back to sleep.

When the ice cream was gone, Louisa showed Francine to a small downstairs room with a single bed, a desk, a chair and a lamp. It might have been a dining room years ago, but now Louisa kept her computer there. It would make a nice office, overlooking the backyard the way it did, if she could think of a home business. She'd never gotten around to pricing the pearls, so her online sales venture had never begun. She never wanted to part with the treasures she found on her garage sale scavenger hunts, anyway. And she had two jobs for now.

Once she'd pointed Francine to the bathroom, Louisa locked the front door. And the downstairs windows. The early July night was not really hot, and she did not care if it was. She'd never be able to sleep with the house open, feeling so vulnerable, and so responsible suddenly for two other lives.

She couldn't sleep anyway. Her mind was in chaos, to say nothing of the caffeine. The day and night kept rewinding through her head like a broken tape.

You just never knew about a man, she concluded an hour later. Here you pledge your life and your love, and he turns out to be a conscienceless creep, or a drunk, a womanizer, a mailbox batterer. Then again, Dante's wife had turned out to be unfaithful, to his entire sex, so maybe disloyalty was not limited to men.

People changed, changed their minds. So how did anyone stay married? For that matter, why did anyone get married in the first place? Just look at the divorce rate; the odds weren't good. Louisa thought of how many of her college friends were already on their second husbands. Then she thought of her mother and Aunt Vinnie, whose husbands had died. The statistics on widows versus widowers, women outliving men, was not encouraging either. One way or another, a lot of women ended up alone, so what was the point of the heartbreak along the way?

Life was hard. Love was harder, so why

did people keep trying? Louisa asked herself, tangled in her sheets. Maybe they were all gamblers, looking for the long shot. Or optimists, desperately wanting to believe in that happily ever after. Wasn't that why publishers put out so many books with handsome hunks on the covers? They gave their readers a small escape from reality, and a little trust that happy endings were still out there.

Trust, that's what it took, she thought, finally feeling drowsy. Trust, and luck.

She was not having much of the latter this night, or sleep, either. Francine snored, Champ had wind, and the house was hot with everything shut up.

She could not have slept through the truck barreling down her quiet block, anyway. The dog growled, but didn't get off the bed. Louisa did, to see where a truck could be going at this time of night, on the dead end street. She had been thinking of Dante, she remembered, half-asleep, and thought, hoped, dreamed, dreaded that he might have come by with her clothes after all. His truck was old, but never as decrepit or as loud as the one that turned around past the Mahoneys' and parked across her driveway, bumping the front fender against the poor old oak tree at the corner of her property. Now she couldn't drive away without knocking over the new fence, but she had no intention of fleeing her own house. What, leave Teddy and his mother unprotected? She'd never forgive herself, and knew Dante would never forgive her either, not that Mr. Rivera's opinions mattered all that much, of course. She had no intention of going downstairs, however. She could just picture Dante shaking his head at that idiocy.

Louisa had no doubts as to the identity of this new visitor. She leaned out her bedroom window and called down, loudly enough to be heard by the lout, she hoped, but not loudly enough to wake the neighbors, or Francine. "Go away, Fred."

"Not without my son. It's a holiday and I get to see him."

"The Fourth of July was yesterday. It's already the fifth. Go home."

"No, I came to see my boy."

"What makes you think he's here, anyway?"

"That crazy old Vinnie said my Fran was playing with the nice little Waldon girls over at Whaler's Drive, that's what."

"Well, Francine's not here now. No one is but me and my dog. My big, protective guard dog."

"I don't hear any watchdog barking."

"He's trained to attack silently, without warning."

"Call him off. I only want to see for myself that my family's not holed up in your place. Let me come look, then I'll go."

"No way. Go home."

"Why not? What are you hiding in there? Dante? Bets at the Breakaway give him the edge. It's close, though. Rivera's rich, but his money's tied up in real estate. Old man Bradford's rolling in dough, and he can't live long, they say, so that might be the better deal. Especially for a city broad. Dante ain't going to fix up no Manhattan duplex like the old man already has. Dante wouldn't do it for Susan; he ain't going to do it for a skinny merink like you. He can't be much in the sack, anyway, or his wife wouldn't of turned, so you might as well go for the sure bet."

Louisa would have slammed the window shut, if she thought he'd go away. "How dare you! My life is no business of yours!"

"It is if you've got my kid. Abduction, that's what you've gone and committed, taking the boy without parental consent. And you're an immoral influence on a little boy's mind, too. I'll tell the judge you were screwing around right in front of my son.

Everyone knows you're carrying on with both of the sons of bitches."

"No one knows anything, but be my guest. You go ahead and talk to the judge. Be sure to tell him how you were out disturbing the peace, driving while intoxicated, and — what are you doing? — carrying a weapon."

Fred had taken an aluminum bat out of his truck. He started swiping at the tree. Leaves were flying, and bark chips shattering. "Fran!" he yelled.

Lights went on next door. Dante's renters were going to complain. Louisa had lost him one month's rent already, and didn't want to cost him another. "If you do not stop that racket this instant, I am going to call the police."

Fred stopped taking batting practice on the oak. He sat on the grass beneath Louisa's window, in the light from her front porch, and put his head in his hands. "What am I going to do?"

He was a big man, Louisa could see, thick-waisted and beefy. He needed a shave, and a haircut too. His shirt was half in his pants and half out, and his jeans were torn across at one knee. He looked like a man desperately in need of a caring hand, not hers or Francine's of course, but

Louisa did feel sorry for him. He seemed lost and defeated.

"Go home, Fred, and get some sleep," she called down, in what she hoped were friendly tones. "Francine will talk to you in the morning."

"She is here then!"

Oops. "No, I spoke to her, that's all. She says she wants to come to an agreement with you, not fight like this. It's bad for Teddy."

Fred didn't move, but started pounding the bat on the ground — hammering Louisa's marigolds.

"Stop that! If the police come and find you with a weapon, they'll have to press charges." Louisa was guessing at the legalities, but willing to commit perjury for the sake of her flowers.

" 'S not a weapon. I bought the bat for my boy. A surprise."

"Little League season is over. He won't need it until next year."

"He needs the practice."

No amount of practice was going to get Teddy an athletic scholarship, certainly not with a bat that had seen better days, and calmer nights.

Fred was going on: "I bought it before they could take everything I owned. It'll be the last thing I can buy for my own kid."

At least he wasn't shouting. The neighbors had turned off their lights and gone back to bed, which Louisa wished she could do, too. Fred seemed in no hurry to move. In fact, he looked as well-rooted as the oak. Louisa sighed. If talking to him kept the lummox calm, she'd keep talking, but she wasn't going to let him think he was the victim here. "For Pete's sake, they're only taking child support out of your wages, not your life's blood. If you'd paid on time no one would have to —"

"Not them. The feds. I, uh, messed up my taxes."

"So you'll pay the penalty. No big deal."

"No, it's worse'n that. I never told them about the money from selling the house when Fran and me split up. Or the money from hauling lobster pots. Or the time I won big at the track. Or when my sister's kid Arlen was doing day trading and we all cashed in a bundle before he tanked."

"You haven't been paying your taxes at all?"

"No one would of known if I hadn't had to show the forms to Fran's lawyer, for the divorce. He turned me in, the bastard."

"They would have caught up with you sooner or later. It's all on computers, except for the lobsters, I'd guess, unless you had to register for a permit."

"Damn computers are taking over the world. It's come to how an honest man can't even make a buck without some twerp at a keyboard in Wisconsin putting his hand in your pocket."

"I hate to say it, but I can't help thinking that an honest man would have declared all that money and paid taxes on it, like the rest of us."

"The rest of who? Everyone cheats on the IRS."

"I don't." Well, she wouldn't have declared any money she made on those pearls, but that was a moot question.

Fred was maundering on: "It's too late now anyway. They're taking my boat and my camper, my season pass to Aqueduct Raceway, everything but my tools and my truck. Then they might come get me. They might get Francine too, even though I told them she didn't know anything about any of it."

"And she never saw a dime of it either, I bet." Louisa was scribbling on a piece of paper from the pad where she made her lists of things to do. She tossed it out the window in Fred's direction. "Here, that's the number of a good tax attorney."

"I can't afford no high-priced lawyers."

"This one will work for free. You call and tell him Louisa sent you. He owes me. He'll make them work out a payment system or something. That's what he does all day, and he's good at it. The IRS isn't going to make an example out of a poor shnook like you; they just want their money. If they put you in jail, what will Francine and Teddy do? They'd have to sign up for social services, which would cost the government more money. So would keeping you in prison. They'd much rather let you work off your debts."

Fred didn't want to hear about working the rest of his life for Uncle Sam. "Nah, Fran won't have to go on welfare. Big brother Dante will take care of them."

"He's her cousin."

"Same thing, the way he's always around, and how she thinks he walks on water. The s.o.b.'s got money and brains, she was always telling me. Her mother was always saying how I should be more like him. My own mother told me, too. Try harder, be more ambitious, get ahead like Dante. Bull. How could I compete with that?"

"He's her cousin," Louisa repeated. "There's no race, no competition. She married you, didn't she?" Why, Louisa would never be able to figure out. Her neck was getting a crick in it from looking down at the lush on her lawn, so she said, "Go home, call Howard in the morning. He'll be able to do something about the mess."

Fred listened to her, amazingly enough, and lurched to his feet, leaving the baseball bat behind, thank goodness. He got in his truck, started it up on the second try, and put it in gear. Unfortunately, he should have put it in reverse. Louisa thought the old oak might have rocked from the impact. The truck sure did. Smoke rose from its radiator, and pieces of metal thunked into the road, startling the peepers and crickets into silence.

Louisa leaned so far out the window she had to clamp her hands on the wooden frame, which was soft with dry rot. "Are you all right?"

"Better'n my truck."

"Should I call you a cab?" she offered, still not knowing if any ran at night.

"Nah. I'll sleep in the truck. Won't be the first time, or the last. Fran can take me home in the morning."

"Francine's not here!"

He shrugged. "Then you can."

With his truck across her driveway? Louisa couldn't get her car out — much less retrieve her clothes from the side of Mr. Bradford's pool. That was small potatoes, she acknowledged, compared to the troubles Francine was going to face in the morning. Fran's car could be driven away from the Mahoneys' tonight, but she'd have to go right past Fred. Who knew what mayhem he'd commit at the sight of his wife driving away, leaving him stuck, next to Louisa's mailbox?

Besides, poor Francine was sleeping soundly in the downstairs room, emotionally and physically exhausted. Louisa did not want to wake her. If Francine stayed through the night, though, Teddy would wake up to see his father slumped over a steering wheel, stinking of booze. Fred had to go.

Louisa thought of calling Dante, despite Francine's wishes, but realized the other woman was right. Fred was so bitter toward his wife's cousin, he might explode if Dante tried to get him out of the truck. Dante seemed fitter, but Fred outweighed him, and Louisa bet Fred fought dirty, too. That would be a worse thing for Teddy to see: his two male role models brawling in the flower beds. Louisa's flower beds.

The neighbors would see too.

Besides, she'd already asked Dante to pull her chestnuts out of the fire once today. He'd found her dog; that was enough. Any more and he was going to think Louisa was a clingy, helpless woman — the kind he hated — and not a reasonable, intelligent, decisive female who could solve her own problems.

So she called Alvin.

Chapter Twenty-Six

Louisa made blueberry pancakes the next morning. Actually, the microwave had made them, from the freezer, but she'd added the blueberries to the syrup. She was proud enough when Teddy ate the whole stack.

Francine had left early for her Saturday half-day at the bank, so she could check on her mother and change her clothes at home. She'd leave a message for Dante to pick the boy up at Louisa's, if Louisa did not mind. Louisa didn't. Teddy could help her walk the dog, she told Francine, and help her find more of those shiny jingle shells she needed to fill a glass lamp. The lamp had come from a yard sale, of course, filled with dried beans. Who would want beans in their living room?

Fred, maybe. There was no sign of him in the morning, only a few beheaded or flattened marigolds, new scrapes on the oak tree, tire ruts on the street-side grass, and a few shards of glass Louisa swept up before Champ could cut his feet on them.

Good riddance, Francine said, when

Louisa explained what had transpired last night while the others slept. Louisa hadn't slept at all, thinking of love, sex, marriage, and her clothes in the pool. It was way too late to worry about them now. Either they had been discovered, or the pool guys were doing a lousy job. Louisa was in no hurry to find out which.

Mr. Bradford didn't need her today, because he was having lunch with an old friend. She'd have to stop by the hill later, to check the messages and see what function they were to attend that evening, so she could figure what to wear. They saw many of the same people every weekend, and they had all seen most of her clothes. Now the pool guys had too. What was the worst that could happen? Mr. Bradford could fire her for conduct unbecoming a lady, or the gardener would be laughing. Well, she thought her job was secure because no one else could read Mr. Bradford's handwritten notes, and she'd been laughed at by everyone else in the world, so why not give the yard workers a chuckle? She was almost getting used to being the comic relief in this town. Maybe in a few months, or years, she'd be able to laugh at herself.

Meantime, she could go to yard sales as

soon as Teddy left. When they got back from the dog walk, Louisa took her newspaper clippings, a pad, pen and the local map out to the porch.

"Do you know where Seaview Avenue is?" she asked Teddy, who was throwing a tennis ball for Champ in the front yard. Either he was getting better at throwing, or Champ was a better catcher than the kids on the ball team, but they were having a great time. Louisa didn't even worry about her old, half-rotten windows.

"Sure, James lives there. Julie lives around the corner. She's in sixth grade."

"That's a big help. How do you get there from here?"

"On the school bus?"

"Thanks." She went back to the small print on the big map. If nothing else, she was learning her way around Paumonok Harbor. Some people went on house or garden tours; she took the tag sale route. She bet she saw more of the way people really lived, too.

When the tennis ball was so slobbered on that Teddy didn't want to throw it anymore, he came to sit beside Louisa on the porch steps. He asked if she wanted to come along with him and Uncle Dante to Montauk. They were having a library sale there.

Louisa worked at a library, and had Mr. Bradford's extensive collection at her fingertips. The last thing she needed was to spend her money on books.

Teddy was going on: "The bakery here gives them all of yesterday's stuff, and we have to deliver it. It's fun. You should come."

Day-old baked goods and musty library discards? That didn't sound appealing to Louisa. "I don't know, Teddy."

"I didn't think it would be cool either at first. But when we went last year, Uncle Dante let me pick out books my mother never would have let me."

Louisa didn't believe in censorship, but Teddy was just a little boy. Dante should have known better. "What kind of books?" she asked, frowning.

"Scary ones. I didn't get any nightmares, either. Except maybe a little. They have more books there than our whole library, I bet."

Mrs. Terwilliger had a closet full of books, culled from the shelves or donated, that would go out for sale in August. Louisa had already been enlisted to cashier. One book sale a summer was enough.

"They have a yard sale section," Teddy added, slyly.

Louisa almost felt her ears perk up, like Champ's when he heard the refrigerator door open. She did not want to thrust herself into Dante's company, though. He already thought she was crazy. Pushy and crazy was too much. "Well, I am still not sure. Maybe your uncle wants to spend the day with you. You know, man to man. I'd be in the way."

Teddy's look was eloquent. "Who are you kidding, Aunt Louisa?" He was young, but he already knew the rules of the road: kids sat in the backseat, always. "I'll ask him when he comes."

When he came, Dante had a shopping bag in his hand. Louisa smiled. "What, we get first pick of the stale muffins?"

He smiled back, winked at Teddy, but handed her the bag. Louisa looked in and saw her clothes, all dry and neatly folded, her sweatshirt and shorts, her blouse and bra and pink panties on top. Her first thought was: Dante Rivera had handled her underwear. Her second was: Thank goodness no one else had.

"What is it, Aunt Louisa?" Teddy wanted to know.

"Just some stuff I left up at Mr. Bradford's last night," she replied, hurriedly shoving the bag inside the house and

322

cursing the blush stealing across her cheeks. Embarrassment was a not infrequent occurrence when she was around Mr. Dante Rivera. She supposed she could get used to that too.

"Thank you," she said, in as composed tones as her rattled wits would permit. He was grinning now, and that was yet another thing she could not seem to grow accustomed to. The sight of his devilish dimples still stole her breath away.

Teddy was hopping around, eager to go. "Did they donate any of those fancy cookies this year, the ones with the icing? Are we going to go out for lunch afterward? Can Louisa come?"

"I was just going to ask her, sport, if you'd be quiet a minute." He turned to Louisa. "I think you'd enjoy it, a real taste of small-town America at its best. Everyone pitching in, having a grand time for a good cause."

"It's very kind of the bakery here in the Harbor to donate stuff for the next town," she said. "And you to deliver it."

He shrugged that off. "They let Mrs. Terwilliger have anything she wants for our library, after the first rush of sales. Everyone helps everyone else. So will you come? Teddy and I need help carrying, don't we, sport?"

How could she refuse? And why should she? Teddy was a great chaperon, and she hadn't been out to Montauk in years.

She'd forgotten how different the resort town was from its neighbors. Paumonok was slow and sleepy, like an old spaniel curled up in the sun. East Hampton was like an Afghan hound, busy preening, prancing, and posing for the cover of *People* magazine. But Montauk was a lolloping black Lab, tongue hanging out, no leash, no rules except being home for supper.

They drove down the hill on Montauk Highway and there it was, blue blue ocean water so close you could touch it, and yellow motels, red and green kayaks for rent at the gas stations, surf boards on top of half the cars, lines at the miniature golf course, lines at the pancake place, lines at the town office where newcomers were trying to get parking permits. There were people on bikes and skates, pushing baby carriages, dragging beach umbrellas. Montauk was a tourist town, and proud of it. There might be elegant mansions on the hills to rival Mr. Bradford's, but the downtown was color and crowds and traffic chaos, at least on a July weekend. Louisa supposed Montauk would be as deserted as the other towns come the middle of the winter, but for now it was bustling.

The library sale was on the village green in the center of town, and Teddy was right. It was huge, and mobbed. "Don't even think about it," Dante warned, almost reading her mind and the dollar signs in her eyes. "Paumonok Harbor could never pull this off. We don't have half the volunteers — there must be over a hundred in those blue shirts — and we don't have the tourists, either. Montauk has a ton of motels while we have mostly second-home owners or renters."

After they each carried a box of pastries over to the baked goods tables, Dante told Louisa and Teddy to start shopping while he made another trip or two from the truck. He pointed Louisa in the direction of the white elephant section and the book compound, which was so filled with cartons that they overflowed the tables and ranged against the fence on the ground.

So many books, so little time. That's what a T-shirt had printed on it, so Louisa bought it for Mr. Bradford while she got her bearings. He mightn't wear it, but he'd appreciate the saying, and the fact that she bought it for him. Then she went to the yard sale area and bought a teakettle painted to look like a cow, just because it made her smile, a blue candle holder with only a tiny chip, a wicker wastebasket to match her porch rocker, a set of dish towels with fish on them, and a bird feeder that needed a couple of nails. Before she could worry about where to put the stuff so she could look at the books, Dante was there, taking the bags from her to put in the truck.

"Will they be safe in the back?" she asked.

He looked at the beat-up bird feeder. "I don't think you have to worry about anyone stealing this cr— this stuff. And this is Montauk, remember, not Manhattan."

Teddy had won a cardboard airplane and a stuffed bear, and he'd bought a seedling butterfly bush to bring home to his grandmother.

"They have plants?" Louisa went there next, and then had to wait for Dante to find her, to carry all the pots and planters. He grumbled that all the good books would be sold by the time he got to look at them, but gathered her nursery stock for another trip to the truck.

Louisa and Teddy went into the book section, where they were given plastic bags. "They weigh the books, like they do the fish down at the docks," Teddy explained, pointing to the hanging scales.

How could Louisa resist? She found a bird identification guide — how could she feed the birds if she didn't know their names? And a couple of cookbooks for beginners, a crossword puzzle dictionary, a guide to houseplants since her yard was getting too crowded, and a book on how to arrange flowers, for when she got enough to need arranging. She added a writing guide, a dictionary and two grammar books, for when she worked at home. Someone handed her another bag so she moved on to the fiction, and filled that one with mysteries and old best-sellers and romance novels.

Dante came back and groaned about his poor aching back, but he was smiling, and she was too busy filling another bag to care. "This way I won't have to worry about getting sand in the library books," she told him, "or bending down the corners."

He looked at the top books in the bag and raised an eyebrow. "You read this?"

She'd thought twice about that cover, with the girl's skirt hiked halfway up her thigh, and the guy's hand pushing it higher, but, hey, the price was so cheap . . . She threw *Moby Dick* and *The Once and Future King* on top of it. "They're fun, and they make me happy."

"What more can you ask?" he said, filling a bag of his own with a couple of science fiction books, with the green alien's hand halfway up the space woman's thigh. Then he went off to find a book on wooden boats, one with architectural house plans, a chronology of the Civil War, and *Computers for Dummies.*

"I thought you were some hotshot tech wizard," Louisa said, wandering back toward the reference section to see if there was a thesaurus.

"This is for Aunt Vinnie. I'm trying to drag her into the twenty-first century, but she doesn't want to learn."

"Show her the solitaire games. Trust me, she'll figure out how to use the mouse fast enough."

Teddy did not have much in his bag. All the good scary books were gone, and mostly picture books were left. Louisa took him over to the nature section and found James Herriot and some other animal stories, and then they found an easy art book on drawing cartoons, and a Yankees yearbook that was only one year old. He started reading statistics that made her wonder if it was written in Greek, which reminded her she wanted a Spanish-English dictionary for Marta.

Dante carried the bags away to the scales while she and Teddy kept scavenging.

"This is heaven!" she said, joining him on the check-out line when neither she nor Teddy could carry one more book. "Thank you so much for bringing me."

"My pleasure," he said, and meant it. Seeing Louisa so happy made him feel like a king himself — no, like a wizard. He'd brought that glow to her cheeks and that sparkle to her green eyes, and that simple joy in the day. For once she wasn't worried about her house or her dog or her pride or where their relationship was going. They were here, and that was enough for now. It was enough for him, too.

He refused to let her pay for the books. "You're our guest, remember? Besides, this is one cheap date. A hot dog and bunch of books."

Louisa wiped mustard off her chin. "This is a date?"

He didn't answer, but pointed to the quilt the library ladies were raffling off. Louisa took only one chance, because it would look lovely on her bed, but too lovely to let Champ sleep on. Dante took three whole books of tickets. "They work hard."

Teddy declared he was far too old to

have his face painted, but when Dante insisted, Louisa let a giggling teenager paint a butterfly on her cheek. It itched like crazy, but his smile made her feel that she could fly too. She knew she was grinning like an idiot and didn't care.

If there was music she would have danced, she was so happy.

Afterward, they drove out to see the lighthouse, mandatory, Dante swore, for anyone visiting the Point. Teddy told her that he was tall enough to climb to the very top of the light now, but Louisa did not think she needed to see Connecticut from such a height, or the narrow stairs to get there. Seeing the landmark was enough.

Acting as tour guide, Teddy told her all about the cattle ranch they passed, and how they used to have buffalo there, but the bull trampled someone, so they got rid of them. Dante pointed out the handsome library that would benefit from the day's profits, and the smallest airport she'd ever seen. He took them to the harbor area next, for an ice cream cone. They sat on a dock built right on the water, watching boats coming in and out of the jetties, and watching people toss french fries to the seagulls.

On the way out of Montauk, Dante

pulled onto a sand path, put the truck into four-wheel drive, and drove straight onto the beach. Other than a few tire tracks and some fishermen, they had the beach to themselves, with the sun and the surf and the dunes in the distance. Teddy stayed in the truck with his new Yankees book, but Dante and Louisa kicked off their shoes and walked along the water's edge. Holding hands just seemed the natural thing to do.

"This might be the nicest day of my life," Louisa said when they finally headed back, just before they reached her street.

Dante's too. She wasn't leaving.

Chapter Twenty-Seven

"How do you know he asked me to stay?" Louisa got out of the truck before Dante could come around to open her door, after they'd dropped Teddy off at his house. She was definitely not going to invite Dante inside. She had not been intending to, claiming she had to get ready for the evening, whatever the function was, figuring that was safer. Why ruin a lovely day with what might be a disaster? Now she was certainly not going to, not when he and the whole town were gossiping about her again. She started gathering her bags and boxes and plants from the back of the truck. When he came to help, she said, "This town is like an old party line telephone, where everyone knows everyone else's business."

"Not everyone. Mr. Bradford told me he asked you to stay on when the book is done."

"And I said no, but he asked me to think about it, saying September was too far away to make decisions now."

That sly old fox, Dante thought to himself, letting him believe it was a done deal.

"Have you been thinking about it?"

"Yes, and I haven't changed my mind yet, although not much time has gone by. Mr. Bradford is a pleasure to work with, once you get his morning coffee into him. He is generous and fun, with the most brilliant mind I have ever encountered. He can talk about anything, and every day is a new experience."

"But?"

"But not everyone wants new experiences all the time. Sometimes the familiar is lovely too. Roots, knowing where you belong, that kind of thing. You have to understand, because you are planted here."

Dante was not sure if she meant that as a criticism or a compliment. He carried another pile of her magpie's hoard to the front door, where she was letting the dog out. "I travel too, you know. I am not some turnip stuck in one place."

"Yes, you vacation whenever you wish. I'd like to also, some, someday. That's the point. If I accepted Mr. Bradford's offer and went with him after the summer, I would be living his life, not mine. I'd be following him, not leading, not even walking at his side. If he decided to do a book signing in Toronto or Timbuktu, I'd have to go along. That would be my job, and my responsibility, to make the trip pleasant for him. I wouldn't mind seeing to the hotel reservations and the limousine from the airport, calling to be sure his books arrived on time, but what if I'd rather be in Paris or Peru, or right here, watching my daffodils come up? I find I love having a place of my own, somewhere to putter around, at my own whims, my own speed."

"You've just been in apartments too long. Trust me, houses can be anchors tied to your neck, too."

"But I have to find that out for myself. We moved into an apartment after my father died. Then I lived in one set of rooms after another through college and later, until I moved in with Howard. It is time for me to put down my own roots."

"In Paumonok Harbor?" he asked, doubt in his voice.

"Maybe. Maybe I'll hate it when Mr. Bradford is gone and I have no social life and no income, but maybe I won't. Maybe it will be as bleak and barren as everyone tells me. But maybe it will be peaceful and inspiring, with awesome scenery and wild stormy seas. I'll have the companion dog thing, if I can afford to volunteer, and bird-watching."

He laughed. "You don't know a gold-finch from a grunion."

She patted the book on top of one bag. "But I can learn, can't I?"

"You can do anything, I guess." He put another box down on her front stoop, waiting to see if she asked him in. She didn't, but he was reluctant to go. "What will you do for a job?"

She shrugged. "I find I like writing, so maybe I'll ask at the local newspaper or magazines. There's still the possibility of finding a van Gogh at one of the yard sales and making a killing at the online auctions. And I can do a lot of Mr. Bradford's work on the Internet too, so maybe he'll keep me as a long-distance associate."

"He'd keep you as a lot more."

She pushed a box of plants out of the sun, until she could water them or get them in the ground. With her back to him, so he could not see the hurt on her face, Louisa said, "I will not become his mistress, no matter how much he offers. He did not ask."

"I didn't mean you should become a kept woman for the money. I meant he might have married you. Wives can't up and quit, you know."

"Marriage? To Mr. Bradford?" Louisa

almost dropped the bird feeder he handed her.

"That's not so far-fetched. He really likes you."

"And I really like him, in a respectful kind of way. He's older than my father would have been, and I look on him almost like that."

"Don't let him hear you say he's a paternal figure," Dante said. "It'll ruin his self-image."

"What? He thinks he's a young stud on the town?" She made a derisive sound. "No, he knows he's a distinguished older gentleman, not about to embarrass himself with a wife maitre d's mistake for his granddaughter. Besides, he's already had a trophy bride. His second wife was that actress, remember? He needed two chapters of his book to describe the three years they spent together. I made him cut it down from four. He'd never make that mistake twice."

Dante wasn't so sure. A woman like Louisa could turn a man's head around and inside out. Look at him, hanging around rearranging her piles of books on the porch, hoping she'd invite him inside. "He wants you with him."

Louisa followed Champ toward the

backyard, looking for a good tree to hang the feeder where she could see it from her office. Dante followed her.

"What about what I want?" she asked. "I don't even know what that is, so how can he? If I ever do decide to get married again, that is, if I ever decide to get engaged again, I would want more than to be my husband's shadow, his helper. I'd want to be his friend and his . . . his inamorata."

Dante jerked his thumb back toward the porch and the books. "You really shouldn't read that crap."

"Why, because it gives me ideas of how a man could love a woman selflessly, devotedly, eternally? If I ever got married, that's what I'd want, not some tepid affection built on familiarity or even respect. I'd want the ground to shake and the world to spin whenever we were together, for both of us. Yes, there should be heaving bosoms and heated loins, but not just good sex. I know lust fades, but real passion, for each other, and no one else, that lasts. I'd want to be wanted for me, not for what I could do for someone else. Do you understand? That's what I'd want. In a nice house. With flowers. Forever."

"That's a tall order, Louie. I mean, the heated loins part is easy enough, and the flowers. The rest? The forever part, that . . . What did you call it? Real passion? That's one rare bird."

"Then I can live on my own." She stood on tiptoes to lift the feeder to the highest branch she could reach.

"How are you going to fill it, goofy?"

"A person can build a nice life for herself without a man," Louisa insisted, straining to get the old feeder down, sorry she bought the wretched thing altogether. "But what about you?" she asked, shifting the ball — "No, Champ, I can't play now" — into his court. "You're no poster boy for wedded bliss yourself."

"I'm thinking about it. Marriage mightn't be so bad, with the right person. If I could find that true passion of yours, then I might be tempted too. Bachelorhood gets tiresome after awhile. That's what Mr. Bradford says, anyway," he hurriedly added, the conversation coming too close to home.

"I make his life easier, that's all," she said, looking for a different tree. "He'll get tired of my nagging about his diet and his cigars soon enough, then he'll be sorry he asked me to stay on. We work well together now, but what if we disagree about the next chapter of his book? He wants my honest opinion, but what if I tell him it stinks? Not that it would or could, but what if? Or would I have to lie to keep him happy? Agree with everything he says?"

Louie, hiding her feelings? Dante could not see how. Every emotion was stamped across her face — when her back was not turned. When it was, like now, the hard set of her shoulders spoke volumes, all outraged at the idea. Her rear end, in those white shorts, bending to reassure the dog he was still her favorite, said something else, but that was a different conversation.

"I won't play the Howard game," she was saying, "not anymore. So Mr. Bradford will get tired of me long before the book is finished, you'll see. He'll be relieved to go on to the city, then Hilton Head and the lectures, without an old fishwife. He'll find a pretty new art history graduate student to answer his mail, and a chauffeur to drive him around." She stuck the feeder on a new branch.

"Too low. Cats will come stalk your birds. And maybe you underestimate Mr. Bradford's affections?"

"Champ will keep them away." She did not answer his other comment.

"How do you know he won't chase the birds too?"

She turned to face him. "Why do you keep asking me such hard questions? I never said I had all the answers. Everyone knows I screwed up. Maybe I can get it right, someday. Until then . . ."

Dante tightened the screw at the top of the feeder, twisted the loop, and fixed it on a different tree, where the birds would have shelter if they needed, but with no nearby branches for the squirrels to climb down. "Until then, maybe you'd like to practice the heaving bosom part?"

She fled inside, the chicken, but Dante didn't care. He had time now, time for both of them to figure out what they wanted.

Louisa wanted Mr. Perfect, not just Mr. Right, a hero who'd step out of one of her romance novels and sweep her off her feet. He'd make up for all the How-comes in the world, worshiping every freckle, wrinkle, and extra pound. No, he'd adore her so much he wouldn't notice any blemish or defect or romantic tripe spewing from her rosy lips. He'd give her fireworks for forty years.

Yeah, when pigs flew.

Her would-be beloved had no balls, like her dog. The heroes on book covers never did. They just had padded crotches. So why was Dante jealous of a paperback paramour? Her Lord of Lust wouldn't stick by her or stand up to her or love her the way Louie deserved to be loved, by a real man who just happened to have enough faults of his own to disqualify him from herohood.

But now Dante had time to change her mind. He had over two months to let Louisa see that not all men were like that fcckless fiancé, or make-believe. He could do it . . . if that was what he wanted to do.

Oh, he wanted her, all right, with every fiber of his aching, unfulfilled body. But forever? Louisa Waldon was no one-summer stand. She was all or nothing, and Dante told himself he was drowning somewhere in between.

He knew what he didn't want: another dependent. Louisa could lean on him anytime — she fit against him in all the right places — but forever? What if he were just suffering a bad case of the hots that cooled off in September's chill? He wasn't about to jump into any kind of relationship based on lust. Without anything to build on but physical attraction, that house had one shaky foundation. No way was it going to last through the first storm.

Why, he might eventually get tired of

that smile that was like sunshine when she was happy, or those eyes that went from spring green to emerald, depending on the light. Who knew, he might get tired of her silly sweetness and her gutsy independence. Sure. He might get tired of breathing, too.

Still, he needed time to be positive, to — Who was he kidding? He needed time to make her forget about both that bastard Blowhard and her blasted fantasy lover. He needed to make her want to stay.

He needed to read a couple of those love stories.

Chapter Twenty-Eight

Mr. Bradford was disgruntled. Here it was, halfway through August, and he had delayed finishing the book as long as he could. Once it was done he'd have no excuse to stay on in the country, no excuse not to move back to Manhattan, then on to Hilton Head, no excuse not to leave Louisa behind. That was not what he wanted, and Mr. Bradford was not used to not getting what he wanted. So he was grouchy, grumpy, and gloomy.

She was good for him. She made him look forward to each day, something he hadn't done in years. She made him value his memories, instead of viewing them as boring and trite. She made an old man look forward as well as back.

He'd be good to her, too, the silly twit. Money, travel, fine art, jewelry, fancy clothes, and her name in his will. She'd be set and secure for life. What more could a woman want or need? A grand passion? If Louisa hadn't found it with her priceless prick Howard, she could find it when he, Wesley Bradford, was gone, with a higher class of cad.

That should have been the end of it, a done deal, and would have been with any other female. Not with Louisa, with her scruples and stubbornness. Then again, if she weren't as obstinate as an ass and as starry-eyed as a sixteen-year-old, she wouldn't be half as much fun, or half as good at getting him organized. He almost regretted that she wasn't intimidated by his fame or influenced by his money. The little fool didn't know what was good for her — or care what was good for him. She was, damn it.

Mr. Bradford was a picky man who hated loose ends and messy threads. Louisa kept everything tidy for him, but she was unraveling right before his eyes. He knew why, too: Dante Rivera.

Curse Dante, and curse him for being young and good-looking, physically fit and a decent man to boot. Mr. Bradford used to like him, until Dante decided to stop playing the field and settle on Bradford's turf.

If that's what he was doing. The situation made no sense to Louisa's boss and would-be benefactor. If this courtship were a painting, it should hang facing the wall. In a garage.

Dante wasn't wining and dining the

young woman, Mr. Bradford knew, because he, himself, was keeping her as close as he could. He had her drive him to more vacuous cocktail parties than he could stomach. He saw a lot of bad movies, worse art, weak theatricals and wimpy poetry readings just to keep her out of Dante's clutches. Mr. Bradford was exhausted, and Louisa was still not convinced to leave Paumonok Harbor with him.

So what was Rivera doing to keep her all dewy-looking when he came into the room? Not much, that Mr. Bradford could see. Louisa laughed at his own jokes, listened attentively to his stories, but she did not change from a candle to a chandelier, the way she did for Dante. Damn him.

No matter what he could offer materially, Mr. Bradford knew he couldn't compete with that. Why, he could practically smell the physical attraction between those two idiots. Half the time he needed to ratchet up the air conditioning when they were in the same room. But Louisa did not have the contented look of a satisfied female, and Dante did not stop drooling over her. What in Sam Hill were they waiting for?

Mr. Bradford figured that once they got

it on, they'd get over it. Louisa would have her fling, then move on — with her employer. She'd stop building air castles on Dante's real estate and she'd go back to being the best darned aide he'd ever had.

So why not? Why didn't she tell her boss she had plans for Wednesday night, or Tuesday afternoon? Why didn't she show up late for work some morning, with a smile on her face and razor burn on her neck?

Unless she was the one playing hard to get. Mr. Bradford hoped Louisa wasn't fool enough to be holding out for a ring, because Dante just wasn't the marrying kind. She'd only be hurt again, which was the last thing Mr. Bradford wanted. He was truly fond of her and would hate to see her heartbroken. On the other hand, the sooner it happened, the sooner she'd sign on to go south. He couldn't figure it out, and hated being confused as much as he hated being thwarted . . . or having to get used to replacement assistants.

Louisa and Dante spent Saturdays together, he knew, going to yard sales in the mornings, of all things — as if Dante Rivera couldn't buy up entire estates. And they usually had young Teddy along, according to Marta. Louisa would come back and tell him where they'd been afterward, raving about the nature preserve where chickadees and tufted titmice ate sunflower seeds out of her hand, and the Whaling Museum in Sag Harbor with its intricate scrimshaw work. They went on a cemetery tour, taking rubbings from gravestones, the thought of which gave Mr. Bradford a splitting headache. He did not need reminding of his own mortality, or anyone else's.

They went to overpriced antique sales, church fairs, carnivals, and craft shows. It was all tourist stuff, and Louisa seemed to be loving every minute of it.

Bah! Mr. Bradford could show her Paris and Italy, all the great museums of the world, including private collections no one else got to see — and she was happy looking at the Clothesline Art Show at Guild Hall.

Maybe her tastes weren't refined enough for his way of life, after all. Mr. Bradford tried to convince himself of that, anyway. Hadn't she gone to a Tupperware party with Dante's cousin, and maternity clothes shopping with his ex-wife? Next she'd be going to a demolition derby with that tattooed savage, the one who might have amounted to something if there'd been free art classes for him when he was young.

Louisa would be wasting her life here the same way, Mr. Bradford thought. She ought to be flapping her wings, not building a birdhouse to spend the winter. He didn't think she was infatuated enough, or fool enough, to think Dante Rivera was going to be sharing that love nest.

In all the years Mr. Bradford had known Dante, except for a few months right after the divorce, he'd never seen the younger man with anything but elegant, sophisticated, successful-in-their-own-right women. And he'd never seen Dante with any of them more than three times. He'd take his pleasure — giving it too, by the disappointed sighs around the social set — and move on.

So why the devil wasn't Rivera strapping on his skates? What was he waiting for, Mr. Bradford's blessings? They'd be taking rubbings off his headstone first! If Dante didn't want the girl, by heaven, he should — No, Dante wanted her. A blind man could see that. And Dante Rivera was about as randy as any man in his prime, rumors about his ex-wife's dissatisfaction notwithstanding. As for Louisa, she could turn on a lamp, much less a limpy. She was giving Mr. Bradford urges he hadn't felt since his stroke — or before, to be absolutely accurate.

So what was going on? If they had the hots for each other, which he'd swear they did, why weren't they stealing private moments together, acting like the healthy young animals they were? Mr. Bradford was prepared to envy them, but they didn't seem prepared to enter into an affair. If they didn't start, they'd never finish, damn them. Not knowing why they were acting like polite but panting strangers was more annoying than having his assistant playing house, or houseboat, with his landlord. Too bad he couldn't simply ask.

Well, he had asked, but Marta had no answers. She just tapped her temple, muttered "loco" and went back to dicing tomatoes.

Instead of working on the next scene of his life's work, Mr. Bradford was staring at his appealing, attractive, downright adorable secretary, wondering why she was sitting at her desk instead of screwing around. Bah!

Funny, Louisa was asking herself the same question, with almost the same aggravation. No, she was definitely more frustrated.

Was something wrong with Dante? Gads, was something wrong with her? She changed her perfume, bought a pound of breath mints, let her hair grow longer. She stopped wearing long pants and wore shorts or skirts — the shorter the better. She stopped wearing a bra half the time! How could she be any more seductive? A tattoo? She settled for a henna band around her ankle at one of the fairs they attended.

She invited him in for coffee. He'd had too much caffeine, he said. She asked him for lunch. He was going out of town. She stepped closer. He stepped back. She'd rub against his thigh, damn it, but Teddy was between them in the truck.

Yet she'd caught him watching her a couple of times, as hungry-looking as a grizzly bear at salmon spawning. She could tell when a man wanted her, and Dante Rivera wanted her big time, almost as much as she wanted him.

She'd changed her mind about sleeping with him. Nothing might come of it, she understood that, but no seedling was going to flower without a little encouragement. If it withered, well, at least she'd tried. And she was an adult, Louisa had decided, one who ought to be able to satisfy her own cravings without complications. She had chocolate whenever she wanted. Why not sex?

The last month or so had been glorious — and the weather was not half bad, either. She loved her work, the intellectual stimulation of Mr. Bradford and his friends and the tranquility of the library. She adored Teddy and counted Francine as her friend now. She enjoyed the country fairs as much as the posh parties. She had her house and her garden, her dog, and now her backyard birds. Mostly, there was Dante.

If he wasn't in her bed, at least he was on her roof. He and Rico finished putting on the new shingles, with her help. They might have finished two days sooner without her assistance, but, hey, it was her house. Then they fixed the gutters she hadn't known were broken, and started on the rotten windows.

He took her with him and Teddy to look at new houses, and with Aunt Vinnie to look at the sunsets. He invited Louisa everywhere, but never alone.

Of course she was glad, Louisa told herself. She did not want any roll in the hay — or in the bay — with anyone. She had principles. But she had hope, again.

Warmth was growing between them, understanding, a real friendship. She appreciated that, but now the warmth wasn't enough. She wanted the heat, too.

Maybe he valued their friendship as much as she did, and did not want to take any chances of ruining it. The jerk.

Maybe, when she'd said she wanted the ground to shake, he'd been intimidated. Some men worried about their performance, she knew, afraid, perhaps, of not meeting their partner's standards. Dante Rivera N.G. in B.? No way. Shoot, the earth quivered when he merely smiled at her with that wanting look. If he ever —

She dropped the box with her boss's manuscript, all 410 completed pages so far.

Mr. Bradford decided to make one last try arranging her life while she was rearranging his on paper. He didn't like losing, but he didn't like seeing Louisa so troubled even more. If she didn't want to leave Paumonok Harbor, he'd accept that. He would not, however, accept leaving her dangling on Dante's string. If he couldn't convince her to accept his final offer, Mr. Bradford decided, he'd throw the two of them together like cats in a sack, and make them face up to the truth. They'd be good together, and even he, jealous old coot that he was, could see it. He had to laugh at himself, acting the irate father, planning a shotgun wedding. If he couldn't have the girl, though, he'd make sure the next best man did — if that's what she wanted. If Dante Rivera would make Louisa happy, well, Mr. Bradford was not going to stand in her way. Neither was Dante Rivera, if an old matchmaker could help it.

"What if I doubled your salary?" he asked, enjoying the view as she bent over, gathering up the book. "Would you come with me this winter then?"

Louisa was putting the pages in numbered order. "You already pay me twice as much as I'm worth."

"What if I rented a house for you nearby, if it's living with me that bothers you, or what people might say?"

"I like my own house." She shuffled the papers, searching for the chapter she'd been looking for, before she started thinking of Dante and bed in the same breath. "Here, this is the section I meant. You are just repeating yourself now. You said most of it before."

"I've said everything before. And done it. I'm tired of the whole thing. How about a swim in the ocean?"

"The surf is too rough today, and there are jellyfish along the bay beach. I saw them this morning when I took the dog there. Besides, we need to finish this chapter. You've been fussing with it for weeks now, for no good reason."

He'd had a damned good reason, Mr. Bradford thought. Maybe he'd be glad to get rid of her after all, though, if she was turning into a shrew. He chewed on his unlit cigar. "There's only a chapter or two after that, so stop trying to rush me. We'll make the deadline. And if we don't by a couple of weeks, what are they going to do? Not publish the book they've already paid half for? Everyone gets extensions."

"And everyone hates them. You know your agent told me they're already working on the cover and they have a publishing date."

He brushed that petty business aside. "Have you thought about what you'll do when I leave?"

"I'll miss you."

"Nice." And no word about Dante. "But what will you do for money? You do remember things like heat and lights and food, don't you, while planning your cozy rustic winter?"

"Of course I remember, down to the penny. I bought an electric heater to fill in for the fireplace, and I've been putting most of my salary in the bank. What I've saved on dinners alone by going out with you every night can get me through 'til January, I figure."

"And then?"

She aligned the book just so, in its box. "I don't know."

"You're not counting on Dante, are you?"

She dropped the box again. "Of course not. Everyone knows his mind is made up. He'll never get married again."

"Until he finds the woman to change his mind for him."

Louisa kicked at the empty box, sending Mr. Bradford's life to the four corners of the office in her frustration. "I am not planning my life around anyone else's. Not yours. Not his. So there. If I run out of money, so be it. Something will turn up."

Something did.

Howard.

Chapter Twenty-Nine

"Go on, get out of here," Mr. Bradford told her. "I can think better without you looking over my shoulder."

Louisa checked the appointments book. "Are you sure? We are supposed to have dinner with the Baldwins tonight."

"I'm tired of them, and tired of eating out."

"Do you want me to get something from the deli?"

"Marta can scramble me some eggs. Go on. And don't come back tomorrow. I need a day off from this crud."

Louisa put the manuscript back on the corner of his desk. "Are you angry with me?"

Mr. Bradford took his glasses off and leaned back against his chair. "No, I am angry with myself. I'm just tired, Louisa. Go. Walk on the beach, weed your garden. Sit and read a book. I'll see you on Friday."

Louisa looked at him closely, checking for signs of illness. "Do you feel all right, though?"

"Yes, little mother, I am fine. I'll go to sleep early tonight and stay in bed late tomorrow. We've been trotting too hard, that's all. Sometimes I forget I'm not a young man anymore."

"You're not old, either," she said loyally.

He was too old for her. "Go."

Louisa went, and made a list on her way home of all the chores she could accomplish with so much free time. The lawn, the attic, the little bedroom — or a book on the beach. Champ voted for the beach. He'd been working hard too, practicing his new training lessons, guarding the bird feeder from prowling cats, keeping the house free of moths.

They went to the beach.

The next morning Louisa woke up early full of ambition. After she brushed her teeth the bathroom floor was full of water. So much for her lists.

They went to the hardware store.

Anyone could change a washer. That's what the book said. The high school kid with the bad complexion working at the hardware store for the summer said she had to know the size. Louisa had thrown him off the computer at the library for trying to locate chat rooms and porn sites, so he was not liable to be really helpful. In fact, he looked downright happy to tell her that old sinks were never standard, and they mightn't even carry the size she needed, once she got her sink apart.

Well, if she had to drive to the next town, so be it. She was going to fix the leaking sink, come hell or the already high water. She could do it. She had a book.

She turned the water off under the sink, with pride in her prescience. Then she tried to unscrew the hot water handle. The faucet was so corroded she couldn't find the screwdriver slot, so she tried the cold water. After a pitched battle, with her climbing into the sink for leverage, she won, but still had to get the washer off. The screwdriver or the pliers? Louisa found an old tweezers, almost as rusted as the washer. Aha! She was as inventive as she was wise.

When she'd gathered the crumpled pieces onto a paper towel, she realized she couldn't take that to the hardware store. She went back to her book, discovered that there was a special tool just for lifting sink washers, which the pimply, porn-chasing kid at the counter might have told her. Too bad it was her friend Bill's day off.

Leaving the hot water faucet dripping with WD40, hoping to loosen the screw, she went back to the store. New tool at hand, she returned to the attack. The faucet broke. The new tool worked, though, pulling the washer out of the debris. Now she had a washer for size, and no fixture to put it in.

The book didn't say anything about how to change a whole unit. She went back to the twerp with the tools.

He was waiting for her, grinning.

"I decided I'd like a shiny new fixture instead of that ratty old one. What are my choices?"

"We got three plumbers in town. Which phone number do you want?"

"I want —"

"Need help?"

Louisa knew that voice, and the shiver it caused down her back and down to her toes. Dante was holding an orange extension cord. He was wearing old jeans, low on his hips, and a red tucked-in T-shirt with Paumonok Harbor written on it. He looked like a Christmas present to Louisa. Before she could deny she was desperate — for anything he might be offering — the kid announced that she'd turned a crummy washer into a catastrophe.

Dante nodded. "Old houses are hell. You start with something simple and find a week's work underneath. I'll come look at it, all right?"

"Now?"

"You can't use it before I get there, right?"

Did she have dirt on her face that needed washing? She stopped herself from scrubbing at her cheeks, and from sticking her tongue out at the hardware half-wit. She smiled sweetly at Dante and said that would be lovely, she'd meet him at her house.

She raced home, then rushed to change her grungy plumbing clothes, comb her hair, and wash up at the kitchen sink. Then she remembered: he'd be working in her bathroom. She tore up the stairs with a plastic bag and swept her makeup and moisturizers and night masks into it. She crammed the bag into the vanity — where he'd be turning the water back on once he'd fixed the faucets. She grabbed the bag and tossed her tampons, panty liners and anti-yeast infection ingredients into it, then shoved that, seams splitting and all, under her bed.

She made it down the stairs, only breathing slightly heavier than normal, in time to hold the door while he carried in a heavy toolbox. Well, she breathed heavily whenever he was around, so maybe he'd think that was normal. Or that she was an asthmatic.

"Are you sure you can fix this?" she asked when he frowned at the chaos she'd wrought at the washbasin.

"It's not rocket science." He put his tools on the closed toilet seat and opened the lid. With that equipment, he could most likely fix a rocket, too, Louisa thought.

"Water off?"

Her chest swelled. She wasn't a total incompetent. She pointed to the vanity, where nothing remained but neat stacks of toilet paper and towels. Then her dog trotted into the tiny bathroom, with one of those plastic disposable douche bottles he'd retrieved from under the bed. Gentleman that he was, Dante pretended not to see her blush, or beat the dog over the head until he dropped his new toy. She slammed shut the bedroom door, the dog on the outside of it, and came back, standing as far from Dante as the narrow space permitted.

"Is the water off at the source?"

She looked blankly at him.

"At the main. You know, where the water comes into the house? Old pipes can snap when you work on them, and you don't want a worse mess."

The water main was in the crawl space under the kitchen, along with the oil tank and the hot water heater. Louisa knew because she'd watched old man Redstone turn the water on when she arrived. The half cellar was down rickety dark steps, and was full of cobwebs, mouse droppings, and even an empty snake skin. "Oh, I'm sure the shutoff up here is enough."

Dante took his flashlight and went. He came back grimy, which Louisa thought never looked so good before, and got to work.

He grunted and grumbled, wiped her WD40 on his pants and her guest towel, the one with pansies on it, from a yard sale, of course. He got dirtier and sweatier, in that little bathroom with its one tiny window, trying to free the old fixture that must have been here since the '38 hurricane. He had a streak of grease down one cheek and torn knuckles on one hand. She clapped when he finally pulled the base off, making it all worthwhile.

"I'll go into town for a new one, all right?"

Louisa really didn't want to face the acned airhead at the hardware store for the fourth time that morning. She also did not want to admit she had no idea what to buy. "Sure, just put everything on my account. I'll make us some lunch in the meantime. Tuna fish okay?" Lunch was the least she could do, and sandwiches were the most, considering her nonexistent culinary skills. Not even she could mess up tuna fish.

Dante smiled. "My favorite." It wasn't, but so what?

While he was gone Louisa got to work. She set the kitchen table with a dark blue tablecloth, two white dishes with blue fish on them, cloth napkins with little lighthouses, and glasses with seashells, all from her Saturday morning bargain hunting. Everyone on the East End had nautical stuff to get rid of, it seemed. Then she went to her garden and came back with a bouquet to put in the blue pottery vase, leaving one daisy to droop over the almost unnoticeable chip. She was busy admiring her lovely table setting when she remembered she needed food, too.

She had just about decided how much mayonnaise to add and was debating onions, when she heard a car pull up in front of the house. Dante's truck was a lot louder, and he could not be back yet anyway, so she went to look.

A silver-gray two-seater Jag was parked on the grass verge, where Dante's truck had just been. The idea of these two vehicles occupying the same space, much less the same street, was ludicrous. One was worth a small fortune, one was not worth driving to the junkyard. On the other hand, you couldn't take the Jag to the beach. You most likely couldn't take it anywhere, worried that it would get stolen or scratched. You certainly couldn't do a week's worth of grocery shopping, not with your dog in the sports car. In fact, the Jag looked like it belonged in East Hampton, where the celebrity watchers could wonder at its owner, way more than in little Paumonok Harbor. Here the star was the guy who caught the biggest striped bass.

Louisa figured someone had finally bought the Mahoneys' place — maybe mistaking the location for something south of the highway and suitably snobbish — and had parked on her side, where the grass was mowed. With that car, they'd be looking to tear down the old cottage and build a modern mansion that wouldn't fit the neighborhood, only their self-image. They wouldn't care, not with a car that screamed "Look at Me."

Already despising her snooty new neighbors, Louisa stood in her front doorway, waiting to see what kind of pompous prig got out of the car. The driver opened his door.

He was more unwelcome than a fatuous fame-seeker, more despicable than a destroyer of neighborhoods, more loathsome than a luxury-flaunting loser.

He was a miserable, mean-spirited, mud-crawling maggot. In a silver-gray, open-neck Polo shirt, to match his silver-gray, ostentatious car, complete with teeny tiny polo player to match his teeny tiny heart.

"Hello, Howard."

Chapter Thirty

He walked up to her, but stopped before he reached the porch, taking stock. "The old house looks a lot better than I remember."

"I've been working hard, fixing it."

"And there's no need to ask how you are. You are looking delightful, as always, only more so."

He wasn't. His sandy hair seemed thinner than Louisa recalled, and his waist appeared thicker. He should have left his shirt untucked and worn a hat. He should have worn sunscreen, too, for his nose was unbecomingly red. He must have believed the UV rays wouldn't dare bother him — and that his head-to-toe scrutiny wouldn't bother Louisa. It did. "I have been working on the plumbing. What are you doing here?"

He did not stop staring. "Whatever you are doing certainly agrees with you. I like your new hairdo."

That was odd. Louisa remembered him always insisting she keep her impossibly straight hair long, no matter how difficult it was to manage, or how much time she had to devote to it, like an unruly pet. "It's easier short. What are you doing here?"

"I was in the neighborhood."

Not even the neighbors were in the neighborhood. The Mahoneys never came, and Dante's renters on the other side were only for July. "You were here, in Paumonok Harbor?"

"Close enough to visit."

He'd never wanted to visit it before. He'd always referred to the village as Poor Man's Harbor. It was too quiet, too empty, too far off the beaten path for him. The house was too crowded the times they'd stayed with her sister and her husband, and he was appalled to be sharing the bathroom with them. A few years ago, when he and Louisa had driven out on their own, he'd been bored the entire three-day weekend. The restaurants were not up to his standards, the tennis courts were full of children and the driving range was full of senior citizens. He did not want to swim, fish, or walk on the beach. And the TV reception stank, since they weren't hooked up to cable then. Too primitive, he'd declared, refusing to go again. Mostly, Paumonok Harbor was too unfashionable.

People used to say that someone was

from the wrong side of the tracks. In the flossy Hamptons, the wrong side was north of the highway. South had the oceanfront estates, the open farming vistas, the horse ranches. North was where the working people lived. North of the highway, where the land was cheaper, they put the recycling centers and the industrial parks, the skateboard rinks and the volleyball courts.

Now that most of the prime real estate to the south had been bought up and built on, the lines of privilege were not nearly as well-defined, but Paumonok Harbor still remained out of the favored loop. Not only was the Harbor north of the highway, but it was over the Long Island Rail Road tracks too. No celebrities lived here, unless you considered an aging art critic to be worthy of stargazing. The paparazzi, day-trippers, groupies and house-sharing groupers couldn't even find the place, for which most of the inhabitants thanked heaven. Howard had been embarrassed to admit visiting such an unfashionable location.

"What did you say you were doing here?"

"Siegal" — one of the law firm's partners — "has a place in Water Mill. He invited me out for a weekend of golf. A benefit tournament starting tomorrow. We played an early round today."

Dante was playing in the tournament, Louisa thought. She'd heard him mention it to Mr. Bradford. Gads, what if they were in a foursome together? That was too dreadful to contemplate. "So?" she asked. "So why aren't you back kissing up to the boss?"

Howard wasn't insulted. He didn't see anything wrong with trying to ingratiate himself with his employer. How else was he going to make partner? "He's got some committee meeting at Southampton College this afternoon, so I was free. And I heard you were out here."

"I've been here for over three months."

"Yes, well, I didn't think you'd want to see me."

Louisa made no reply.

"Listen, do you think we could go inside? I feel silly standing out on the lawn, talking to you up on the porch."

And his nose was getting more sunburned. Hmm. Petty vengeance aside, Louisa did not want Howard in her house. She already had that snake skin in the crawl space. "The plumber's gone to town for parts, but he'll be back, and the house is a mess until he does. I guess I can bring some iced tea out here."

"Great," he said, coming up and sitting in her rocking chair, the only seat on the porch. Champ came over from the backyard then, to sniff the newcomer. Howard did not pet him, despite the wagging tail. "What, they don't even have leash laws in this godforsaken place?"

"They don't need them. Champ's no stray, he's my dog. I think we've taken care of his flea problem, but you'll find out. That's his chair."

Howard was sitting on the top step when she got back with two paper cups — what, waste her good yard sale china on the slug? — of iced tea, with no ice. She took the rocker. "You still didn't say why you came."

He took a swallow of his drink. "I wanted to thank you."

"For being a good little girl and not suing your ass off for breach of promise?"

He choked on the tea. Louisa thought of pounding him on the back, but she was afraid she mightn't stop there.

"Um, for that, yes, and for leaving the check and the ring."

"I didn't want anything of yours, including your gratitude."

"You're not making this easy, are you?"

"Why should I?"

He cleared his throat and shifted on the steps. "Well, you've got it, my thanks, that is. The little Porsche model is a beauty, and the license plates were a nice touch. You always had a great sense of humor. I brought it into the office and Siegal was so impressed that he almost wanted to fire me and hire you back."

"I wouldn't have gone."

"Yes, but now he thinks better of me, because I could laugh at it, too. I wasn't in his good graces after you started e-mailing your friends at the office."

"I wonder why that was? Maybe because I told them you'd lied when you said it was a mutual decision to call off the wedding? Or because they heard you'd left me standing at the catering hall, with all the bills?"

Howard was crumpling up his paper cup. "I thought it was for the best, so you didn't appear to be rejected."

"Or so you didn't appear to be a cad? I heard that two of the secretaries refuse to do your filing and none of them will fetch your coffee."

"They're getting over it, now that you and I are friends."

Now Louisa swallowed wrong. "Friends?"

"You sent me the car. You sent me that

pro bono client, Fred Minell. I don't know if you heard about the company's new public relations policy, but Siegal was happy I was working on a charity case. It took me three days of my own time to straighten Fred out. I got him fixed up with the Feds, a credit agency, and a financial manager. And I might have found him a better-paying job. Siegal was impressed, I can tell you."

"I'm sure his wife and son will be too."

"What? Oh, yeah, them. Anyway, I thought enough time has passed, water under the bridge and all that, that we could talk."

Louisa was rocking so hard the rest of the iced tea sloshed out of her cup. "We have nothing to say to each other."

"Come on, you were sending me messages. The car, the client. I figured that meant you wanted me to call."

"I was sending you a headache." Maybe, though, in some perverse way, she did expect Howard to respond in some manner. Maybe she needed to face him once and for all and air some of her outrage and enmity. Louisa stroked the dog, who had come to lick the spilled tea, while she thought about it. When she stopped rocking Champ leaned reassuringly against her leg, and she could feel some of the hostility fading away — until Howard opened his mouth again.

"Fred said you were working for some old coot, shtupping some other guy who fixes houses, or both of them. Good grief, Louisa."

"An old coot? A guy who fixes houses? Is that what Fred said? And you believed him, a cheating, lying, drunken gambler who doesn't support his own kid?"

"He is working on his problems. And he didn't think much of your two boyfriends, either."

"They're not my boyfriends."

Howard ignored her protests, the way he had always done. "You can do much better, darling."

"Like you?" Champ sidled away at her tone of voice, as if he were afraid he'd done something wrong. She started rocking again, fast enough to make the old wicker squeak. "But I already had you, didn't I? I don't see how I could do any worse."

"There's no call to get nasty."

"No? Should I wait until after you apologize for not telling me you didn't want to marry me? Or after you say you're sorry you made a fool out of me? Or maybe when you show some regret for costing me my job, my money, my self-esteem?"

In typical Howard fashion, he focused on the finances. "Now wait a minute. I did try to give you a check."

"But you didn't try to resend it, once the immediate shock was past. You didn't try to see if I was all right. You didn't care if I dropped off the face of the earth — until I sent messages to people you work with."

Howard was on his feet, tossing his crumpled cup at her feet. His face was red, not just his nose, and he was shouting. "Now you listen to me. I —"

"Is everything all right here, Louie?"

Neither one of them had heard Dante drive up, slam his truck door, or greet Champ. He was speaking to Louisa, but he was looking at Howard, the new faucet unit in one hand, a pipe wrench in the other.

She made the introductions. "Howard, this is Dante Rivera. He fixes things. Dante, meet Howard Silver. He breaks things."

Howard nodded briefly, then turned away from the sweaty, greasy, unshaven clod to ask, " 'Louie'?"

"Everything is fine, Dante. We can have lunch in a minute."

"You're sure?"

"Positive."

Champ followed Dante into the house. As soon as Dante was gone, Howard asked, "So are you screwing him?"

"You're disgusting. He's fixing the sink. Are we done here?" She stood up, as if to follow Dante.

Howard ran his hand through his hair. "Listen, darling. I am sorry, and not just for thinking you'd sleep with a plumber. The whole wedding mess was not well done of me, I admit it. I just couldn't face you, I was that ashamed. But I knew it was wrong to go on with the ceremony. We had problems."

"You had the problems, Howard. The Porsche, the money, your mother."

"Why don't we leave my mother out of this? You never liked her."

"You liked her too much. But that's no skin off my nose." Which was well-protected by a hat. "By the way, did you ever get the Porsche repaired?"

"No. It's in Mother's garage. I can't find anyone to repair it for what the insurance company thinks it's worth."

"I want it."

"You thought it was a ridiculous luxury."

"I still do. But I have a mechanic friend who does super bodywork. He can fix it and we can split the money when it gets sold. I think you owe me that much."

For once Howard bypassed the money. "You have more friends like that?" He waved his hand toward the screen door, where Dante had gone. "Gads, you've fallen far."

"Far enough to recognize an honest man, no matter what he does for a living or what he's wearing or driving. I'm a slow learner, but I'm working on it. What are you working on, Howard? Your golf handicap?"

"Please, I don't want to fight. You just deserve better. You're a wonderful woman, darling, beautiful inside and out. Everyone says so. You've got great people skills. You should see the new personnel director they hired to fill your job." He shuddered. "The people she hires can't even follow simple directions. We miss you. I miss you."

"And it took you three months to realize that?"

"I guess I'm a slow learner too. Please try to understand, I was just afraid of that final, permanent step. We'd been together so long, but the wedding would have put a seal on it. I wouldn't have any more bachelor flings, no casual affairs, unless I cheated on you, of course, which I wouldn't do once I said 'I do.' "

Louisa tried to untangle that speech.

"Did you cheat on me before the wedding, then? I wondered if there was more to it than the Porsche."

Howard was twisting the ring he wore on his pinkie finger.

Louisa held up a hand. "No, don't answer me. I have little enough respect for you already. But it's funny, I thought you were too busy to get bored with only one woman."

"It took me this long to realize that it's more boring, and more time-consuming, without one."

"You mean no one takes your laundry to the dry cleaners, or sees that your house is clean, so you have to tend to those pesky chores?"

"Mother takes care of those things."

"I'm sure she does."

He frowned. "That's not what I meant. It's boring to tell your life story to a new date every weekend, tiresome to wait to see if something clicks. Christ, then there's the first time in bed together, with all that anxiety to perform, and —"

"You? I didn't think you cared enough about sex to be anxious."

He pretended not to hear that his long-term lover believed he was indifferent to lovemaking. "I thought we could . . . You know . . ."

The rocker slammed to a halt. "Have relations?"

"No. Maybe date, be friends again, that kind of thing."

"We were never friends, Howard. We were like an old married couple, used to each other, leaning on each other. There was no closeness, no spark, no camaraderie. Just familiarity."

"I loved you."

"Not as much as you loved your car, though."

"You loved me," he insisted.

"Did I? Maybe. Or maybe I wanted to fulfill my girlhood dreams of getting married. Maybe I just didn't know any better. I do now."

"I think I deserve a second chance, to make it up to you. I helped your friend Fred, didn't I? And I'll hand over the title to the Porsche, if your other friend comes to get it, naturally. But think, darling. Boat mechanics, auto-body repairmen, plumbers — you need me!"

"You forgot about the old man."

"Him too. And I need a date for some big shindig at Southampton College next weekend."

"Ah, the bottom line, finally."

"All the partners are going to be there.

The firm is sponsoring a new professorship or something, naming a chair for some old fart. It's more of that public relations garbage I told you about, and because they all have summer houses out here. I can't just make a donation, either. I have to show up, and not alone. They like you, Siegal and the others do, and I wouldn't look like such a bastard if you came with me. They'd be happy to see we were friends again."

"But we're not friends, Howard. And I am already going to the President's Ball at the college."

Howard stepped back. "You are?" He looked at her in her cutoff jeans, with the grease and rust stains on her legs, the freckles on her cheeks. Then he looked at her house, noting the rotting window frames. "Living here? Like this? Tickets cost a fortune."

"I know. I saw the invitation."

"So who's your escort?" he asked with a sneer. They both heard Dante and the dog coming down the stairs, whistling. "Your handyman special?"

"No, Howard. I'm going with the old fart, the guest of honor."

Chapter Thirty-One

"Regrets?" Dante asked, coming out onto the porch to stand behind Louisa, watching the silver Jag pull away.

"Yes, that I didn't have the pipe wrench in my hand."

"That's all?"

"Oh, there were a few more things I wanted to mention about his character, or lack thereof, but I think I hit all the high spots."

"Was it good for you?"

She smiled. "Better than sex."

Maybe better than sex with Howard, Dante thought, but she hadn't much to measure by. Yet.

The conversation, which he could hear from the bathroom window right above the porch, worked for Dante. He put his arms around Louisa's shoulders and gently pulled her back against him, kneading her tense shoulders. As she relaxed, he could feel bands of steel falling away from his own chest, as if someone had cut the cage bars and his very soul could fly again. His spirits went soaring. She'd dumped Horton. She didn't want him, didn't like him, didn't want anything more to do with him. She was over him. Louisa Waldon was an independent woman now, standing in no man's shadow. She was free, and so was Dante. "Do you know what you need?"

"Not a new sink, please."

"No, yours is working perfectly now. What you need is an afternoon off, away from the house, away from your jobs and responsibilities."

"That's how Mr. Bradford felt, too."

"He was right, especially now. You need a break, and a nice dinner afterward."

She was drained, though. Dante's strong hands on her neck and shoulders felt heavenly, but standing there was taking about all the energy she had. "I don't feel like going out any more today. I've dealt with enough difficult people for one morning, without facing crowds and traffic."

"But I don't intend to go socializing, or out for dinner. I'm cooking at the houseboat. The catch is, you've got to catch your own meal. Come fishing with me this afternoon, Louie?"

"I haven't been since I was a kid. We used to go out on one of the big party boats from Montauk. I didn't like it much.

It was crowded, noisy, and smelly. And it left the dock at some godawful hour of the morning."

"My boat's nothing like that, and we'll leave when we're ready."

Louisa was enjoying his touch too much to think about going anywhere. "Howard and I went on a cruise last year. I didn't like that a whole lot, either."

He kept rubbing her shoulders. "Why not?"

"Everyone ate too much and gambled too much, but when we'd go ashore we'd see the poorest people you can imagine, with children begging on the streets. How could anyone enjoy the extravagant opulence of the cruise ship in the face of such poverty? Howard said we were helping the local economy, but it ruined the trip for me."

"I promise we won't see anything but seagulls looking for handouts."

"Hmm." She tilted her head so he could rub a particularly stiff spot on her neck. "My father used to take my sister and me rowing along the shore in a little dinghy. We had to wear life preservers because the boat could tip over. You do have life jackets, don't you?"

"Of course, but you won't need one. My

boat doesn't tip, and we're not going out of sight of land. The fluke are right in the bay now, big ones. Doormats, they're called, and you've never eaten better fish than a fresh fillet, broiled with crabmeat stuffing."

"You can cook too? I mean, besides fixing things." And making a woman feel as if she were a handful of clay he was shaping into something precious and lovely.

"Simple meals. The local corn is at the farm stand, and the first real tomatoes are out, for a salad. Say you'll come, Louie. You'll like it fine, I promise."

He wasn't promising a boat ride and a meal, and they both knew it. His massage of her neck and shoulders had gone from muscle-relaxing to muscle-melting. Alone, on his houseboat, with a man whose touch made her knees weak? "I thought Teddy was going with Francine to buy new sneakers today."

"Teddy is not invited."

He was so close his breath made the hair near her ear flutter, and that wasn't the only thing that stirred. She could feel his interest burgeoning behind her. Alone, with the lapping of the water against the hull, and the moon for illumination?

"What about Champ?"

"I don't have a life jacket his size. It'll be just you and me, a couple of fishing poles, an easy dinner. No pressure."

Alone in the dark with Dante — no pressure? Hah! "I'll need a shower first." And to shave her legs, tweeze her eyebrows, slather on that expensive body lotion . . .

He nearly pushed her into the house. "Grab a sweatshirt for later. It might get cold out on the water. I'll wash up down here and put the tools away."

"Oh, and eat lunch. I started to make the sandwiches. Everything's on the counter in the kitchen."

"What about you?"

"I'm not hungry." She was, but not for tuna fish, not by a long shot. She missed his touch already. "Too much aggravation, I guess. I'll wait for my fish dinner."

Louisa took a moment to admire her new bathroom faucets, until she realized the shiny chrome didn't cover the decades of grunge around the handles. Aunt Vinnie would know how to get rid of the stains and scum. She'd worry about that tomorrow.

Dante fed half his sandwich to the dog, out of guilt for leaving him behind. "Not tonight, pal. You've had her for months. Tonight is mine." He'd worry about the rest of it tomorrow.

On the drive to the docks, Louisa asked, "You are coming to the ball at the college, aren't you?"

He looked over at her, at the stop sign. "What, you think you need reinforcements?"

In total honesty, since that seemed appropriate right now, Louisa answered, "Yes. I'd like to have another friendly face nearby."

"I'll be there. I wouldn't miss Mr. Bradford's big night, or dancing with the prettiest woman at the party."

"What, is your ex-wife going too?"

He laughed. "She wasn't invited."

"You won't, um, be driving this, will you?" Louisa's wave encompassed the pickup, with its dents and rust and stained upholstery.

"What, are you afraid it's not up to the Jag?"

"I'm afraid you'll be sent home by the valet parkers."

"Don't worry, I'll take the car. I'll even wash it first."

Louisa remembered that he'd said he had a car in the garage. "Why don't you ever drive it?"

He grinned, showing those dimples. "Real men drive real trucks, not those SUV station wagons."

If he wanted to prove his manhood, Louisa could think of a lot better ways . . . and she was thinking of nothing else. She figured she just might get to see some proof of Dante's virility tonight, and she wasn't thinking trucks.

"I'm getting a new truck at the end of the summer, anyway. Or after the striped bass surf-casting season at the latest. I love this one, but there's no denying the seat covers don't come clean anymore, and once the windows are rolled up, well, you wouldn't want to ride in it."

She didn't want to ride in it now, but Dante had wanted her to come along when he made a couple of stops, canceling appointments, picking up salad ingredients and wine and bait. He wasn't giving her a chance to change her mind, it seemed.

While they waited on the check-out line at the supermarket, Louisa said, "Howard mentioned something about a new job for Francine's husband, Fred. Do you know anything about that?"

"I know some people at the Jersey shipyards. That might be best for everyone, giving him a fresh start, giving Fran some breathing room."

"She's thinking of asking Alvin to move into your aunt's house. Will you mind?"

"It's not for me to mind, one way or the other, as long as he keeps going to meetings. She says Alvin's rent money could help pay for college tuition, which she refuses to take from me, even as a loan, and he'll trade looking after Aunt Vinnie and Teddy sometimes, for home-cooked meals."

"She likes him."

"I think she just wants to see the rest of his tattoos."

Louisa could relate to that. There were a lot of things she wanted to see more of. The rickety dock at the end of a dirt road, with four boats tied to it, wasn't one of them.

"You keep your boat here, instead of the marina?"

"It's more private."

Louisa was thankful for that, she supposed, that the entire town wouldn't know she was going out for an afternoon cruise with Dante. Then a bald guy came out of the little shed near the dock. Dante introduced him as the man who looked after the boat. "Want me to come along, Mr. Rivera?"

"Not today, Rick, I brought my own first mate."

First mate? First mating? Louisa could

feel her cheeks burning.

"I can see you did, Mr. Rivera. I can see you did." The whole town would know soon enough.

The boat was not what Louisa expected. She thought he'd own one of those sleek cigarette boats or a gleaming sports fisherman draped with outrigging. Instead he led her to a smallish black cabin cruiser.

"Isn't she a beauty?" he asked. "She's a classic, an old Hubert Johnson wooden lapstrake. They're always black, you know."

She didn't, of course. Or what lapstrake was, or who Hubert Johnson might have been.

"I had to rebuild her from scratch, due to the dry rot. New engines, of course. And I totally refitted the cabin. These old babies didn't have any of the modern conveniences. The teak's original, though, most of it, anyway. You can't destroy that stuff."

While he went on about the marvels of his boat, Louisa had to wonder what was it about men and their toys. Howard and his Porsche, Alvin and that motorized masterpiece, now Dante and his old boat. No, Dante didn't seem so obsessed; he just liked repairing things. For a minute she worried that he was trying to repair her, that he'd invited her to come fishing because he thought she was broken. Nope. She wouldn't let her doubts bob to the surface. They both knew she didn't need fixing.

He went around, stowing supplies, checking the boat's readiness under mysterious hatches, showing her where the life jackets were stowed. He even took one orange vest out of its cubby, leaning it near her. "Just to give you confidence."

She'd have a lot more confidence in one of those big fiberglass yachts moored at the marina.

"I named her *Celia*, after my mother," he was saying.

Uh-oh, more shades of Howard, Louisa thought, trying to stay out of his way. But at least he hadn't named the boat after his first wife.

Rick helped Dante cast off, then jumped back onto the dock, nimbly for an old guy, and they headed out into the bay.

"It's a little rougher than I thought," Dante apologized for the ground swells, "but that's no problem."

Not for Dante or the boat, it wasn't. Louisa felt her stomach complain. She hadn't had any lunch, she told herself. That was all.

Soon enough, Dante cut the engines. "We drift for fluke." He handed her a pole and started to unknot a plastic bag.

"What's that?"

"Squid." He started slicing the things into strips.

"Is it alive?"

"No. Don't tell me you're getting squeamish."

Okay, she wouldn't tell him, but that slimy, smelly, inky stuff was not making her stomach feel any better.

"You eat fish, don't you?" he asked as he threaded a loop of the squid onto a hook and handed her the fishing pole.

"Yes, but it's in nice little chunks on plates."

"Well, supper will be, too. After we catch it."

He showed her how to let the sinker weight hit the bottom, then jig the pole up and down to make the fluke think the hooked bait was still swimming. Every ten minutes or so he'd tell her to reel in, then he'd start the engines, steer them back where they'd started, and set the boat to drifting in the current again — right where Louisa could breathe the boat's exhaust . . . and the mildewy smell of the life preserver, the stink of the squid. The swells were hitting the boat broadside, not front — not bow, that was — first, which was not helping matters. She had to hold on to the side of the boat to keep her balance.

Louisa didn't pick up her pole for the next drift. "I think I'll let you catch dinner," she said, trying to smile for Dante.

Dante grinned back at her, almost bursting into song. An afternoon fishing, an evening of lovemaking, separated by a good meal. Fluking and fooling around. He felt like Maria in *The Sound of Music*. These were definitely a few of his favorite things. Then Carly Simon started singing in his head, "Anticipa-ation." Yup, driving him crazy, but a good kind of crazy, the kind that couldn't keep a smile from his lips.

No nephew, no dog, no work. No distractions, detours or doubts, just Louisa and him. Heaven. This afternoon was the fishes'. Tonight was his. "Maybe we'll quit soon if we don't get any fluke. It's cheating, but I can see where you might be getting bored."

She was looking over the side of the boat, watching the seaweed drift past. Then she was leaning over the side of the boat.

"Oh hell." There went her breakfast — and his hopes for a romantic interlude. She was limp and green and too weak to stand, much less survive the vigorous lovemaking he'd been planning. Dante cursed the whole ride back to the dock, and the drive back to her house.

Louisa managed to lift her head from the seat back when they reached her street. "I don't know why you're so angry," she told him. "I missed the boat, didn't I?"

Chapter Thirty-Two

No man looked bad in a tuxedo. That was a given. Mr. Bradford looked like a distinguished elder statesman in his, the lion in winter with a red rosebud in his lapel.

Dante looked . . . gorgeous. Oh, boy, did he ever. Tall, dark and handsome took on new meaning for Louisa, and the meaning was Drool, ladies, he's mine. Or he was going to be, as soon as Louisa could manage. He put every other man in the shade, in the crowded room at the opening reception of the college ball, like a single star on a murky night. Louisa couldn't take her eyes off him during the cocktail hour, after he greeted them and moved on, but not too far away. Three hundred people must have been in that hall and the tent outside, half of them wearing tuxedos, but she always knew where Dante was. If she had any trouble picking him out of the crowd, she merely had to look to see who was staring at her. Actually, a lot of men were staring at her, but she only noticed Dante.

Louisa had not seen much of him after

the fishing fiasco, partly because she was working twice as hard to make up for lost time with Mr. Bradford and his book. She knew Dante was busy with the charity golf tournament, besides. Now she couldn't see enough of him. If he did not make another move soon, she was prepared to invite him for dinner at her house, on dry land to . . . to thank him for help with the roof. Yes, that was a good excuse. And she'd say her stove was broken, as an excuse for bringing in Chinese food. Why take chances?

Dante had stayed away, thinking. A woman who couldn't cook was one thing. One who didn't know Mickey Mantle from Mickey Mouse was another. But a girl who got seasick? What about long lazy afternoons on his boat? Damn, what about heated nights on his houseboat? Granted it was solid as a rock and tied at the dock, but what if she hated it? Then he saw her walk into the reception on Mr. Bradford's arm, and he stopped thinking. He'd sell his boat — Hell, he'd sell his soul — to make her his. He would have snatched her away then and there — her look said she was willing enough — except for Mr. Bradford and the college dignitaries. He pretended to socialize, instead, feeling anything but social or civilized.

Louisa was wearing a long black, drapey chiffon gown with a slit up the side, way up the side. The fabric of her clinging gown was so sheer it could have fit through the gold bracelet she wore on her wrist. It was the dress she'd bought to celebrate her New Year's Eve engagement to Howard, when he'd given her the diamond ring from Tiffany's. Now she wore a diamond pendant on a gold chain, one Mr. Bradford had presented to her early that afternoon.

"I was going to save it as a bonus for when the book was finished," he'd said. "But you should be wearing it tonight, especially if that fool is going to be there."

"Howard?"

"Not that fool. The other one."

He refused to explain further, but Louisa didn't care. The necklace was exquisite, and she felt like a princess in it and the silky, swishing gown. For once, even her hair cooperated. It was long enough now that Janie Vogel had been able to gather the sides into some fancy twist at the back of her head, held with a clip covered with three red rosebuds to match the one in Mr. Bradford's lapel.

"It won't come undone in the middle of the night, will it?" she'd asked.

"In the middle of the dance?" Janie had

replied. "No way. In the middle of the night?" She'd winked at a woman with silver foil on her head. "That's between you and Dante."

So much for thinking that the gossip hadn't traveled past the dirt road dock. Louisa had ignored the ladies' smirks. "I am going to the ball with Mr. Bradford."

"Honey, word is you ain't going nowhere with the old man."

Where was Mr. Bradford, in fact? Louisa stopped staring at Dante long enough to find her employer surrounded by well-wishers from the college, greeting one of the lady trustees like an old friend.

He didn't need her. Howard did. Her former fiancé bustled over toward Louisa, towing a reluctant blonde with larger than normal lips, boobs, and eye pupils. Howard gave Louisa a cursory look, obviously not recalling her gown. He was more interested in Dante, anyway. He jerked his head across the room, where Dante was talking to Mr. Siegal, head of Howard's accounting law firm. "Isn't that your plumber?"

"Dante? Didn't you come across him during the golf tournament? I heard his foursome came in second."

Howard didn't care who won, if it wasn't

him. His foursome had not placed in the top ten. "What the hell is he doing here?"

"He is honoring my beloved boss and my good friend, Mr. Wesley Bradford, like almost everyone else, I suppose. Other than that, I believe he is speaking to your boss, who begged me to introduce him, after he begged me to come back to work, that is. I do recall Mr. Siegal mentioning how the law firm would love to get the Rivera Corporation account. Dante would love to get some of the company's new PR money for the Harbor's new community center. He's the chairperson of the building committee, you know, and the chief benefactor. I heard Dante and Mr. Siegal making a golf date for next weekend. Or were they going fishing on Dante's yacht?"

"He's that Rivera?" Howard looked almost as green as Louisa had on the boat, as Dante came toward them. "Your plumber?"

"Oh, he's a lot more than that," she said, turning her back on him to go into dinner between Dante and Mr. Bradford.

They sat at the head table with the college president and her husband, the dean of the art department and his wife, the senior partners at Howard's law firm and their wives or girlfriends, Mr. Bradford's agent with his fourth wife, who was younger than Louisa, and that handsome woman of a certain age who was one of the college trustees. She and Mr. Bradford had known each other for ages, it seemed, but not well enough that Ms. Martin appeared in his book.

Dante sat on Louisa's other side, his thigh pressed against hers, his arm brushing against hers when he reached for his fork. She didn't taste the soup or hear the opening speeches.

Then it was Mr. Bradford's turn. He was charming, eloquent and witty as he thanked the college, the law firm, and all his friends for coming. He was proud to have a new professorship in the art department named after him, he told the gathering after dessert, because no one could ever have enough art in their lives, especially young people. If one student went on to be an artist, he would be thrilled. If one went on to truly appreciate great art, he would be equally as happy.

"Mostly I want to thank you for giving me this honor now, while I can take pride and pleasure in it. Too often men of arts and letters have to wait to die to be recognized. What good does a posthumous statue do anyone? Your heirs will only stash it away in the attic, if they don't sell it first. But this honor, this great act of generosity you are bestowing on me by using my name, gives me great joy here" — he patted his heart — "and especially now, with my good friends surrounding me." He circled the room with his hand, but looked at Dante and Louisa. "Thank you, my dears, and may you always find great beauty in your own lives, the way I have in mine. Oh, and be sure to read my autobiography when it comes out."

After a standing ovation, everyone wanted to shake Mr. Bradford's hand and congratulate him. Dante patted Louisa's back while she dabbed at the tears in her eyes with his handkerchief, leaving mascara streaks on it.

After coffee and cordials, Mr. Bradford grumbled about having to dance, but he took the floor with Louisa because everyone was waiting for him to start the ball. He swore that was the last time he put on a show, but he relented and asked Ms. Martin, but not for the fast dance the orchestra was playing. A man with a new, lofty distinction had to maintain a degree of dignity, he insisted.

Louisa danced it with Dante, regretting

the tempo and the dance style that kept them from touching. She might have been dancing with the man next to her, his toupee flapping, for all the closeness. She did have Dante's promised "Later" to keep her smiling at her next partner, and the ones after that.

She kept glancing back. He danced with the college president and Ms. Martin, then settled in, it appeared, next to two of the law partners to discuss business, or maybe golf. Mr. Bradford was still accepting congratulations and good wishes, with Ms. Martin at his side, so Louisa accepted a dance with Mr. Bradford's agent, whose hand wandered only an inch or two into overfamiliarity.

Howard intercepted her after that song, before she could return with the much-married agent to her table.

"What, did you lose your date?" Louisa asked, knowing she was being catty. "I'd think she'd be easy to find in that gold dress."

He looked disgusted. "She's in the ladies' room. Again. God only knows what she's doing there."

Enhancing her mood, to match her lips and boobs, Louisa thought, but she didn't say it out loud. If Howard wanted to date a woman whose dabbling in controlled substances could get him disbarred, so be it. That was on his head, or up his nose. She made to step past Howard but he held her arm. "You could have told me about Rivera, you know. I could have made some points with the boss."

"And you could have been nicer to someone I said was a friend. Instead you treated the kindest man in Paumonok Harbor — maybe the richest, too — as if he was the scum in the sink, instead of doing me the favor of fixing it."

"Yeah, well Fred said —"

"And you aren't the one finding Fred a new job, either. Dante is. So you lied to me, besides everything else."

"Give me a break, here. I didn't know who he was, all right?"

"Because you were too wrapped up in yourself and your own interests to ask."

Howard decided talking was getting him nowhere but in trouble. "Let's dance."

"Sorry. My feet hurt."

He pulled her toward the dance floor anyway. "But they're starting a waltz. You know we perform it well together. Didn't we take those dumb ballroom dancing lessons before the wedding?"

"There was no wedding, Howard. And there will be no dance."

He did not let go of her arm. "I thought you were over all that crap. I apologized, didn't I?"

"You —" Louisa did not get to finish, as someone reached between her and Howard, pushing his hand away.

"My dance, I believe?" Dante said, his head tilted slightly, his eyes narrowed slightly, his fist clenched, slightly. Louisa floated to his side, letting his arm around her waist guide her toward the dance floor.

"Hey, I thought your feet hurt," Howard called after her.

"Funny, I thought you didn't care."

Dante threw back, over his shoulder, "Good night, Homer."

The dance was everything Louisa could have wished — except they were dressed, in front of hundreds of people, and her feet really did hurt.

"Hmm," Dante whispered on a sigh, after inhaling the scent of the roses in her hair. "Maybe we could go out for a drink, later, after you take Mr. Bradford home?"

"I have some wine in the refrigerator."

"That's even better."

They finished the dance in silence because nothing else needed to be said, not until they were alone.

What seemed like an eternity later, although it could only have been a few dances, when some of the party-goers had gone, Mr. Bradford decided he could take his leave too. Without Louisa. Dante could take her home in his car, he declared with a look toward the younger man, who nodded, grinning like a fool.

"Rosemary — that's Ms. Martin — will drop me back here later, to fetch the Mercedes."

He was going home with the college trustee? Louisa swallowed, getting used to the idea. "But you don't like to drive in the dark."

Mr. Bradford raised his eyebrow. "Who says it'll still be dark by then? Stop worrying like a mother hen, my dear. I'll be fine. Better than fine. I intend to cap this lovely evening off with a wondrous night, and I suggest you do the same. Time goes by too fast to waste. None of us is getting any younger, you know, and such golden opportunities come few and far between, if at all." He pulled the flower from his lapel and tossed it to Dante. "Gather ye rosebuds, and all that," he said, as he headed toward the door where his new old friend was waiting.

"I think we have just been given his blessings," Dante said as they both stared after Mr. Bradford while he waved good-bye to everyone on his way out. Now Louisa had nothing to feel guilty about, nothing to regret.

"For . . . for tonight?"

"For whatever we want, tonight and tomorrow," he told her, "and all the tomorrows to come."

"I like the sound of that, Mr. Rivera. I really do."

They decided to have one more dance together, a slow one, after Louisa kicked her high heels off. There was no hurry; they'd have all night, at least. Now the other dancers and watchers didn't bother them. No one else even existed, in the world of their two bodies pressed against each other, touching everywhere as they barely swayed in time to the music. The dance was a prelude, they both knew, a tease, a tender torment that would make the real dance that much more enjoyable.

One of his hands was on her rear end, the other on her neck. One of hers was under his jacket, while the other toyed with the curls on the back of his head. Their lips met because they had to, and neither cared that the music had stopped minutes ago.

The silence didn't bother them. Neither did the chuckles. The sirens did.

Chapter Thirty-Three

A security guard came into the room and looked around for the college president. She headed toward Dante and Louisa.

"Oh, no!" Louisa cried, but Dante put his arms around her to listen.

As far as anyone could tell so far, Mr. Bradford got behind the wheel of Ms. Martin's big white SUV when the valet brought it forward. He hit the gas instead of the brake, however, crashing into the car ahead of them. When Mr. Bradford got out to look, the guard reported, he collapsed right in the roadway. The ambulance had already come, and the campus patrol car had followed with Ms. Martin, who had been shaken up by the collision.

"Be happy it happened here and not in Paumonok Harbor," Dante told Louisa as they hurried out, her shoes in his hand. "The hospital is only minutes away from the college, instead of the forty it takes from home."

"And there's not much traffic this time of night, is there?"

"He'll be fine," Dante said, squeezing her shoulder as he helped her into the car the valet brought. He turned her away from the tow trucks that were already trying to separate the white SUV from the smaller car it had demolished. Glass and metal and radiator fluid were everywhere.

There was no question of Louisa's driving Mr. Bradford's Mercedes to the hospital on her own. She didn't know the way, her hands were shaking, and she needed Dante.

She didn't notice what kind of car he had. It was a black luxury something that couldn't go fast enough to suit her. Dante handed her his cell phone and told her to call Marta, telling her to place an emergency call to Mr. Bradford's physician, and another to his agent, who had left earlier in the evening. He had to be prepared in case they needed an extension in the book's deadline. "Tell Marta not to call Mr. Bradford's sister yet, until we know more."

Louisa was happy to have something to do, rather than worry and wonder how Dante could stay so calm. "How soon before we're there?"

"Soon."

But not soon enough. No deadline extension was going to be long enough.

Mr. Bradford was gone.

Dante told the nurse at the emergency room desk that they were Mr. Bradford's niece and nephew, and he was the health care provider listed on the forms anyway. There were no decisions for the proxy to make, but they did get to talk to the doctor who was on call that night.

They'd tried, the doctor said. The emergency medical technicians had tried in the ambulance, and they had tried at the hospital, but they couldn't bring the gentleman back. The damage to his brain was so severe, he would have had no life anyway. They could not tell if Mr. Bradford had a stroke as a result of the accident, or if the coming stroke had caused the crash.

Dante asked about Ms. Martin. She was shaken up, understandably, and needed a few stitches from the collision, but her sister was already on the way to drive her home.

"At least he didn't die in that poor woman's bed," Dante said, "although Mr. Bradford might have liked that, I suppose."

No. Mr. Bradford could not be gone. Louisa simply refused to accept that. He had to be all right. He had to be coming out of the back rooms in his tuxedo, telling her to stop fussing over him.

The nurse at the reception desk was looking away, the doctor was saying how sorry he was.

Mr. Bradford wasn't coming. Just like Howard hadn't come to the wedding. Louisa started to shake. Dante led her to an empty corridor where she could cry in private, wrapped in his arms.

She sobbed against his chest. "I should have —"

"No!" he said, a catch in his own voice. "Do not start feeling responsible. You were his assistant, not his nursemaid, and there would have been nothing you could have done were you with him, were he at home. You heard the doctor, it was a massive stroke this time. Would you have wanted him to lie in a hospital bed for weeks or months, with respirators and feeding tubes?"

She shook her head no, which was a good thing, because Dante would not have let that happen, on Mr. Bradford's express written wishes.

He went on: "He was having the best time of his life, and who could ask for a better time to go? You heard him say this was his finest moment. All that recognition, a pretty woman on his arm, his friends rejoicing for him. Be happy for him now, Louie, because he didn't die too soon."

"He could have died later, after his book came out!"

"Yes, but I think he knew. He spent half the summer rewriting his will and setting up trusts. He wasn't leaving anything up to chance, right down to the music he wanted played at the funeral."

"He was good at details, just not so good at timing. A few more weeks and the book would have been finished, at least."

"I think that's what kept him going so long. And you."

She started crying again, but stopped when someone handed Dante a plastic bag with Mr. Bradford's belongings in it: his watch and keys and wallet, his glasses and hearing aid and his dentures.

"I didn't know he had false teeth," Louisa said, but she took the bag from Dante and clutched it to her chest as if holding Mr. Bradford to the earth a little longer.

Meanwhile Dante had gone to sign papers, to speak with the receptionist about notifying the nephews, the funeral parlor, the newspapers. He came back and guided Louisa out to the parking lot.

Someone leaped out of a taxicab before they could reach the car.

"Howard? You came? That was so nice of you to care enough to —"

"Of course I care. It was my car the old man plowed into, and over. No one at the college had his insurance card, or that woman's either."

"His insurance?" Louisa echoed.

"That's right. Someone has to pay for my new car, don't they? You're a jinx, Louisa, that's what you are. Every time you're around, something gets wrecked. My mother was right: I'm a lot better off without you."

"He's dead," Louisa said, while Dante was making growling noises.

"Dead? That's too bad. But the insurance company will still pay."

Louisa handed Dante the bag of belongings. She bent down and scraped up a handful of dirt from the patch of garden next to them. Howard backed up, fearing she was going to throw it in his face. Instead Louisa crumbled the loose soil in her hand, then let it trickle from her fingers back to the ground at her feet. "That's what you are, Howard," she said, stepping on the little pile on her way to Dante's car. "Dirt. Nothing but dirt."

They drove to Osprey Hill, after stopping to pick up Champ and a change of clothes for Louisa. After hugging and crying with Marta and Rico, Dante and Louisa started to make phone calls and arrangements. A lot could wait for the morning, but they could make lists together tonight, rather than being alone in their grief. Louisa was glad to be doing something, glad not to think. She was glad to be with Dante, a rock to lean on.

The next week was overwhelming, but organized. Mr. Bradford had decided to be cremated, his ashes to be taken out to sea on Dante's boat later. Louisa vowed to go, no matter how many seasick pills she had to take. Meantime, there would be no wake or interment or funeral as such. Instead they held a memorial service at the funeral parlor in East Hampton, with half the population of Paumonok Harbor mixing with celebrities and dignitaries from the entire East End. The place was filled with flowers, two framed pictures of Mr. Bradford, and an architect's rendering of the proposed Wesley Bradford Memorial Arts Center. A fund was established at the bank, and donations were pouring in.

Afterward, almost everyone came back to Osprey Hill to celebrate Mr. Bradford's life, not mourn his death. They told stories of his generosity and kindness, his wisdom and erudition — and his sharp tongue and his intolerance of ignorance. They ate his food, catered so Marta could grieve, and drank his wine, and threw the flowers into the bay.

Two days later another memorial was held in New York City. Everyone in the arts world attended, along with politicians and publishers. Louisa sat next to Mr. Siegal, her former boss, who was wondering about the estate's disposition. Howard did not attend.

Dante spoke briefly, mentioning the arts center, Mr. Bradford's love of the sea, his hopes for future generations, and his gratitude to Louisa Waldon for the last, joyous months. Louisa was crying again, of course.

At the end of the week there would be yet a third tribute, this one in Hilton Head, with Mr. Bradford's nephews and his sister, if she could be taken from the nursing home. Louisa chose not to go. Dante had to, both as old friend and executor of the will. He was going to stay on there for awhile, Dante told Louisa before he left, to start the legalities of selling that house and apportioning the art collection there between the nephews.

"What about all these paintings and drawings?" Louisa wanted to know, standing in the living room of Osprey Hill.

"These? They're mine, although Mr. Bradford helped me decide on some of the purchases. They stay with the house, of course. I'll be moving back in here when I return. I was planning on staying on the houseboat through September, but I don't like leaving Marta alone here so long, when people might think the place is empty. I figure I'll be gone two weeks or so. With any luck, I can get it all done and not have to go back. Are you sure you won't come with me?"

Louisa couldn't go, no matter how inviting a trip with Dante sounded. She'd be too busy finishing Mr. Bradford's book. His editor and his agent had agreed — after Dante had made some phone calls — to let her complete the work.

"Why would they trust me to write the last chapters?" Louisa was thrilled, and appalled.

"You said all the notes were there, right? And everyone knew how much he depended on you to rewrite the previous chapters, so what would be more natural? They had too much money invested already to just junk the project, and besides, I am executor of the will, remember? I'm in charge of the trust that holds the rights to the book and all its earnings. I told them you can do it."

Louisa vowed to do the best job she could, to make Dante proud, and to earn the incredible fee they were paying her. Louisa would have done the work for nothing, as her tribute to Mr. Bradford, but this was a whole lot better. She'd be getting a quarter of the acceptance advance, a tiny part of the royalties, and her name in little print on the cover of the book.

She wouldn't have to worry about finding a job or making the rest of the repairs on her house. Without paying rent, without needing a new wardrobe every changing season, without eating out every night, she could make that money last until next summer, at least. Mr. Bradford's literary agent had even hinted of more work to come, if the publishers were happy with the completed manuscript.

They'd be happy, or she'd die trying.

Louisa had never worked so hard in her life between the book, keeping track of the donations and the thank-you letters, and helping Marta and Rico pack up Mr. Bradford's belongings. They had to decide what should go to the hospital thrift shop, what might have sentimental value to his sister and nephews, and which books belonged to Dante or should be donated to the library.

She still made time for Teddy, who was missing his uncle as well as Mr. Bradford, who had been like a crusty old grandfather to him. She didn't neglect her dog either, taking Champ for long walks on the beach, where she thought of Mr. Bradford swimming and Dante fishing, the tides changing, and the seasons.

Fall was coming, the tourists were leaving, school was starting, and Dante did not come back. Louisa kept so busy she barely had time to miss him. Except for every other minute, every other thought that entered her head.

He'd come back, she told herself. He had to; he practically owned the town. He had responsibilities, properties to oversee, an arts center to build, striped bass to catch. He'd come back when his business and Mr. Bradford's was done. That's what he promised, when he called. The question was, would he come back to Louisa?

Dante did come back to Paumonok Harbor, at least, but not until the hurricane was on its way.

Chapter Thirty-Four

Elvira was raging up the Eastern seaboard, headed straight for Long Island. Dante was raging up and down Louisa's living room.

"You came back."

He looked at Louisa as if she were crazy. Crazier than he already thought she was, that is. "Of course I came back. I live here." He'd been home for a day, boarding up windows all over town. He'd tried to get here sooner, starting as soon as the weather forecasters had a firmer idea of the storm's path. His flights had been cancelled, though, diverted and delayed, until he'd finally bought a whole new truck, bigger and stronger than his old one. He'd picked a red one off the lot first, thinking about Louisa's flower gardens and her orange sandals. She seemed to like bright colors. Then he thought about her in that evening gown and almost changed his mind for a black one. No, he'd never get home thinking about her in that dress, or out of it. He took the red truck. And thought about her anyway.

He'd driven north, through the fringes of the storm that was headed in the same direction. Now he was here, exhausted, worried, and furious.

"Masking tape? You think masking tape is going to protect your house from hundred mile an hour winds or more? That's the precaution you've taken?"

"Of course not. I have water and candles and a battery radio and a flashlight, just what the newspaper recommended. I took all the hanging planters down and brought in the porch furniture so it didn't blow away or crash into a window." She did not mention the bottle of over-the-counter sleeping pills she'd bought, hoping to sleep through the worst of the storm. It was either sleep or face the panic that was threatening to reduce her to a quivering mass of incoherence and incompetence. The TV newspeople were forecasting doom, showing the disastrous remnants of every hurricane and flood since Noah, it seemed. The radios were reveling in their warnings to have extra batteries. Bill at the hardware store told her the power had been out for a week in an ice storm two years ago. The supermarket was out of bottled water.

Now Louisa thought she'd rather face the hurricane than Dante, who did not seem impressed by her preparations. He slammed his fist against a wall, which shook, proving how frail her house truly was, as if she didn't know it.

She tried to sound confident. Dante admired strength. So what if her spine was made out of sponge? "I, ah, also bought peanut butter and crackers in case I can't cook for a few days."

"You can't cook period, but that's not the point. You can't stay here."

"I am not leaving my house. You know how hard I've worked on it. Besides, if the power goes out someone has to be here to eat the melting ice cream."

He was not amused at her feeble attempt at humor. "Damn it, there's nothing between you and Gardiner's Bay except for a narrow stand of scrub oak and honeysuckle vines. That's little enough protection from the wind, and nothing against the storm surge. The hurricane is due to come ashore right at high tide. Your house could be underwater if it's not swept out to the bay, or carried straight across Montauk Highway to the ocean. Half the town could be lost if the water breaches the dunes, or if the beaches are so eroded they can't hold it back."

She couldn't accept the idea that her

house, her refuge, her cocoon of security, might disappear. Her tomato plants and her marigolds, maybe, but not her house. "No way. This place has been here for years."

"We haven't had a bad storm in years, either, and the beaches aren't as wide as they used to be. Besides, you won't have a choice. The police and firemen come around and evacuate this area. It's just too low, and too hard to get to if someone needs rescuing. The volunteers from the ambulance department can't be expected to jeopardize their own lives trying to get here in an emergency. Ambulances aren't built for high water, and you wouldn't be able to call them anyway, if the phone lines go down."

"Yes, I would. Remember, you told me to take Mr. Bradford's cell phone so I could answer his calls."

He'd told her to take the phone so he could check on her wherever she was, so he could hear her voice. "Cell phones don't always work when transmitters go dead too. That doesn't matter. You can't stay here alone."

"Then stay with me." There, she'd said it, what she'd been hoping for since the first word of the approaching storm. Heck, it was the only thing she'd been thinking of since he left: having him come back here, to her.

"I can't. I have too many other responsibilities."

"I . . . see." She saw that she was merely another concern of his, another duty, another obligation to look after. "Then consider me warned and go on about your knight errantry. I'll take my chances here."

"I can't leave you like that, Louie. It's just too dangerous and I would worry too much. I need to know you're safe. I need you where I can find you."

He needed her? "Thank you. I missed you too."

Dante pulled her into a hard embrace and kissed her, quickly. "You can't imagine how much. I'd show you, but there's no time."

"I can guess how much you missed me between your busy social calendar." Louisa could not keep the resentment from her tone. She'd been pining for him while he'd been playing golf. She'd been answering sad condolence letters that enclosed donations for the arts center, while he'd been going to movies every night. Not that she was jealous or anything, wondering who he was with. "Not that it's any of my business, of course."

"I was doing estate stuff, putting the Hilton Head house and its contents into the hands of the right people. I only played a couple of rounds of golf while I waited for the appraisers to come. Then it made sense to take care of the City apartment while I was waiting for the papers to go through. I figured I might as well kill some time seeing films that will never get out here, rather than watching reruns on TV. Mr. Bradford doesn't have the sports networks on his cable, so I couldn't even watch the Yankees. I only went to one game with Mr. Bradford's agent. I was shuttling back and forth for ages, it seemed, until I decided to let your friend Siegal handle some of the local, legal stuff. Now I don't have to go back to either place. Besides, I called all the time, didn't I?"

That was how she knew he hadn't been sitting around, missing her. He had called frequently, going over endless details concerning Mr. Bradford's estate and checking on the progress of the book. Not that he doubted her, he swore.

No matter what he said, Louisa knew Dante was worried; he'd put his reputation on the line for her. She intended to make him proud. Mr. Bradford had given her freedom, she owed him her best, too. As for what Dante had given her . . .

"You never said you missed me."

Over the phone? Without knowing how she felt? Didn't she understand he'd called so often just to listen to her say his name? Exasperated, he said, "Well, I did miss you. I thought about you all the time. And I was sorry I had to leave you so soon after the memorials, knowing how fond you were of Mr. Bradford, but I needed to make sure his sister was all right, not tossed into some sinkhole of a nursing home. Once I saw that she was living in luxury in a retirement center, and her sons were taking care of her, I decided to get as much done in one trip as possible. I didn't want to have to keep going back, and you sounded okay."

"I didn't need you to stay and comfort me. I managed."

"Of course you did. I knew you could, that's why I left. You're one tough cookie, but you're not tough enough to fight a hurricane, Louie. Please don't fight me, either. I don't have time to argue. You have to get out of here."

Because he cared, and because she was terrified, Louisa said, "Okay, I'll go to Osprey Hill. Your house."

"What, with all that glass? I don't trust

the new aluminum track shutters. Or that overhanging eave on the top floor. Besides, there's only one driveway up to the top of the hill, and it's lined with trees that can fall. The road at the bottom floods during every heavy thunderstorm from the runoff. The place will be an island if we get half as much rain as they are predicting. Your car would never make it through."

Louisa stared at her bare feet. "You don't want me there."

"Not without me, I don't. You'd be all alone. Marta has already left to stay at a friend's house in town."

Alone in that huge house, in the dark? With things rattling around? "Where are you going to be?"

"Heaven knows. I doubt I'll be finished battening everything down until dark, so I might have to stay in whichever house I finish last if there's no time to get back to town, or if the roads to Osprey Hill are blocked. I'll try to get to the school then, where Francine and Aunt Vinnie and Teddy will be. They'll have lights and food and cots and radios. That's where you should be too. With them."

It was already raining here, with the center of the storm hours away, not due to touch land until after midnight. Dante had been working since daybreak, hauling ply-wood for Rico and his crew to hammer over windows of all the houses Rivera Realty controlled. They were next door now, and it looked like they would have to do Louisa's windows as soon as they were done. Dante still had his ex-wife's office and his aunt Vinnie's house to fortify, then he had to secure his houseboat, see if the boatyard had hauled the *Celia* out of the water as he'd instructed, make sure Francine got the family over to the evacuation shelter, and check on his own house on the hill. The yard crew said they'd put everything loose into the garage and drained the pool so it did not overflow, but Dante wanted to move the art collection to a safer room, and make sure the backup generator was in working order. He was hoping to wait Elvira out there, watching the storm as long as he could. There was nothing like a hurricane's raw, elemental power — but it was not safe enough for Louisa.

"Please say you'll go to the school so I don't have to worry about you."

"What about my worries? You'd be fool enough to drive in the middle of the storm if you thought something needed doing, or someone needed rescuing. I wouldn't put it past you to sit in your pretty new truck next to the beach, watching the surf."

He smiled because she was reading his thoughts. "Hurricanes have their own excitement, but I am not crazy. And I know this place better than anyone." And he had too much to look forward to when the hurricane was past. "I won't take chances."

"But you really will come to the shelter?"

"As soon as I can."

He kissed her good-bye when Rico started dragging plywood boards over and started hammering them in to her rotten window frames. Now she'd need new windows more than ever. The kiss made her want Dante more than ever, but they both knew he couldn't stay.

"Soon," he promised.

Louisa still had a few hours after the men left. Her house was shuttered and dark, with an abandoned look to it already that left Louisa feeling chilled and even more anxious, now that Dante had gone. The wind was picking up, whipping the branches of the old oak at the corner, and the rain was coming down harder. At least she did not have to worry about the roof leaking — only that it stayed on the house. She unplugged the microwave and the TV, on Dante's advice, and carried her computer into the downstairs bathroom, at the back of the house.

Now that she was leaving, she had to pack. She gathered a bunch of clothes into a suitcase, along with towels and blankets, her makeup and her jewelry. She never took off Mr. Bradford's diamond pendant, but she gathered Howard's pearls, too, on the far chance that she ran out of money and had to pawn them. She filled a tote bag with her emergency supplies, chocolate and breakfast bars and fruit, and enough dog food to keep Champ for a week, just in case her house wasn't there in the morning.

"It will be," she told the dog as she turned and locked the door, reassuring herself, if not her pet, who did not want to go out into the rain. "We'll be back."

As she drove through Main Street she thought she was in one of those western ghost towns. The shops were all boarded over and no one was on the roads. The few cars that passed had surf boards tied to the roofs, the idiots. Everyone else was already home, making last-minute preparations, or at the school, the church, or the firehouse.

The windshield wipers of Louisa's car were working furiously, and leaves and a few small branches were tumbling in the roadway. The radio was saying she still had time. Her white-knuckled hands clenched the steering wheel.

Louisa drove to Osprey Hill. She'd made backup copies of all the computer files, of course — but they were all stupidly in the same place, in Mr. Bradford's office. Dante had said his house wasn't invincible either. What kind of dummy put all her eggs into one fragile basket? Louisa needed to take a copy of the nearly completed manuscript with her, on a disc at least, just in case.

She let herself and Champ in through the back door, the only one not protected by a locked-down metal covering. She put on every light she could so the house did not seem so dark and scary. She put on the TV so she couldn't hear the wind rattling those aluminum shutters.

After checking the storm's progress on the Internet, Louisa uploaded Mr. Bradford's autobiography and sent it to herself in an E-mail. Even if all the power went dead and the computers crashed, the book would be out there in cyberspace. She made another CD of the book too, and put it in her pocketbook. Checking the weather station again, she decided to print out another paper copy to take with her. If she had to stay at the school for any time, at least she could be editing the manuscript. The laser printer could do the whole book in less than an hour.

When she'd done everything she could think of to protect Mr. Bradford's work and hers — and delay leaving, hoping Dante would come — she unplugged everything. Then she clipped Champ's leash on his collar, just to make sure he didn't take fright and run off. She wrapped the book in a plastic bag and made a dash for her car, ending up soaked despite her raincoat.

She hadn't expected the day to grow so dark, so quickly. Or the wind to make her car sway. Dante was right: she'd feel better with Francine, Teddy and the rest of the town for company. The sooner she reached the school, the better. Maybe Dante would be there by now.

Chapter Thirty-Five

Dante was almost ashamed to admit it, but he was enjoying himself. He could feel the adrenaline rush through him, if not the testosterone. This was man versus nature, primitive and raw, guts against Goliath. Man might lose, but not without a damned good fight.

Dante's property was as secure as he could make it. His family was safe. Louisa was . . . worried about him. He was warmed, despite the mounting wind and the driving rain.

Finally someone was not dependent on him, not waiting for him to make the decisions, take out the trash, pay the bills, pick up the pieces. Not his Louie.

She was a person in her own right. She didn't need him or his money, but she wanted him anyway. Now he was finally rich, where it really mattered. What was a measly hurricane compared to the storm inside him, raging to make love to her, with her, to make her love him?

The measly hurricane was picking up strength as it got closer to shore. They would have done better if the trees were not still leafed out, making the branches wetter, heavier, more liable to break or pull up the roots altogether. Smaller, more exposed trees were already toppling as the soaked ground grew too muddy to hold them upright. A few cable TV lines were broken loose, whipping in the wind. A garbage can rolled down the street. It was time to get to shelter.

The Hill, by himself? It had a garage for his new truck, but it did not have Louisa. He drove up there, checking everything one last time. The puddles were almost to the bottom of the hubcaps, higher when he left a short time later.

The school? It had no garage — and no Louisa either.

They shouldn't have stopped naming hurricanes solely after women.

His was the only car on the road as he headed toward Whaler's Drive, leaning forward to try to see out of the windshield. The wipers couldn't keep up with the rain or the bits of leaves that were plastered against the glass by the wind. The headlamps barely brightened a car length ahead of him. More wires were down, but he couldn't see any sparks.

Sure enough, though, lights were on at

Louisa's house. Dante left the truck parked in the road in front of her house, intending to grab her and get out.

The wind whipped the screen door out of his hands, smashing it back against the house. Good, he thought. He felt like smashing something himself.

Then Louisa opened the door. Sheets of rainwater drove into the house, and a gust of wind shook the overhead chandelier but didn't extinguish the candle burning in a glass lantern.

She pulled him inside, throwing herself at his dripping wet foul weather gear as if she wanted to burrow inside. "You came! You came!"

Dante set her aside and manhandled the front door shut against the gale. "You didn't leave," he said, disgust and aggravation tinging his words. "After you agreed that you would."

She was shaking, so he opened his arms again. She was already wet, so what did it matter?

"I did go. I really did," she babbled against his chest. "But they wouldn't take Champ. They said they barely had space at the school for all the people, so no pets were allowed except little ones in carrying cages. They said dogs might get upset by

431

all the confusion and the crowds and bite someone. Champ never would!"

"Of course not."

"And they said the dogs might mess inside."

"I know, Champ never would."

"The firehouse was for emergency workers, and a bunch of people hooked up to oxygen tanks. They told me to try the church, but they wouldn't take animals, either. I couldn't leave him in the car by himself, could I? So I brought him home. But you know how afraid he is of firecrackers and thunder. I just couldn't leave him alone here, after you said it wasn't safe. Now we can go to Osprey Hill."

She was crying in worry and in relief, so he stroked her back. "Too late, sweetheart. There are wires going down all over, and trees too."

"I know. The cable TV is out. I can't get any local news on the radio either, only static."

"I'm sorry I didn't know about the dog thing. I would have thought of something else, or kept you with me at the Hill."

"So we'll have to stay here? What about the flood?"

"We'll just have to go upstairs if the water comes in."

"But what if the roof goes?" Louisa had been imagining every kind of disaster she could, including the entire house crumbling around her ears. She'd been hugging the poor dog for the last hour. Now Champ was as wet from her tears as Louisa was from Dante's jacket.

He stepped back and took off his yellow slicker. "If you're afraid the roof won't hold, then we should camp out in the crawl space."

"With the spiders and snakes? I'll take my chances with the roof."

Dante dried his hair with the towel she handed him, wondering if they'd be better off in the vacant rental house next door. He knew the structure there was sound, at least.

That's when the lights flickered twice and went out. Now it was too late to make any moves. "Okay, Girl Scout. Show me what you've got."

Louisa had matches in her pocket, so she went around lighting the rest of the candles, all carefully placed on saucers, away from the paneled walls and curtains. The candlelight would have been romantic, except that they kept flickering in the drafts in the old house. She handed Dante the flashlight and the radio, to see if he could

433

get it to receive anything.

"I have hot tea in a thermos, too," she told him.

He led the way to the kitchen with the flashlight, which was already growing dimmer. He didn't want to ask if she had more batteries. "Tea sounds great."

The next wind gust sounded like a jet engine landing on her house. The walls were shuddering. So was Louisa. She forgot about his tea.

"I . . . I think we should go upstairs."

"There's no water coming in."

"I don't care. I don't want to sit here waiting! I want to get into bed and pull the covers over my head."

Funny, Dante thought, he'd rather go outside and face the storm head-on than wait for the house to collapse on top of him. Louisa was frightened, though, and he'd never leave her. "Isn't there a bed in that back room? The one you made your office?" He did think the roof would hold, but there was no knowing with old houses and hurricanes. "There'll be less movement down here, and that room's on the back side of the storm." He saw no reason to tell her that the wind would turn and come back from a different direction, after the eye passed over.

"Yes," she said with relief, pulling him toward the office room, the lantern in her other hand. "We'll be safe here. See? Champ is already under the bed."

Safe? On a narrow bed with a woman begging to be held? "I don't think this is such a good idea, Louie."

"It's the best idea I've heard all day. Come on, get comfortable." She was already tearing at her jeans.

"That's not going to make me comfortable." In fact, his imagination was making him anything but. The wind, the storm, the danger — and a gorgeous woman in a T-shirt and panties? Oh, boy.

"Dante, I need you next to me. I need to block out the hurricane."

He thought he knew what she was asking, but he had to make sure. "I can't promise not to want more than you want to give."

"How do you know how much I want? Do I have to spell it out? I want you. All of you. Now." She reached for the buttons of his shirt.

"Just because you're scared and I'm nearby?"

"Don't be dense. I wouldn't jump the electric company guy if he came to turn the lights back on."

Dante finished unbuttoning his shirt, but paused at the zipper of his pants. "What if one of the hot young firemen came by in a tank to evacuate you?"

"Nope. Not even him. I only want you, Dante Rivera."

She was crawling under the covers, waiting for him. The wind wasn't as loud back here. His breathing was. "Louie, you know I want you."

She lowered her eyes as he lowered his pants. "That's pretty obvious."

"But I can't do this, this way."

She leaned down and pulled a silver-foil packet out of her jeans pocket.

He smiled, took two, more optimistic packets from his pocket, but shook his head.

"What, you want to make love on the floor?"

"I want to make love. That's the point. I don't want comfort sex. I mean, it would be nice, and help pass a long night in the best possible way, but it wouldn't be enough. I think I love you, Louisa Waldon."

"Of course you do, silly. It just took you a long time to figure it out."

He sat on the bed, on top of the covers, with a corner of the sheet over his lap. "Let me get this straight. You knew it before I did?"

"Even if I didn't believe it, everyone else in the town did. They all told me so. They know I love you too."

"You do?"

"I think I've loved you since the day you stood up to that dog-napper. I just had to wait to see if you were for real."

"And I had to see if you'd stick around."

"I'm not going anywhere. Are you?"

He reached over and brushed the hair away from her face. "Not without you. Except maybe fishing."

"Good. I have a lot of work to do."

"That's fine. Someone has to support that expensive yard sale habit of yours. Speaking of expensive, I signed that paper of Susan's. I won't be claiming her baby, or supporting it, in case you were worried."

"I wasn't worried. I know you'll do the right thing for everybody, no matter what."

Which called for a long kiss, which would have led to where they were both longing to go, but Dante put his foot down, literally. He sat up on the bed, one leg on the floor so he was almost on bended knee, and took her hand. "Will you marry me, Louisa Waldon? I don't have a ring yet, but I have a new key ring for the truck in my jacket pocket."

"Isn't it too soon?"

"I'd rather that than too late, like Mr. Bradford."

"Are you sure?"

"Positive. Are you?"

"How soon?" she asked in reply. "I'm telling you now, I won't stand for any long engagement. I won't give you time to change your mind. And I don't want any big wedding, either."

"We ought to be able to get the license and line up Judge Chmelecki in two days. How's that?"

"Okay, but I'm not letting you out of my sight until then."

"I'm not going anywhere," he echoed her words. "Except into bed."

The bed was far too narrow for two people, but they managed. The hurricane roared and the dog whimpered. The rain pelted and the house creaked. They didn't hear any of it, only words of love, sighs, and purrs of pleasure.

Louisa was everything Dante had ever dreamed of in a woman, and so much more. More softness, more warmth, more responsiveness. More Louisa, who threw her heart into everything she did. He caught it, and carried her with him to new heights, new depths, new closeness that had nothing to do with the single bed.

Louisa knew Dante was generous, but she'd never imagined any man could be so unselfish, so gentle and so strong at the same time. He loved her, and he made love to her with an intensity she'd never known, making sure she was as enraptured as he was. She couldn't get bored or seasick like she'd done with Howard. There wasn't time, the first time, they were both so ready. She knew she never would, the second time. Dante would never let her, keeping her at the fever edge of completion with his hands and his mouth and his words of love. He kept her with him, urgent, needing, pulsing, pounding.

She cried out in ecstasy.

For a minute Dante thought she'd shouted Howard's name, but then Louisa shouted it again. "It did! It did!"

"What did?" he asked, gasping, their bodies still joined.

"The earth! It moved. I knew it would."

He kissed her eyelids, first one and then the other. "Thank you, sweetheart. But that was the hurricane, not me."

They both listened, catching their breaths.

"It's quiet!" Louisa wriggled until Dante shifted positions so she was lying on top of him. "We made it! The hurricane is past and we didn't get washed away or blown to kingdom come." She kissed him fast and hard. "We lived through it and the house is still standing." She paused. "We are still going to get married, aren't we?"

"Hell, yes. Do you think I'd part with a woman who makes love like that? I hate to tell you this, though, but this calm is the eye of the storm passing over. It'll come back, maybe stronger."

"Stronger?"

He was stroking her back, loving the feel of that slope at the bottom of her spine, the softness of her rear end, the dewy feel of her skin after lovemaking. He nodded. "Stronger."

She could hear the wind howling again already. "Then maybe we better do that again."

"That?"

She trailed kisses down his cheek and his neck and on to his chest. "That."

"Again?" Dante wasn't sure he could, until she rubbed against his lower body. He rose to the occasion, letting her set the pace this time, happy to have her on top so his hands were free to explore her perfect breasts, the tiny curls where their bodies met, the no longer private places hidden there. "Have I told you lately how much I love you?" he gasped.

"Not for . . . five . . . minutes . . . or so."

"I do. More than —"

BOOM!

Dante was off the bed so fast Louisa landed on the floor. He grabbed up his pants and the dim flashlight and ran toward the front of the house. The house hadn't collapsed, so Louisa took the time to find a robe and reassure the dog with a pet. "What was that?" she asked, coming to join him by the front door he'd just closed again.

"I think the old oak tree at the corner finally went over. On my truck."

"Oh, no! Your brand-new truck?"

He took her hand and led her back to the little bedroom. "My brand-new flat pile of scrap metal, I'd guess."

"I really am a jinx, then! Howard's Porsche, and then his new Jag, Fred's jalopy, and now your lovely new truck. It's all my fault for making you come here when you would have parked it somewhere safe. You would have put it in the garage at the Hill or the field at —"

He stopped her agonizing with a long kiss, then said, "Hush, sweetheart, it's no one's fault. You're not a jinx. You're the best thing that ever happened to me. Disaster-prone, maybe, but the best."

"And you're not mad?"

"Hey, I'm not Howard."

"Howard who?"

He pulled her into his arms, then onto the bed. "It's a truck, Louie, only a truck. But you, you're my life, my love, soon my wife. Now come, let's make the earth shake again."

"I thought that was the hurricane?"

"What hurricane?"

Author's Note

Paumonok is the Native American word for Long Island, meaning fish, or fish-shaped. There is no village of Paumonok Harbor, however. I plunked it, school, bank, library and bayside boatyard, at the eastern end of Long Island's South Fork Hamptons, halfway between Montauk and Amagansett, which are decidedly real. None of the characters in *Love, Louisa* are based on the characters of either place.

About the Author

Author of more than thirty romance novels, BARBARA METZGER is the proud recipient of two *Romantic Times* Career Achievement Awards and a RITA from the Romance Writers of America. When not writing romances or reading them, she paints, gardens, volunteers at the local library, and goes beachcombing on the beautiful Long Island shore with her little dog Hero. She loves to hear from her readers, through her publisher or her Web site:

www.BarbaraMetzger.com.

The employees of Thorndike Press hope you have enjoyed this Large Print book. All our Thorndike and Wheeler Large Print titles are designed for easy reading, and all our books are made to last. Other Thorndike Press Large Print books are available at your library, through selected bookstores, or directly from us.

For information about titles, please call:

(800) 223-1244

or visit our Web site at:

www.gale.com/thorndike
www.gale.com/wheeler

To share your comments, please write:

Publisher
Thorndike Press
295 Kennedy Memorial Drive
Waterville, ME   04901